BLACK BEANS & VICE

A SUPPER CLUB MYSTERY

BLACK BEANS & VICE

J. B. STANLEY

WHEELER
CHIVERS

This Large Print edition is published by Wheeler Publishing, Waterville, Maine, USA and by AudioGO Ltd, Bath, England.
Wheeler Publishing, a part of Gale, Cengage Learning.

LIBRARY OF CONGRESS CATALOGING-IN-PUBLICATION DATA

Stanley, J. B.
    Black beans & vice / by J. B. Stanley.
      p. cm. — (Wheeler Publishing large print cozy mystery) (A supper club mystery)
    ISBN-13: 978-1-4104-3183-7 (pbk.)
    ISBN-10: 1-4104-3183-5 (pbk.)
    1. Henry, James (Fictitious character)—Fiction. 2. Cooking—Fiction. 3. Murder—Investigation—Fiction. 4. Large type books. I. Title. II. Title: Black beans and vice.
PS3619.T3655B57 2011
813'.6—dc22   2010046038

BRITISH LIBRARY CATALOGUING-IN-PUBLICATION DATA AVAILABLE

Published in 2011 in the U.S. by arrangement with Midnight Ink, an imprint of Llewellyn Publications, Woodbury, MN 55125-2989 USA.
Published in 2011 in the U.K. by arrangement with Llewellyn Worldwide Ltd.

U.K. Hardcover: 978 1 445 83618 8 (Chivers Large Print)
U.K. Softcover: 978 1 445 83619 5 (Camden Large Print)

"I have from an early age abjured the use of meat, and the time will come when men such as I will look upon the murder of animals as they now look upon the murder of men."

— LEONARDO DA VINCI

To Jessica Faust of Book Ends:
Vegetarian, Über-agent, Friend

ONE:
BLACK JELLY BEANS

Grams of
Sugar
14

Head librarian James Henry held the brochure as though the glossy, trifold paper covered with photographs of happy, healthy people might suddenly ignite in his hands. "You want us to get *hypnotized?*" he asked, his voice rather shrill.

High school art teacher Lindy Perez nodded calmly. "Hypnotherapy is a *very* effective weight loss method. Or so I've read. There are loads of testimonials on the Internet."

Tossing the brochure on the surface of the circulation desk, James reached for a glass bowl filled with jellybeans. Picking out two black ones, he popped the candies into his mouth and chewed thoughtfully. "I'm having a moment of déjà vu, Lindy," he declared once his mouth was empty. "It doesn't seem too long ago that I met you right here for the first time. You had schemes then too, remember, and you were seeking permission to hang a flyer on the bulletin board —"

"In search of folks to join a dieter's supper club!" Lindy finished for him, her brown eyes glimmering at the memory. "You were mighty nervous about becoming a member back then too, and look how *that's* turned out!"

James couldn't help but grin. "One of the best decisions of my life, no doubt about it. What would I do without all of you? You're my best friends." He gestured at the brochure. "Still, this is a bit out there. I could picture Gillian appearing at one of our meetings with this brochure, but not you, the ever-so-sensible Lindy Perez. You're too level-headed to be reaching for these mumbo-jumbo straws."

Lindy's eyes flashed and James shrank back a little, worried that his friend was about to demonstrate her infrequent but fierce Brazilian temper. "I may be Ms. Practical, but I've also gained fifteen pounds over the last three months. I was maintaining my weight until your stepmother's sister had to go and get herself murdered. After that, PLOP!" Lindy smacked her palms together. "I fell off the wagon in a *big* way. Now, I'd like to gain control over the way I eat once and for all. I'm sick and tired of food controlling *me,* James, and I am *not* looking for another diet plan." She pointed a finger at her temple. "We're never going to change our bodies until we fix what's going on in here."

"And a hypnotherapist can do that?" James was doubtful.

Lindy nodded enthusiastically. "What's the one thing you can't seem to resist? When you go on a diet, what food do you miss most?"

"Cheese puffs," James answered right away. "And in a close second, anything made with sugar." He held up another jellybean. "Like these, for instance."

"Exactly!" Lindy cried and several library patrons sent frowns in her direction. "Sorry," she whispered and gave a self-effacing wave to those browsing the new-release section.

"We're *all* addicted to sugar. Candy, cake, soda, ice cream, cookies —"

James held out his hand. "Enough! Do

you want me to drool all over the barcode scanner? I don't think it's waterproof."

Lindy picked up the brochure and gave it a triumphant wave. "See? Sugar is ruling you even as we speak. How many of those jellybeans have you had?"

Embarrassed, James shrugged. "Um, I don't know. Enough to turn my tongue black?"

"Pick a number," Lindy insisted.

"Well, since I've only been eating one color out of five possible shades and I bought a jumbo-sized bag, I'd say twenty-five."

"Okay! Let me give you a brief lesson in mathematics. I might be an art teacher, but I can demonstrate some basic addition that will have your black tongue hanging on the floor." Lindy dashed over to the shelving cart, grabbed a few books, and pushed them against James' soft paunch. He automatically reached out to grab them. "Feel those books? Would you say they weigh somewhere between two and three pounds?" Lindy asked expectantly.

James tested the weight by bobbing the tomes up and down. "I'd say that's accurate."

"*That's* how much sugar the average American eats *every* week! Sugar weakens

12

our immune system, rots our teeth, and makes us fat!" Lindy looked down at the ground, her face flushed, and murmured. "I think it's why Luis isn't proposing. He's watched me grow bigger and bigger over the past few months. I've stopped going to the gym and my portions are the size of a linebacker's. He must believe I have no self-discipline, no self-respect. He might even wonder how big I'm gonna get after having a few kids. With that unpleasant visual, it's no wonder he's had second thoughts about popping the question."

"Oh, Lindy." James put an arm around his friend's shoulder and squeezed. He hated to see sadness etched on her face. "Anyone worth his salt would be lucky to call you his wife. You're smart, kind, funny, and easy on the eye. And Luis is not so shallow that he'd stop loving you because you put on a few pounds. You wouldn't be in love with *him* if he were. Have you two talked about your future recently?"

Sighing, Lindy nodded. "He wants me to fly to Mexico to meet his mama when school is out. His treat, of course."

"There you go!" James proclaimed boisterously. "He's taking you home to Mother. You're halfway up the aisle already."

"Yeah, *if* she likes me!" Lindy snorted.

"I'm not her first choice, remember? That honor goes to the daughter of her best friend. Luis' mama set her sights on that girl to be her daughter-in-law, so how am I, an outsider to their community and a woman who is half-Southern American, half-Brazilian, supposed to compete with Miss Mexico 2010?"

Leading Lindy to the lobby door, James said, "You're going to dazzle her just like you dazzle everyone you meet."

"Well, I only have two months to *look* like a priceless diamond, so I'm going to book us an appointment with the hypnotherapist. She can explain the process to all of us at once. Do you have Eliot this weekend?"

At the mention of his son's name, James felt a rush of pleasure that seemed to increase in intensity whenever he thought of his little boy. Six months ago, James hadn't even known he had a child, but when his ex-wife introduced him to a sweet and shy four-year-old named Eliot Henry, James had fallen instantly in love. Since then, James had been spending most of his free time with his son and every time Eliot ran into his arms, James felt as though his heart would burst with joy all over again.

"Jane's taking Eliot to visit her parents in Tennessee for the better part of spring break," James said. "I was invited to go along, and while Jane and I are really enjoying getting reacquainted, I'm not *quite* ready to spend five days with my former in-laws yet. So I'm completely available to be put under a spell."

Lindy swiped at him with the hypnotherapy brochure. "You'd better not show up at the consultation with that kind of attitude, Mister."

"Yes, Ms. Perez." James used a high, squeaky voice to mimic one of Lindy's students. "I will be on my best behavior. Just don't expect me to get acupuncture next if this experiment fails. I have no desire to resemble a human pin cushion."

Backing up a few steps, Lindy helped herself to a handful of jellybeans and smiled self-effacingly. "A few for the road. And don't worry about the other lifestyle gurus at the Wellness Village. We can bypass the masseuses, acupuncturists, and yoga masters. We're only interested in one therapist: the woman who is going to kick our sugar craving for good!"

Visualizing the new complex south of town, which consisted of six offices built to resemble a row of small cottages surrounding a courtyard, James grew pensive. "You know," he told Lindy as she reached for the front door, "if we let Gillian near that place we may never see her again."

Lindy laughed. "Then we should tell Lucy to bring along a pair of handcuffs. She'd better cuff Bennett to Gillian because it's going to take a miracle from the Almighty to get our favorite mailman within a mile of those pink and purple 'health' houses!"

"Yes, I believe it's quite likely he'll balk at the idea of being hypnotized, especially in a setting that looks like it was teleported straight from Disneyland." James gave Lindy his sternest look. "The first sign of an oversized mouse wearing gloves and suspenders and I'm leaving."

"The only oversized creatures there," Lindy answered with a wry snort, "will be *us!*"

Later that week, James met Bennett at the local YMCA. It had been a long time since the two friends had worked out together and they spent the first few minutes in the weight-training alcove simply studying their images in the mirror and frowning. While they meticulously examined their protruding bellies and flaccid limbs, a pair of younger men with hard, streamlined bodies entered the room.

After greeting James and Bennett with

friendly waves, the two men opened a notebook and began to discuss their goals for the day's workout. They discussed and debated a variety of different exercises until an agreement was reached in which each man would complete five rounds of three hundred jump ropes, twenty-five weighted front squats, and fifteen shoulder presses. The men gathered their equipment, picked up their jump ropes, and synchronized their watches.

"Ready?" the first one asked in a business-like tone.

"Let's do it," the second responded. When the subtle beep of his watch indicated the commencement of the stopwatch feature, the two twentysomethings began to jump.

James and Bennett, who up to this point had been gathering a haphazard pile of impressive-looking dumbbells in an attempt to appear as fit and strong as the new arrivals, paused to watch. The jump ropes whirled so quickly that the blue plastic cords blurred in the air. The men held their bodies rigid, their wrists circling with incredible speed as the jump rope passed under their feet again and again. Their even, fast rhythm never altered and neither of the men missed a jump or got tangled in the rope. Not once. The sound in the room was like that of a small helicopter in hover mode.

"Hey, man. How about some bicep curls?" Bennett suggested after finally turning away from the athletic jumpers.

"Yeah. Let's go *heavy*," James stated in a deeper voice than usual. He and Bennett selected the largest dumbbells from the rack. As James curled the weight toward his shoulder, he compressed his lips to bite back a groan. He couldn't believe how weak he'd become.

And that's my strong arm! he thought woefully.

After two pathetic reps, he switched to his left arm. Meanwhile, Bennett was focused on lifting a forty-five-pound Olympic bar in one motion from the middle of his thighs to over his head. Normally, he would conduct this motion with slow deliberation, being careful to maintain correct form, but the intense pace of the younger men encouraged him to increase his speed. Now, Bennett raised and lowered the bar as fast as he could, his back rounding dangerously. Suddenly, the bar became unbalanced. With an anguished yelp, Bennett dropped it directly onto his shoe.

"AAARRRGH!" He shouted in pain and began to hop on one foot. In his awkward dance of agony, he ended up bumping into

James. The weight of the heavy dumbbell in James' left hand lurched, forcing him to pitch forward. In order to keep his grip on the weight, he reached across his body with his right hand and as he did so, he twisted his entire torso in an awkward, unfamiliar motion that painfully wrenched his back.

"OOOOO!" James howled and immediately sank down on the carpeted floor. Digging his fingers into his lower back, he moaned and winced in acute discomfort. Bennett plopped down alongside him, took off his sneaker and white tube sock, and gingerly bent the toes on his right foot to make sure none were broken.

Eventually, when James was able to speak, he turned to his friend. "Are you hurt?"

Bennett eased his sock back on. "I don't think my little piggies are gonna be runnin' all the way home for a real long time."

Feeling clumsy, weak, and old, James glanced in the mirror and was relieved to see that the younger men were far too busy lifting superhuman amounts of weight to have noticed their inelegant collapse.

"So much for our workout," Bennett mopped his face with a dish towel. "It's gonna take me twice as long to deliver the mail tomorrow, since I'm gonna be limpin' every time I've gotta carry a box to someone's door."

"And I'll be the Hunchback of the Shenandoah Public Library," James answered with shame. "Bennett. I think this may be a sign that we should give Lindy's hypnotherapist a shot. We're clearly floundering on our own."

Bennett mulled the proposition over as he retied his shoe. James witnessed his friend's internal debate as Bennett's expression changed from a frown to a look of hopefulness and back to a frown again. "You really believe this woman can change our minds without turnin' us into zombies or makin' us — I dunno — squawk like parrots whenever we stop at a red light?" He wiggled a finger at James. " 'Cause I sit through an awful lot of lights every day."

James clapped Bennett on the back, though the motion made him grimace in pain. "Don't worry, my friend. I doubt anyone intends to turn you into parrot."

Sighing with visible relief, Bennett helped James rise to his feet. The two friends hobbled toward the locker room just as the younger men removed their shirts and began to jump rope again.

Bennett gazed at their rippled abs, the bulging muscles in their arms, and their rock-hard pectorals. "Okay, man, I'm in.

Let this woman brainwash me. If I end up lookin' half as good as those two, she can even sneak the parrot squawks in."

Sharp stings exploded across James' lower back and he placed his palm on the wall for support. "Don't make me laugh!" He remonstrated. "It hurts too much!"

The next day, the five friends gathered in the parking lot of the new Wellness Village. Lucy Hanover, dressed in her brown and beige sheriff's deputy uniform, stood with her hands on her hips, looking rather nervous. To her left, owner of The Yuppie Puppy Pet Grooming and Pet Palaces (custom designed pet homes) Gillian O'Malley rubbed her hands together in buoyant expectation. She gazed at the sign reading, "Your Map To Good Health," her expression bordering on rapture.

Lindy pointed at the map. "Harmony York's office is in Health House Number Four. This way." She began to march down a cobblestone pathway.

"Harmony?" Bennett spluttered. "That's her real name? Oh man, she's gonna be one of those Flower Child-types."

Gillian looped her arm around his and beamed. "Not *only* is it a lovely name but I find it *very* symbolic. Isn't our goal to rebalance our bodies and minds? To create an inner harmony? I have *complete* faith that we are not meeting a woman named Harmony by coincidence. This is the cosmos working on our behalf, my friends!"

"Pink Health Houses! Hrmph! Where's the yellow brick road," Bennett grumbled, clearly apprehensive. "I never thought I'd wanna be whisked away by a flyin' monkey before, but if I see a chimp with wings, I'm gonna wave him down and get the hell outta here!"

Gillian nearly yanked his arm off as she dragged him up the path toward one of the purple cottages bordered by a garden of riotous and fragrant wildflowers.

Next to the light blue front door, a simple placard bearing the name, *A Better State of Mind,* hung by a gold chain. Letting Lindy take the lead, the rest of the supper club members entered the waiting room and took in their surroundings.

"Something smells funny," Lucy whispered, and James pointed at a burning stick of incense in the far corner. The opposite corner was occupied by a small wall fountain, which gurgled pleasantly at a slightly lower volume than the instrumental music being piped into the space through a set of speakers resembling gray stones.

"Do I detect the sound of pan pipes?" James murmured softly in hopes of making Lucy grin. Ever since Jane and Eliot had become such a significant part of his life, Lucy had become more distant around James. She was always polite, but he knew that she was still coming to terms with the reality that any chance of rekindling their romance had evaporated.

Not only did Lucy place law enforcement at the center of her life, but she also wanted to be free of dependents other than her trio of gargantuan German Shepherds. Still, James knew that although the gift of fatherhood had changed him forever (and for the good), Lucy viewed his new circumstance as a personal slight. He felt completely fulfilled and as of this point, she did not. Because he understood the crushing weight of loneliness and the sorrowful feeling of having been rejected, James tried to make his former flame smile whenever he could.

Unaffected by his attempt at humor, Lucy skirted around the plush mauve sofa and approached the coffee table. She investigated each magazine closely but James knew she wasn't really interested in the office's reading material. She was merely nervous and was looking for clues as to Harmony York's personality. Eying a small, gold-painted Buddha on the receptionist's desk, James had to admit he shared Lucy's trepidation.

He settled down on the sofa with a copy of *Body + Soul Magazine* and had just flipped to an article on the best workout for one's body shape when a pretty woman in her mid-twenties entered the room from deeper within the cottage.

"Namaste!" She said and, folding her palms together, bowed her upper body. A curtain of shiny brown hair fell over her shoulders as she did so. Gillian immediately returned the greeting while the rest of the supper club members merely smiled idiotically.

"My name is Skye," the young woman said. "I'm Harmony's assistant."

Bennett rolled his eyes at the name and Lindy quickly stepped in front of him. "You're the one I spoke with on the phone. Thanks for mailing me the brochure. It sure convinced us to give this a try."

Skye swept her arm around the room in an encompassing gesture. "I'm afraid we don't offer group hypnotherapy. Are you *all* here for the consultation?"

"Yes," Lindy answered firmly. "We have the same goal and since the first session is free, I figured we'd save Harmony's time by coming together." She smiled warmly at her friends. "Besides, we like to support one another when it comes to our issues with food —"

Gillian interrupted, "So it makes sense for us to embark on this exciting new journey as one entity. We believe we'll have better success this way."

Skye digested this rationale for a moment and appeared to have no objections. "Well, let me just tell Harmony that she has five clients waiting for her." She gazed at each of them warmly and then said, "Please, help yourselves to some pure spring water flavored with organic orange slices. I'll be back in one moment."

James watched the poised young lady walk away and then pivoted. "Where is the water?" He found that he was suddenly very thirsty.

Bennett licked his lips and pointed at a stainless steel pitcher on Skye's desk. "Man, I could slurp down a lake right about now. Was that the power of suggestion or what?"

Fortified with glasses of cool and refreshing citrus-flavored water, the five friends made themselves comfortable. They had barely sipped from their recycled cups when Skye returned. "Harmony would be delighted to talk to you together. It would be a tight squeeze in her office so she'll meet with you here, in our Welcome Space."

Skye dipped her head and walked gracefully to her desk. James watched her sit with the straight-backed posture of a ballerina. Her fingers moved with deliberate elegance over the computer keyboard and her face seemed infused with a serene glow. There was an air of calm assurance about her, an unusual trait in one so young. It was as if she already knew the answers to life's most significant questions.

I certainly didn't feel that way when I was twenty-five, James thought.

His attention was distracted by the arrival of Harmony York. James had expected someone with waist-long hair, a flowing skirt, and leather sandals. Someone who dressed, looked, and acted a bit like Gillian. Harmony and Gillian might have been cut from the same cloth, but while Gillian was outfitted in a vibrant tangerine-colored sundress, which echoed the orange shade of her wild, frizzy hair, Harmony wore a plain gray suit and a light blue blouse. Her hair was silver and fashioned in a sleek bob. She was in her late fifties, James guessed, though her age was difficult to approximate as her skin was mostly smooth and shone with the light of good health.

"It's a pleasure to meet all of you." She

went around the room, shaking hands with her five potential clients and asking for their names. She then pulled one of the side chairs positioned near Skye's desk to the center of the room. She sat, smoothed her pants, and studied each and every one of them. Normally, such scrutiny would discomfit James, but Harmony's gentle, almost caressing gaze actually encouraged him to relax.

"Now." She smiled. "Let me tell you what we do here. I will be your therapist and Skye will take care of scheduling, billing, and the creation of your daily listening CDs. I'll explain how those work in a moment. First and foremost, allow me to assure you that anything you tell me will remain in the strictest confidence. During your therapy session, I'll talk to you, but I will also ask you questions. I'll be taking notes on your answers, but none of my movements will interrupt your relaxed state."

Bennett cleared his throat. "So we're not *under?* We know what's happenin' to us?"

"Absolutely," Harmony answered calmly. "This isn't sideshow hypnosis where you're tricked into submitting to another person's suggestions purely for the sake of entertainment. You will enter a deeply relaxed state so that your mind can become incredibly focused and alert while your body rests. I will ask your mind to do something for you and, with repetition, your mind will respond."

Lindy wiggled on her seat in excitement. "Well, like I explained to Skye, we don't want to be controlled by sugar any longer. Can you help our bodies to stop wanting it so doggone badly?"

Harmony laughed. Her voice was low and melodious. It reminded James of the seductive pitch shared by so many female actresses from the forties and fifties. "Yes, if *you're* willing. You see, that's another misconception about hypnosis. You *cannot* be hypnotized unless you're willing to be hypnotized. Some people want to change, but they can't trust enough to let go. I often can't get through to those clients and I have to suggest another method of treatment for them."

"What other things do people get help for besides food issues?" Lucy asked with an edge of skepticism to her voice.

If Harmony picked up on the negative tone, she didn't let it show. "All kinds of things. Many clients want to stop repeating bad habits like smoking, overindulging in alcohol, gambling, drug abuse, and even nail biting. Others seek freedom from phobias such as a fear of flying or of confined spaces. And many want relief from chronic pain, depression, or destructive attitudes."

Gillian, who had been hanging on Harmony's every word, sighed in delight. "Oh, this is so *wonderful!* When can we begin?"

Harmony rose and walked over to Skye's desk. She returned with a cup holder filled with pens and several pieces of paper. "Like everything else, we have to kick things off with paperwork." She distributed two sheets to each of them. "The first is a consent form. This basically states that you understand the meaning of hypnotherapy. If, at any time, you wish to stop your session and leave the hypnotic state, you have the right and the ability to do so. *You* are in control." She grinned as Bennett exhaled audibly in relief. "We will have three sessions together. Every night, as you lay down to sleep, you'll listen to your reinforcement CD. That's the gist of this form."

Lucy's pen hovered over the signature line. "Will any of this be covered by health insurance?"

"I'm afraid not." Harmony shook her head in genuine regret. "Payment is required at the end of every session and I'd prefer, if possible, to receive twenty-four hours advance notice in the event of a cancelation.

Once you sign, feel free to schedule your first session with Skye."

"And what's this? Homework?" Bennett joked as he flourished the second sheet of paper.

Harmony laughed again. "That's just a diagram to show you how hypnosis works. My goal is to bypass the conscious mind, which is where your short-term memory operates, and target the subconscious mind where permanent memory resides."

The five friends studied the drawing for a moment. Gillian actually traced her finger around the rings representing the different levels of the mind. James watched her in amusement, wondering whether she'd try to line up an appointment that very day. "So we're going to *retrain* our mind's memory into believing it doesn't crave sugar?"

Harmony beamed at Gillian as though she were a prize pupil. "Precisely. We're going to rewire your permanent memory in order to get a positive reaction from your short-term memory. In this case, your short-term memory will wonder if you feel like a piece of cake. Your mind will check with your long-term memory and come back with the answer, 'No, I don't want to eat cake. That's no longer a taste I'm interested in.' "

Whipping out her checkbook and pocket calendar, Gillian leapt out of her seat and stood at attention in front of Skye's desk. "When is the next opening? I simply cannot *wait* to begin this inner journey!"

"How's Tuesday at four-thirty?" Skye inquired.

"Sublime!" Gillian shouted.

Bennett rolled his eyes again. "Like a pig in mud," he muttered.

Lindy jabbed him in the arm with her capped pen. "Not the best of analogies there, Romeo."

Having booked her preliminary session, Gillian practically skipped over to Bennett, yanked him out of his sofa seat, and led him over to Skye. "And give him the five-thirty. This way, I can track him down if he gets cold feet at the last moment."

Bennett shot James a look of appeal. "That's right, my friend." James winked. "I want you to think about those *feet*. Especially the one with the bruised toes."

A scowl bloomed on Bennett's face and James knew his friend was picturing their failed workout at the gym. "Five-thirty it is," he told Skye with the forlorn resignation of one being led to the electric chair.

Two:
Sausage and Pepperoni Pizza

Grams of
Sugar
7

James woke in his luxurious king-sized bed in his yellow house on Hickory Hill Lane in a good mood. The sun was shining, he could smell freshly brewed coffee wafting down the hallway, and Eliot and Jane were driving down from Harrisonburg for dinner.

Sliding his feet into his leather slippers, James filled a mug featuring the slogan, "I'm a Librarian: Assume I Know Everything," and took a leisurely walk down the driveway to collect the Saturday paper. Sliding the *Shenandoah Star Ledger* into his robe pocket, he examined the flowerbed at the base of the front porch.

According to last night's garden report on the community television channel, Quincy's Gap and its environs had safely moved beyond the average date for the season's final frost. The announcer proclaimed it officially time to begin spring planting.

"Work hard now and rest all summer," the Master Gardener had suggested.

James decided to heed the expert's advice. He sat at his kitchen table and searched the paper for sales on tulip and daffodil bulbs, azalea bushes, and phlox. After showering and dressing in his yard clothes, a faded William & Mary sweatshirt and jeans that had gone thin in the knees, James hopped into his old white Bronco and headed north.

He deliberately selected one of the two-lane highways, doubling the length of the drive time to the nearest Lowe's, but as he eased the vintage truck around curve after curve, he could feel his spirits rise as the road steepened. In his opinion, there was no place else on earth as beautiful as the Shenandoah Valley. The rugged line of the Blue Ridge Mountains, the wild forests, and the crisp, untainted air had always been a source of strength to James. After driving for twenty-five miles, he pulled over at one of the lookouts and parked the Bronco next to a minivan filled with a vacationing family from Ohio.

He walked to the edge, leaned on the iron rail, and inhaled the scents of spring. The trees were covered with plump buds or newly unfurled leaves, highlighted by dappled sunlight. Everywhere he looked there was a glow of verdant green that only existed at the end of April.

A red-tailed hawk circled overhead and as James watched the raptor adjust its wings to a draft of wind, the bird cried out with a hunter's primeval call.

"This is God's Country," the mother from the minivan spoke to her children breathlessly. James couldn't agree more. He got back in the Bronco and spent the rest of the trip fantasizing about the trips he would take with his son. Like the family at the overlook, he wanted Eliot to see the wonders of his own region. Sure, there'd be a visit to Disneyland too, but it was important to James to foster a sense of state pride in his child and he couldn't imagine a better way to do that than to embark on a series of road trips.

On the other hand, the idea of pitching tents and spending the night in a bug-infested woods didn't appeal to James. Though he hated to admit it, he'd grown rather soft now that he'd entered his middle years and wondered how he could create the intimacy of the camping environment without actually having to resort to sleeping bags, canned food, and the absence of a morning shower.

"Jane will come up with a plan," he said with confidence and then realized that he had included her in his vacation fantasies. Over the past few months, he'd spent every weekend and several weeknights with his ex-wife, but they'd never been alone. Eliot was always present and often, Jackson and Milla were too. James' normally irascible father melted like a pat of butter in the frying pan anytime he was with his grandson and Milla was in danger of spoiling the child completely. She never stopped by the house empty-handed and should Eliot visit her store, Quincy's Whimsies, he was allowed to pick out any candy he wanted from the bulk bins. Eliot knew, for the price of a kiss and a hug, he could procure more sugar than his mother would allow over the course of a week.

At first, Jane smiled indulgently. She had longed for a loving reception from James' family when it came to her only child, but she didn't want Eliot's new grandpare~ become overindulgent. After holdi.

tongue for a month, Jane convinced Milla to settle for giving Eliot two pieces of candy instead of twenty and begged the older woman to ease off on the gift giving unless it was a special occasion. Milla had respectfully promised to obey Eliot's mother, but James knew full well that she slipped Eliot little treats on the sly. Fortunately, Eliot seemed more interested in spending time with his grandparents than in garnering material goods, and since he was a very well-mannered little boy, James decided not to tell Jane about Milla's infractions.

All in all, James and Jane were united when it came to the manner in which they would raise their son. Intent on molding a person of strong character, they had spent several long evenings agreeing on a set of rules for Eliot to obey in both of their homes. The discussions had gone smoothly and James had told his ex more than once that he was extremely impressed by her mothering skills. Jane had blushed at the praise, her pretty face — now fuller and rounder than it had been when they were married — tinged pink with pleasure.

Thinking of her now, James experienced a powerful and unexpected wave of lust. As their friendship had been renewed, reminding James of the year they'd dated before becoming engaged, he recalled all the reasons he'd proposed in the first place. He loved her sense of humor and quick wit, and he enjoyed being able to discuss books with her. Now, however, he felt the desire to touch her as well. Every time he saw Jane he wanted to kiss her. On the lips, the neck, the soft skin on her shoulder.

James knew such feelings would complicate their lives but he couldn't help himself. Jane was no longer the skinny, angular woman he'd wed, but a curvy, soft, and enticing woman of forty. She was growing out her layered bob and now it hung in thick waves of lustrous walnut-brown to her shoulders. How James longed to stroke that hair, to touch the silky locks and then slide his hand down the nape of her lovely neck. Her body, once familiar to him, was now intriguing new territory. One that he was hungry to explore.

"Stop it!" he chided his stimulated libido. "I'm supposed to be focusing on plants!"

But even as he wandered through the rows and rows of vibrant blooms at Lowe's, he tried to recall which flowers Jane preferred. Eliot loved the color yellow, so James selected a flat of daffodils to plant alongside the front walkway. He noticed that Jane often wore a lavender sweater set. In hopes of pleasing her, he picked out a flat of light purple phlox. He skipped the tulips, knowing the deer that routinely meandered through his property would make a quick meal of the bright red and orange flowers. In fact, the Master Gardener on last night's television program had also listed skunks, squirrels, mice, rats, and voles as tulip destroyers and James assumed that his spacious lot harbored these creatures in droves. Instead, he selected a few bleeding hearts for the corner of the porch bed that remained in partial shade, and pushed his loaded cart to the checkout counter.

When the sales associate rang up his purchase and the total flashed upon the register screen, James nearly passed out.

"That's *with* the coupons?" he asked shrilly.

The young woman didn't bother to look up from the register. "Yep. If you're using a credit card, you can slide it now, sir."

Outside, he carefully examined his receipt and saw that the sale had been tendered correctly.

"I wanted my own house," James muttered as he transferred his purchases into the Bronco. "I wanted independence and privacy and to own something other than a bunch of dog-eared paperbacks and comic books. I agreed to humbly accept all the gripes and grievances that go with home ownership. Well, here's a big, fat gripe. Plants cost *way* too much money."

His bright mood a bit dampened by the morning's expenditure, James decided to return home for lunch instead of treating himself to a burger and fries.

I'll have to save for years to afford a vacation for three to Disneyland, James thought sourly. It wasn't as though his bank account grew larger with each paycheck. After all, librarians weren't exactly in the upper echelons of the salary scale and there were always so many bills to pay.

Driving home, James reflected that he had earned a great deal more money as an English professor. He could always return to that field, but such a change could mean moving farther away from Eliot and Jane, his friends and family, and his beloved library.

"No. Quincy's Gap is my home. I'll just have to find ways to trim costs wherever I can," he declared.

James' spirits were eventually restored by a lunch of salami and cheese on sourdough, Granny Smith apple slices, and a generous handful of cheese doodles. Following this feast of comfort foods, he spent the afternoon cleaning leaves and dried stalks from the garden beds, planting his new flowers, and spreading hardwood mulch. Singing along to the local country music station, James delighted in his outdoor work. He didn't mind that his job at the library kept him inside five days a week, but during his time off, he liked nothing better than to walk around his property and make a list of chores that needed to be done over the weekend, eyeing his little yellow house with pride.

"I practically had to chase after you with the danged chain saw to get you to mow the lawn when you were a boy," Jackson had crossly remarked one evening as James described how much he enjoyed yard work. "And *now* look at you! Mr. John Deere himself."

"Don't badger him, dear," Milla had chided. "He still drives to our place to cut the lawn twice a month. You should count your blessings that you have such a fine son."

Jackson had made a noise somewhere between a snort and a huff and had quickly returned his focus to the pot roast James had made.

This evening, James didn't have to concern himself with cooking, as it was the

Henry Family Pizza Night. He was relieved too, because he was feeling the results of an afternoon of physical labor in his lower back and in his hamstrings as well. He also imagined that Jane would be worn out from the drive back from Nashville. The idea of sitting down to a casual supper was sure to appeal to her and James went to extra lengths to tidy up the house before her arrival.

For months, the only pizza place that would deliver to Quincy's Gap was Papa John's. James liked their pizza just fine, but ever since Luigi's Pizzeria had opened two doors down from Quincy's Whimsies, James had felt obliged to patronize Milla's new business neighbor. Besides, Luigi had six children to feed, a fact which he repeated to his customers at every opportunity. Just thinking of the photo of the half-dozen, dark-eyed and adorable kids tacked behind Luigi's cash register made James feel doubly compelled to order any Italian food exclusively from the eatery.

"AH HA!" Luigi shouted when James phoned to place his order. "THE PROFESSOR IS CALLING FOR TWO PEPPERONI AND SAUSAGE PIES AND A CAESAR SALAD, NO?"

James smiled. Luigi didn't seem capable

of calm speech. Everything he said came out as an exuberant yell. One day, he'd reprimanded James for being too soft-spoken on the phone. "I CANNOT HEAR YOUR MUMBLES, MR. LIBRARIAN!" Luigi had hollered.

"I'm calling from the library," James had answered in defense. "I'm accustomed to talking quietly."

"I'VE GOT SIX KIDS, PROFESSOR! THERE IS *NO* QUIET IN MY LIFE, CAPICHE?"

"Yes, Luigi," James now informed the boisterous proprietor using a raised voice. "Can you have the order delivered to my house around six o'clock?"

"CERTAINLY!" Luigi screamed and hung up.

James had just showered and put on a pair of loose-fitting chinos and a long-sleeved collared polo shirt when he heard Eliot's impatient footsteps on the front porch.

"Daddy!" he cried, his freckled nose wrinkling in delight.

James knelt down and opened his arms wide. Eliot flew against his father's chest, permitting a longer embrace than usual. James smelled the aromas of childhood on the boy: fresh grass, Ivory soap, Johnson's Baby Shampoo, and the promise of things to come.

"Did you have a nice time in Nashville?" James asked, reluctantly releasing the squirming child.

Once freed, Eliot stepped aside and commanded, "Say hi to Mommy first."

Smiling, James reached out to Jane and she hugged him and gave him a kiss on the cheek. "We missed you," she said warmly, her eyes echoing the sincerity of the statement. She was wearing her lavender sweater set.

"Five days never seemed so long," James answered and was unable to say more as Eliot demanded his full attention from then on. The four-year-old prattled on and on about his grandparent's house, the day spent at the zoo, the tour of the Grand Ole Opry (which he referred to as the place where the cowboys sang), getting to meet Fay Sunray (whoever she was), and the set of wings he was given by the pilot of their "ginormously *huge* airplane."

"And Granny and Grandpa Steward have a pool! It was warm too, like a bathtub. And I have my own room in their house with tons and tons of toys!"

Jane must have noticed the fleeting expression of envy that crossed James' face. She knew he could never provide Eliot with an equitable amount of material goods or entertainment, but to her, that didn't matter. He had quickly proved to be a loving and devoted father and no amount of money would increase his desire to do right by his son.

"And how many times a day did you say, 'I wish Daddy was here'?" Jane prodded Eliot in the side.

He giggled. "A *million!*"

James shot Jane a grateful look, knowing full well she'd asked their son that question to dispel James' insecurities.

"And I can't believe how gorgeous the flower beds are!" She touched her sweater. "Those purple phlox are my favorite spring flowers. Won't it be nice to sit out on the front porch with a glass of sweet tea come summertime?"

The doorbell rang and Eliot bolted off to see who was waiting on the welcome mat. Jackson and Milla greeted their grandchild as though he'd been away for months. Milla scooped him into her arms and covered the little boy with kisses until Jackson finally intervened.

"Ease up there, Milla! The boy can't even breathe!" he grumbled with false sternness. His eyes were twinkling at the sight of his grandson.

Jane also received a warm hello from Milla, while Jackson remained polite but aloof. James knew that his father wasn't quite ready to accept Jane back without punishing her a little bit for breaking James' heart years ago. Soon after Jane resurfaced in his son's life, Jackson had solemnly counseled James not to trust her and to immediately seek legal advice regarding Eliot's custody.

James had ignored his father's suggestion, however, as Jane had never once denied James the opportunity to spend time with his son. In fact, she was the one who routinely made the drive down from Harrisonburg, where she was a professor at James Madison University, in order for the three of them to be together.

Often, while James and Eliot built Lego towers or Lincoln Log fortresses, she busied herself grading papers, enabling father and son to make the most of their time together. She and James took turns cooking, wanting to gather around the dinner table as a family whenever possible. The result of this schedule was that on weeknights, Jane had to drive home in the dark with Eliot falling asleep to the sound of a children's lullaby CD, arriving home with little time to do anything for herself. Yet she had never complained. Unlike the Jane of old, who was habitually self-centered and impatient, motherhood had softened her heart as much as it had softened her body.

"You're very different now," James had told her one night.

She'd nodded in response and covered his hand with her own. "When we were married I cared about silly things, like what car I drove and whether or not I could fit into a size six dress. I had a great guy and couldn't see you for what you were. I thought our life didn't measure up somehow. I was a fool, James. A fool who didn't understand what defines true happiness. With you and Eliot in my life, I understand the meaning of that word now."

Looking around at his enlarged family, James recalled Jane's words. He too was amazingly content and the feeling scared him a little. Suddenly, after years of being unsure of his future, his life was full of love and hope. What could he do to ensure that nothing changed?

Luigi's arrival interrupted his trepidations. "AH HA!" He boomed as his stout form filled the doorway. "I THINK YOU NO HAVE ENOUGH FOOD FOR ALL THESE PEOPLE, EH?"

James handed him some cash and received

the pizzas and Caesar salad in return. "I've got dessert if we're still hungry. Thank you, Luigi. Have a pleasant evening."

"BUT YOU NO ORDER CHEESE-CAKE FROM *ME!* I'VE GOT SIX KIDS TO FEED!"

"Goodnight!" James called out and shut the door. The adults were all trying to stifle laughs.

"What's so funny?" Eliot inquired. "Does Mr. Luigi think cheesecake is yucky?"

Jane put an arm around her son's shoulders and pivoted him toward the bathroom. "We're laughing because Luigi is what we call a loud talker. Now march down the hall and wash your hands, please."

While Eliot complied, James poured cold bottles of beer into chilled pint glasses. Jane placed slices of pizza on the plastic red and white-checkered plates she'd found at Target and were held in reserve for the Henry Family Pizza Night. Milla distributed napkins and forks for the salad. These tasks were completed over an endless stream of female chatter and by the time Eliot joined his family at the table, his plate had been filled and a glass of cold milk rested on top of his napkin.

After clinking pint glasses together in a toast, everyone tucked into their food. The pizza had a thin, crisp crust, mounds of melted cheese, and tender pieces of pepperoni and sausage. It was perfection.

"I *love* pizza night," James declared after swallowing a bite of crust. At that moment, he looked across the table at Eliot in order to illicit his son's agreement, but Eliot hadn't eaten a bite. Instead, he was performing surgery on his pizza, removing the round, greasy discs of pepperoni and the lumps of brown sausage while trying to keep the cheese intact.

"What are you doing, buddy?" James questioned. "Is there something wrong with your meal?"

Eliot shrugged, but didn't say a word.

Jane frowned and laid down her own slice. "Your father asked you a question, mister."

Tears sprang to Eliot's eyes and though he fought against them, his effort failed and two little rivulets slipped down his cheeks. With trembling lips, he cried, "May I be excused?" and without waiting for permission, scrambled off his chair and ran down the hall. The stunned adults heard the door to his room slam.

"What in Heaven's Name . . . ?" Milla started to rise.

"I'll go," James assured his family. "Please, eat. The pizza will get cold."

Though he was as flummoxed as the rest of them by Eliot's outburst, James was secretly glad to have the opportunity to listen to his son's troubles and provide comfort if possible. Knocking respectfully on the door, James did not wait to be invited in. After all, his son was four years old and too young to merit privacy.

"What's going on, Eliot?"

The boy, who had been lying facedown on his bed, rolled over and sniffed. "I don't want to eat meat anymore, Daddy. Are you gonna make me?"

James had not expected this statement. He was so surprised by Eliot's confession that he had no idea how to reply. "Um, I don't know. Why don't you want to eat meat? You've always eaten it before."

Clearly relieved that his father planned to calmly listen to his reasons, Eliot sat up completely. "Fay Sunray never eats it. She says it's mean to kill animals for food." His eyes threatened to spill over again. "I don't want cows to die so I can have a Happy Meal."

Oh boy, James thought. He was absolutely unprepared to handle the current scenario. *Maybe I should have ordered* Idiot's Guide's to Parenting *for the library,* he mourned. To stall for time, he said, "Can you tell me about Fay Sunray? I don't know her."

"She's on TV," Eliot replied, his expression quickly morphing from despair to adulation. "She sings, and shows us yoga, and explains how to take care of the earth and stuff."

"And she's the one you saw perform when you were in Nashville, right?"

Eliot bounced a little bit on the bed. "Yeah! We went last night. It was *awesome!*"

"I'm sure it was, son." James looked around the room. "Do you have a Fay Sunray book or movie or something I could look at? I'd like to get to know her better."

"Mom bought me the movie, but it hasn't come in the mail yet." Eliot had been greatly cheered by discussing the entertainer. "So I'm not in trouble?"

"No, you're not in trouble," James reassured the boy. "Come back to the table and I'll make you a grilled cheese, okay? We're going to talk about this some more, but I'd like to tell your mother what you told me first."

Shifting nervously, Eliot gave James his most plaintive look. "But she might not like it. Do you have to?"

James nodded solemnly. "Yes I do. Your mother and I are a team, remember? Different houses, same rules."

Eliot stuck his bottom lip out, mustering up the kind of drama favored by the very young. "I wish we had just *one* house. I wish we could be together all the time!"

Surprised by his son's yearning, James put his hand on Eliot's back and gently pushed him toward the door. "You can never tell what the future will bring, kiddo. You can never tell."

THREE:
CHOCOLATE ICED GLAZED DOUGHNUT

Grams of
Sugar
21

Come Monday morning, James was still reeling over his son's decision to become a vegetarian. At a quarter to nine, he unlocked the library's front doors, rolled the cart of sale books gathered by the Friends of the Library out of the supply closet and into the lobby, flipped on the main light switch, and booted up all twenty computers. While the machines hummed and blipped into life, James made a beeline for the parenting books and began to scan the shelves. He was foolishly hoping to find a quick and easy answer on how to handle Eliot's request.

James selected several books with chapters on children and eating, but after reading several paragraphs on how parents should give their progeny a choice about what they'd like to eat before each meal, he began to grow frustrated. James planned dinners ahead of time. He didn't wait to ask Eliot what he was in the mood to eat. He just cooked the boy the same food he was eating and served him a plateful.

He wondered if he'd been handling dinnertime incorrectly. After all, he was fairly new to parenting and had decided to follow the same rules and guidelines established by his parents. But the book in his hands discouraged such old-fashioned child rearing methods.

"You should encourage a child's natural curiosity about foods by providing a colorful plate. Shape their food until it looks fun to eat! For example, you could create a vegetable pizza with a face made of broccoli and mushrooms or use a cookie cutter to encourage your kids to eat a heart-shaped tuna and sprout sandwich. Sometimes children don't like different foods to touch on the plate. Try serving them meals in a Japanese-style divided box or three, colorful bowls," one psychiatrist advised. "If a child still resists sampling something on his plate, you should respect his wishes and take the unappealing food away. Respect and dignity are an integral part of the parent-child relationship."

James chuckled ruefully. "I'd like to read that paragraph to Pop. He'd uncap his pen and write this PhD a scathing letter about how parents are meant to be benevolent dictators and kids are meant to be polite and obedient, not the other way around. I can't even imagine what he'd think about the recommendation to serve Eliot's dinner in a Japanese box!"

In fact, Jackson had given James his own parenting advice a few weeks ago. "You be sure to do the right thing by Eliot," his father had told him. "Don't be too soft. He won't grow into a man if you're a lily-livered father. Draw the line and give him hell when he crosses it. That's what makes a man. Not these long-winded reasons why he can't do this or shouldn't do that. You say, 'because I said so,' and leave it at that. Worked for you and millions of kids before you."

It had taken all Jackson's willpower to remain silent on his grandson's decision to become a vegetarian. He merely shook his head with wonder and gave James a look that said, "You'd better nip this one in the bud."

Jane had also been nonplussed by her son's determination to change his diet. Once Eliot was asleep in James' house and she had driven back to Harrisonburg, she and James had spoken on the phone until late in the night and had decided not to act until they'd each done some research on the nutritional effects of vegetarianism on such a young child.

Tired as he was, James had been unable to fall asleep afterward and so he perused the hypnotherapy brochure until he could practically recite the content verbatim.

"At least I'm prepared for my afternoon session with Harmony," James murmured as he examined another parenting book. "Because I'm not finding an ounce of practical advice on how to handle this situation with Eliot."

At the sound of someone clearing his throat, James pivoted to his left and looked up. Scott Fitzgerald, one half of the well-liked twin brother team working at the library, wore a solemn expression.

"Good morning, Professor." Scott spoke in his "business hours" whisper, though no patrons had entered the building yet.

Francis Fitzgerald stepped around the corner of the stacks and stood shoulder-to-shoulder next to his long and lanky brother.

Running a hand through waves of untamed brown curls, he nodded a sedate hello. Silently, the twins exchanged worried glances and then, as though they had rehearsed the movement in a mirror, each young man reached up to push his tortoise shell glasses farther up the bridge of his nose. If their expressions hadn't been so lugubrious, James would have found the synchronized gesture amusing, but he recognized the signs of impending trouble in the fidgety postures of his two employees.

"Gentlemen. There appears to be a problem." He smiled at the brothers, letting his fondness for them show through his eyes. "We've tackled some tough challenges before, so let me know what we're dealing with and we'll come up with a plan."

Shoulders slumping slightly in relief, Scott held out a sealed envelope. "This is for you. It's from Mrs. Waxman."

James raised his brows in surprise. He certainly hadn't expected an issue to arise around his former middle school teacher. Mrs. Waxman was his only part-time employee. She worked weekday evenings and every Saturday, managing the library as efficiently as she'd once run her classroom. A few months ago, James had become aware that Mrs. Waxman was moving slower and looking more fatigued than she had in the past. She was nearly his father's age and because he was worried that she might be overdoing it by working so many hours, he'd asked her if she'd like to cut back.

"This is my home," she'd responded with heat, waving her arm around the library. "I love this job. No, I do *not* want fewer hours!"

That was the end of the matter as far as James was concerned. Mrs. Waxman knew her limits and since he felt exactly as she did about their work, he'd accepted her answer without argument. But now, as he tore open the letter and digested the first few lines, he saw that even though Mrs. Waxman would never retire by choice, circumstance was now forcing her to do just that.

According to the letter, her younger sister had recently been widowed and was having a difficult time caring for herself due to some complicated health issues. After giving the matter much thought, Mrs. Waxman had come to the decision to move into her sister's condo in Phoenix.

"Therefore, it is with no small measure of regret nor shortage of gratitude that I tender my resignation. This is my official two-week notice," she'd written in her tidy script. "It has been an honor and a joy to work as an employee for the Shenandoah County Library and to share these wonderful years with Francis and Scott and with you, James Henry. For those who believe library work is dull, they have never had the privilege of working in your employ. Thank you for making my Golden Years so fulfilling. I am very proud that I had the chance to know you as a bright young boy and now as a fine man, community leader, and father. I wish you the very best."

Mrs. Waxman's signature became blurred as James' eyes grew misty. He sniffed and simultaneously inhaled a giant breath in an attempt to gain control of his emotions. Folding the letter into a small rectangle, he avoided looking at the twins for a moment in order to fully collect himself.

"What's that song our local Brownie Troop sings at the end of their monthly meetings?" he asked the brothers. "The one about friendship?"

The twins answered in perfect unison. Without the slightest hint of shyness, their bass voices lifted together in song, " 'Make new friends, but keep the old. One is silver and the other gold.' "

James nodded. "That's it. Let's look at this as an opportunity to make a new friend while keeping in touch with an old one. I'll put an ad in the paper first thing. We only have two weeks to find someone to meet our high standards." The brothers didn't seem overly cheered by the idea of a new employee. "You two know as well as anyone how much I dislike change. But the biggest surprise of my life, finding out that I had a son, was also the most wonderful. Who knows? Your new coworker might just be a sci-fi loving, video-game playing bibliophile. She might even be your age. That wouldn't be so horrible, would it?"

As he was already dating Milla's business partner, Willow Singletary, Francis just shrugged, but Scott instantly brightened. "You raise an excellent point, Professor! We have the chance of a lifetime to pick the perfect coworker. Can you put all the requirements you just mentioned in the classified ad?"

James swatted the younger man with a parenting book and all three moved off to begin their daily duties.

After prepping the coffee machine in the break room, James pushed the brew button and went into his office to compose an ad for a part-time librarian.

"Wanted. Part-time library assistant," he spoke to the empty room. He paused, sharpened his pencil, and resumed. "Must be available weeknights from 5 to 8:30 p.m. and Saturdays from 9 a.m. to 6 p.m. High school diploma required. Customer service and computer experience a plus." Placing the eraser nub against his lips, James hesitated again. "How can I say that the suitable candidate should love books, be able to tolerate even the most aggravating patrons with courtesy, and be prepared to soothe anxious toddlers and tangle with surly teenagers? How can I say that each book must be treated like a crown jewel and though the salary isn't very high, it is worth every meager cent to be able to serve the public as we librarians have served them for hundreds of years? The ad would cost a small fortune if I could ask for what I truly wanted!" James tossed the pencil down and sighed.

He then picked up the phone and dialed the main number of the *Shenandoah Star Ledger.* "I'd like to place a classified ad," he told the woman on the other end of the line. When she gave him the go-ahead, he dictated the words and then added a line saying that any interested candidates should phone him for an interview.

"So have you heard the big news, Professor Henry?" the young woman asked breathlessly after their business was concluded.

"Apparently not," James replied pleasantly.

"Your famous ex-girlfriend is back!"

Frown lines furrowed across his brow. "What do you mean? Has she released another book so soon?" He struggled to recall if the library had received a postcard similar to the one he'd been mailed at his father's address announcing the debut of Murphy Alistair's thrilling mystery, *The Body in the Bakery*.

"Not yet. I think the sequel comes out a week before Christmas. But she'll be able to tell you all about her future bestseller in person."

James knew he was being baited, but he couldn't stop himself from asking, "And why would that be the case? I thought she spent most of her time in New York or *on tour?*"

"Not anymore! She's come back to Quincy's Gap!" The girl shouted in triumph. "In fact, she bought *The Star*! She's moved into one of those big old houses off Main Street and is working on her third book. A celebrity! And now she owns the paper where she used to work! Can you believe it?"

The news hit James like a punch in the

gut. It was bad enough that his former flame had written a novel portraying him and the rest of the supper club group as fat and goofy amateur sleuths, bumbling their way through a small-town murder investigation. Whether out of spite for having been dumped by James or merely for the sake of comic exaggeration, his character was especially inept and spineless. Though he'd refused to read the book himself, he'd heard more than enough about it from friends and library patrons to be angry and embarrassed by his fictionalized persona.

"Professor?" The young woman's voice penetrated his unpleasant reverie. "Are you there?"

"Please place the ad as soon as possible," James answered as though he hadn't heard the unpleasant announcement that his ex-girlfriend, local reporter-turned-celebrity novelist, had returned to stir up more strife. "Thank you and have a nice day."

James hung up the phone and walked over to his window. He let his eyes rest on the brilliant green hue of the spring grass bordering the tidy sidewalk and then lifted his gaze toward the parking lot, as though Murphy Alistair was sitting out there in her car, plotting the next chapter in which she would make certain to depict him as a corpulent fool once again.

"Why did she come back?" he asked the pink dogwood blossoms at the edge of his vision. "Half the town hates her because of how she described them in her book." On the other hand, he had to admit that many citizens were pleased with Murphy, citing her novel as the reason so many tourists had flocked to Quincy's Gap over the course of the year. In fact, the number of visitors had nearly doubled, bringing much-needed income to small-business owners. Milla had told James several times that she'd made sales to tourists who'd asked her numerous questions about the "real" people described in *The Body in the Bakery*. Of course, Milla always tactfully replied that she hadn't been around when the actual events occurred, so she couldn't attest to the truth of Ms. Alistair's version.

James turned away from the window and strode out to the circulation desk, his fists balled in irritation. The morning had gone from bad to worse. First, Eliot's declaration, then Mrs. Waxman's unexpected retirement, and now, the return of a troublesome ex-girlfriend.

"Are you okay, Professor?" Francis asked as he passed by with the shelving cart.

A hunger pang awoke in James' belly and

he looked at his watch without really noticing the time. "Hold the fort, Francis. I'll be right back."

"Aye, aye, Captain!" Francis saluted and gave the cart a mighty heave toward the open space where patrons lined up to wait for assistance checking out. Scott darted from behind the Information desk and deftly caught the cart. In a continuous and fluid motion he pushed it toward the Children's Corner while giving his brother a thumbs-up behind his back.

James never left the library during the morning. Occasionally, he'd meet one of the supper club members for a casual lunch at Dolly's Diner or he'd eat a sandwich in the Bronco while running a few quick errands, but he and the twins had a system for handling midmorning coffee breaks. James would brew the coffee around ten o'clock, as he had this morning, and then he'd take a mug into his office to review emails or complete necessary paperwork, such as balancing the budget or placing orders to the library supply company. When he reappeared at the circulation desk, Scott would venture into the break room next. He'd repair a few hard-covers while bolting down a Twinkie and a cup of milky coffee or a Mountain Dew. He'd then switch off with Francis.

In this relaxed manner, all three enjoyed a leisurely morning's work. They never got behind because they all worked during this respite. No one kept track of the length of these sit-down times and no one took advantage of them.

Yet now, James Henry, Head Librarian, was blatantly leaving the building just as the coffee pot finished percolating. Knowing he was unbalancing their perfect system, he jumped into the Bronco and drove northwest to the nearest Wawa. Once inside, he filled up a Styrofoam cup with French Vanilla-flavored coffee, and selected half a dozen doughnuts from the Krispy Kreme display.

"Were these baked this morning?" James asked the clerk.

"Yessir. The truck came in at five-thirty. They were still warm enough to fog up the glass after the deliveryman unloaded them."

James pulled the bag to his chest and inhaled the scents of chocolate, cinnamon, powered sugar, baked dough, and glazed icing. "That's exactly what I wanted to hear."

Inside the privacy of the Bronco, he reached into the bag and pulled out the doughnut on top. At this point, he didn't care which of the six varieties his fingers closed around. Any one of them would do. Unhinging his jaw like a python attempting to swallow his oversized prey whole, James sank his teeth through the layer of chocolate icing and into the soft, cake-like dough. An explosion of sugar coated his teeth, gums, tongue, and the roof of his mouth. For a moment, he was completely lost in the overwhelming power of the sensation. It was heavenly. It was, he admitted silently, a total high.

It took all of forty-five seconds for James to consume the doughnut. He then licked his fingers, took a sip of coffee, and leaned back against the seat with a sigh of contentment.

"I needed that," he murmured, noting how his anxiety had drained away. He immediately felt calmer and more optimistic. Turning the engine on, James pulled out of the Wawa parking lot and headed back to Quincy's Gap. He breezed through the lobby doors as though it was completely typical for him to have left work for a doughnut run. Still, when James raised the white and green Krispy Kreme bag in the air so that Francis could see it over the head of the elderly patron he was assisting, the younger man's eyes sparkled with delight.

James placed the bag in the center of the

round table in the break room, removed a blueberry cake doughnut from the bag, and placed it on his desk blotter for later. Returning to aid the patron waiting at circulation, James looked over his shoulder and smiled as the Fitzgerald brothers circled the pastry bag like sharks, bickering good-naturedly over which treat to enjoy first.

"We'll cut them in half, bro," Scott suggested. "That way we get to try them all."

"Totally!" Francis happily agreed. "Do you think this will become a new tradition? The Monday morning sugar rush?"

After a pause in which James imagined his employee's mouth was crammed with a glazed cruller Scott said, "Nope. The professor is going to be hypnotized after work today, remember? This might be the last time we'll walk into this break room and find one of Milla's cakes or Mrs. Waxman's pies or Mrs. Goodbee's brownies."

Francis groaned. "That would be a total tragedy for us, bro." He sighed. "Well, at least we've got Willow's chocolates to eat at night."

"You got that right!" The brothers exchanged high-fives while James loaded the last two books in the Harry Potter series into a Friends of the Library canvas tote bag. "You're going to enjoy these, Mrs. Gibb."

"Oh, I *know* I will!" The old woman cackled. "I saw the boy who played the movie Harry Potter onstage in England." She lowered her voice to a conspiratorial whisper. "What a play! That boy was as naked as the day he was born! Cute little tush on him too." She patted her tote bag. "It's gonna be real hard to picture him back in the old Hogwart's robes again, but I'll do my best!"

Doing his best to hide a grin, James set to work on the hold and transfer requests until Scott reappeared from the break room. His upper lip was lined with chocolate frosting and a sprinkling of powdered sugar covered the front of his navy polo shirt.

"I don't know how you're going to live without it, Professor. Sugar, I mean. All the best-tasting food is filled with loads of sugar or loads of salt. Your giving that up would be like Francis and me being hypnotized to lose our love of video games."

James indicated his protruding belly. "But video games aren't bad for your health. Being sedentary is, yes, but you boys get plenty of exercise. I need to do this so I can live a fuller life with my son."

Scott nodded. "For what it's worth, Francis and I think it's really cool of you to give this alternative treatment a shot." He fell silent for a moment and then began brushing the flecks of sugar from his shirt. "You've given me something to think about too. Maybe I'm not living a full life either. Francis has been spending more and more time with Willow and they're super happy together. I think they might be the real deal. But me? I waste countless hours trying to complete missions with a bunch of online friends I've never met face-to-face."

"It's a hobby. I don't see any harm in that," James replied kindly, but Scott remained rather distressed.

"But life's about making connections," Scott continued. "For example, there's this person I team up with every night. She even lives around here somewhere, because her User ID is Shenandoah Shutterfly. For an entire year we've sent instant messages about all kinds of stuff, but I don't even know her name."

"Can't you just ask?" James inquired.

Scott shook his head. "That would be poor gaming etiquette, Professor. We're all on there pretending to be brawny barbarians or powerful mages. For example, I've never told anyone I'm a librarian. I've got to stay in character. When I'm playing I become Fitz the Fierce!" He brandished his right arm as though it held a sword.

"Excuse me, Fitz the Fierce," a middle-aged man carrying a thumb drive interrupted. "Could you help me with the computer? I keep on tryin' to open a file and the danged thing won't let me."

Smiling, Scott jutted his arm forward again. "Lead the way, sir. No stubborn Word doc or paltry PDF can withstand the lightning-quick fingers of Fritz the Fierce!"

Between the chocolate-glazed Krispy Kreme and Scott's playacting, James discovered that his bad mood had been wiped away like the powdered sugar from his employee's shirt.

James opened the blue front door of A Better State of Mind's office at half past five that afternoon. He was too nervous to read the selection of magazines stacked on the end table, so he merely sat on the sofa and stared at the bowl of purple crocuses on the credenza near the door.

Skye appeared a few minutes later, carrying a CD in her hand. "Hello, Mr. Henry. Would you like to settle up before your session begins?"

"Sure." James pulled out his wallet and handed Skye a credit card. "Is my friend

70

Bennett in there now?"

"No. He switched appointments with Ms. Perez. She and Harmony have just finished, actually. I just need to label your friend's nighttime CD and then it'll be your turn." She smiled in encouragement.

"I guess you hear many interesting things working this job," James remarked as Skye ran his credit card.

She swiveled abruptly in her chair, her eyes stormy. "I don't listen in on Harmony's sessions, Mr. Henry! They are strictly confidential!"

"Of course! I didn't mean to imply . . ." he trailed off, feeling moronic. He was relieved to hear the sound of Lindy's voice. She called out "thank you," from farther down the hall and when she entered the reception room, she seemed calm and slightly groggy. "How was it?" he whispered anxiously to her.

"Great." Lindy's voice was soft and relaxed. "I feel like I had a long nap, but I heard every word Harmony said." She touched James on the arm. "You're gonna be just fine."

Lindy collected her CD from Skye, and James noticed that his friend continued to speak using a slow, sleepy voice, as though her tongue could not move any faster.

James would have liked to ask Lindy more questions but Harmony glided down the hall. Smiling, she greeted him and asked him to follow her. After giving Lindy a nervous wave, he walked down the hall and into a dimly lit room. As his eyes adjusted, he noticed that a large indigo sofa and a beige recliner took up most of the space. Several small lamps sat on side tables covered with butter yellow cloths. Watercolors of lush gardens hung in a set of three above the sofa, and a pair of midnight blue curtains covered the room's large picture window.

Expecting he'd be lying on the sofa, James was just about to stretch out when Harmony gestured toward the recliner. "Clients are usually most comfortable in the recliner."

As soon as James sat down, he began to relax. He pushed against the chair back and the footrest gently popped up. Harmony reached into a nearby cabinet and removed a cotton throw. She handed it to James. "I keep it a little chilly in here. If you're under a blanket, it helps your body believe that it's rest time."

The blanket smelled of lavender and laundry detergent. James spread it over his legs and wriggled farther into the chair's yielding cushion. Harmony switched on her

CD player and the sounds of instruments and wind chimes piped through the speakers. It wasn't exactly music, as there wasn't a clear melody, but the noises were very tranquil. James recognized the sounds of flutes, running water, and occasionally, the chirping of birds and the gentle clanging of a small metal gong. The overall effect was the feeling of being at repose in some isolated Japanese garden.

"Let's begin by taking several deep breaths." Harmony said. "Breathe in through the nose and out the mouth. One. That's good. Two. Annnnd, three." She smiled as though James had accomplished a great feat. "Well done. Now, if you feel comfortable, go ahead and close your eyes."

James was delighted to oblige. Suddenly, the idea of spending an hour in the recliner, listening to the soothing music and Harmony's melodious voice had become very attractive.

"I'd like you to allow your body to become *very* heavy," Harmony directed quietly. "Your muscles are going to relax. Your body doesn't have to work any more. Imagine instead that you're on a lounge chair by a pool or perhaps by the ocean. There is a gentle breeze blowing across your face and you feel very warm and *very* relaxed."

Snuggled in his blanket, James did feel warm. He gave his shoulders leave to sink farther into the chair cushion.

"Now imagine a current of warm air flowing down your body starting with the top of your head. As it moves down your face, to your neck and your shoulders, you can feel any tension, any stresses or worries that you might have walked in with today just melt away."

For a moment, his concerns about Eliot, finding a replacement for Mrs. Waxman, and Murphy's return flitted through his mind, but he turned away from those thoughts and centered his attention on the vision of a sparkling ocean lined by a pristine white beach and a few stands of palm trees.

"Now the warm, gentle flow of air moves down your arms and down each and every finger. It flows across your chest, over your stomach, over your lower back and your hips, and down each leg. As it moves you feel more and more *relaxed,* while your mind stays focused on the sound of my voice." She inhaled deeply. "And now, as that air moves over your calves and your feet, let any impurities or anxieties flow out with it through your toes. Let your body rest. It feels *very* heavy in the chair, but your mind is very clear; it is actually at a heightened state of awareness."

It was true. James felt as though he had never possessed such mental focus before. He was certain that, if asked, he could suddenly solve complex mathematical algorithms or balance the library budget without a calculator. He believed he could recite every Shakespearean soliloquy he had made his students memorize when he'd been a college professor.

"Take your mind to that pool you've been sitting beside," Harmony continued in her lulling voice. "There's a set of steps leading down to the pool. The water is very warm and inviting and there's a floating lounge chair waiting for you. Try to picture this peaceful place in your mind. Nod if you can see it."

James nodded.

"Okay, now you're going to walk down those steps slowly, one at a time, as I count backward from ten. With every step, your body is going to become *more* and *more* relaxed. Ten . . . nine . . . eight . . . seven . . . six . . . five . . . four . . . three . . . two . . . one. You can rest on that float now, James."

He could practically hear the water lapping at the side of the pool. The sun bathed him with its gentle, nourishing rays and the faintest of breezes cooled his heated skin. It was paradise.

"James." Harmony's voice drifted to him across the pool. "I want you to ask your mind to give up this craving for sugar. I want you to pretend that your mind looks like the inside of a control center. I want you to climb up a ladder into the middle of that control center."

Reluctantly, James switched his visual away from the pool and focused on a wooden ladder.

"You're going to climb up into a room. It's filled with lots and lots of lights. There are lights of every color and there are switches all around you. Walk around your brain's control center and observe it carefully."

Harmony was right. There were buttons and levers and switches. Rows of bare bulbs dangled from the ceiling and the whir of machinery filled the air. Despite the sense of endless industry, the room was neat and tidy.

"Look at the switch closest to you," Harmony commanded firmly. "Put both hands on the switch. This is the machine that sends your brain a message that you want to eat sugar. You're going to turn it off, James. And as you do so, tell your brain

76

that you don't want to crave sugar anymore. You're turning that craving off for good right now. Go ahead and do that, James."

Reaching both hands forward, James gripped the metal level and pushed it downward with all his might. He whispered the orders Harmony had given him to his brain and felt a surge of accomplishment rush through him as he silently and sincerely urged his mind to believe what it was being told.

Next, Harmony directed him to return to the pool. She repeated over and over that he no longer needed sugar, that he was free of his addiction to the substance, and that he'd been released from his craving. Eventually, she led him back up the stairs from the enticing water and asked him to open his eyes.

"That was amazing!" he croaked. "I saw everything as if I actually experienced it! The pool, the float, the control center. But the session was so brief. Are you sure it can work that rapidly?"

Harmony laughed lightly. "Most people lose all sense of time when they're in a highly relaxed state. How long do you think we've been in here?"

James eased himself upward and shrugged. "Twenty minutes?"

"Try fifty minutes," she answered with a smile.

"Wow," he said breathlessly. "So what happens next?"

"You must listen to your CD every night." She held his gaze. "The reinforcement is very important, James. Please don't skip any nights, especially since we've only had one session together. When I see you next Monday we'll see how things are coming along."

James collected his CD from Skye and lazily walked to his Bronco. At home, he ate a healthy meal of roasted chicken breast, green beans, and brown rice. When he opened up the freezer to get some ice cubes for his diet Dr. Pepper, he glanced at the pint of Caramel Crunch ice cream and waited for the desire to compel him to reach for the carton.

"I really don't feel like anything sweet," he stated in astonishment. He then dug out a package of Eliot's snack-sized Oreos, a bag of chocolate-chip morsels, a tin of candied pecans, and a Charleston Chew that he kept hidden in the freezer for an emergency. He examined each of the goodies for several moments, but nothing happened. He didn't want to eat any of them.

Staring at the food, James shook his head

in disbelief and, for the second time that evening, breathed out an amazed, "Wow."

FOUR:
CHICKPEA BURGER

Grams of
Sugar
11

The rest of the workweek passed quickly for James. Between the high school students researching topics for their senior projects and the flood of incoming applications for the part-time librarian position, time buzzed by quickly.

On Thursday, just as James was about to duck into his office to review the paperwork on a fresh batch of candidates, a middle-aged woman with a very long ponytail of ash-blond hair turning to gray walked up to the circulation desk. She had several rolled posters tucked under her right arm.

"I was wondering if you could hang this in the lobby right away?" she inquired with a friendly but determined air. "The Wellness Village is sponsoring a Fresh Food Festival this weekend. I know it's late to be promoting the event, but we don't have much of an advertising budget and are hoping to attract people through word-of-mouth."

James reached for the poster. "May I?"

The woman unfurled one for him and laid it gently on the counter. The central graphic showed a picnic basket overflowing with fruits, vegetables, and a loaf of bread. Each corner was embellished with drawings of a farmer's life. One showed him plowing his field, another featured him selling wares at an outdoor market, the third was a close-up of him handing a little boy a plump peach, and the final picture depicted the farmer sitting down to eat a meal with his family. James thought that the farmer bore a close resemblance to Santa Claus. The red suit had been replaced by denim overalls and a straw hat, but the man had the same kind face and laughing eyes. In addition to the date, time, and location of the event, a stream of text ran around the perimeter of the poster. It read, *Save Our Farms! Buy Fresh! Buy Local!*

James couldn't agree more. Having lived in the Shenandoah Valley most of his life, he rubbed shoulders with members of the agricultural community every day. He believed there were few individuals who worked harder or with more dedication than the farmers he had come to know in his years as head librarian.

"I'd be glad to hang this for you. In fact, if you have any extras I can assure you they'll be prominently displayed in the windows of Quincy's Whimsies and The Yuppie Puppy. Both of those proprietors support the farming community. As do I." James couldn't help but add.

"Thank you!" The woman beamed at him. "My name's Roslyn Rhodes, by the way. I'm a herbal healer and have an office in the Wellness Village." She handed him a business card. Under her name were the words, *Holistic Medicine* and the slogan, *Let Nature Heal You*. Beneath those lines her office phone numbers, address, and hours were listed. James noticed that Roslyn's Health House was right down the path from Harmony's.

For some reason, James wanted to show just how open-minded he was, so he informed Roslyn that he'd received a hypnotherapy treatment on Monday from her neighbor at A Better State of Mind.

"Good for you!" Roslyn's praise was genuine. "I've heard a great deal of positive feedback about Harmony's sessions. She's a lovely person and has been an incredible help putting this festival together." She gave a self-effacing laugh. "We flaky types aren't always in top form when it comes to organization. Ask me about any herb on the face of this green earth and I can tell you all about its properties, but ask me where my checkbook is and I'll be at a total loss!"

James walked Roslyn out to the lobby and the two of them exchanged small talk while he hung the poster. "It says here that we can eat lunch at the festival. My son has recently become a vegetarian. Will there be something else for him to eat besides farm stand fruits and vegetables?"

Roslyn nodded in excitement. "Oh, yes! There will be dozens of wonderful dishes to choose from. Trust me, I've been a vegan for fifteen years and I'm already daydreaming about all the tasty things I'll be sampling on Saturday. Your whole family is in for a treat. Come hungry, my friend."

After Roslyn left, the Fitzgerald twins wandered into the lobby to examine the poster. The two brothers consumed more food than James deemed humanly possible for individuals with such tall, lanky frames and the slightest reference to anything edible caused a glimmer to appear in their hazel eyes.

"Food festival! Sweet!" Francis declared and tried to peer around Scott's shoulder. "What kind? Greek? Italian? Lebanese? Barbeque?"

"Locally grown," Scott answered. "You know what *that* means?"

The brothers exchanged hungry grins and in perfect unison shouted, "Pie!"

Francis elbowed his brother away from the bulletin board and gazed at the poster with a dreamy expression. "Apple Brown Betty, peach crisp, pear crumble."

"Blueberry cream cheese, lemon meringue, chocolate peanut butter pie!" Scott finished the list and then turned to James. "Oops. Sorry, Professor. We didn't mean to torture you."

James gave a light-hearted shrug. "Believe it or not, I'm not drooling onto my tie. Three nights of listening to my hypnotherapy CD has really helped stop those sugar cravings."

"That's good, Professor," Francis said. "Because that's the tie we gave you for Boss' Day last year and it's dry clean only."

Looking down, James picked up the end

of his tie and gave it a shake. "I know. It's my all-time favorite. I became a librarian hoping that one day I could wear a garment that says, 'Don't Make Me Shush You!' and now I can."

Scott poked his brother in the side. "*I* wanted to get you the Librarian Drinking League tie, but Francis said Mrs. Waxman wouldn't approve."

"Probably not," James agreed with a laugh and then sighed. "I'd better get back in there and look over those applications. So far, no one's worthy of even licking Mrs. Waxman's boots, let alone filling them."

As James reviewed applications from college students in search of an easy summer job, retirees who wanted a permanent part-time position but didn't want to work the hours the position required, and a young mother who wanted the job but only if she could bring her three-month-old infant along, he began to despair.

Finally, toward the bottom of the stack, James came across a very promising application. A graduate student from U.V.A. was looking for evening and weekend hours as he had classes every weekday morning. The young man was working toward a Master's in English Literature and was not only well read, but also mentioned that he was interested in pursuing a career in public service. Feeling optimistic, James was just reaching for the phone to schedule an interview when his gaze fell on the application line reading, *Wage Sought.*

The young man had written that he needed to make a minimum of twenty-five dollars an hour to cover his cost of living.

Spluttering, James slammed the phone back into the cradle. "Where are you living? In a mansion? With a butler and a personal chef? The nerve!"

He was just warming up to his indignation when the phone rang. It was Jane calling to assure him that Eliot's pediatrician said that their son could receive all the nutrition he needed from a balanced vegetarian diet.

"As long as he's eating plenty of protein, taking his vitamins, and not subsisting on potato chips and fruit roll-ups, he'll be fine." James heard a hesitation in her voice. "The doctor also seemed to think this was merely a phase. Apparently, it's quite common for kids to experience feelings of guilt about eating animals at some point in their childhood."

"So what do we do?" James asked. "Encourage him or try to convince him that he doesn't need to feel guilty?"

"I think we should support his decision, but we need to sit down with him this weekend and explain animal husbandry a bit. I want him to realize that raising livestock or eating meat does not make a person bad."

Jane's suggestion caused an idea to form in James' mind. "Why don't we let him talk to a farmer? There's a food festival in town this weekend and a bunch of local food producers have been invited to sell their products to the public. After we give Eliot his Livestock 101 talk, we can bring him to the fair."

"Sounds good to me," Jane replied. "But James, we have to be honest with him. You and I both know that animals raised for food consumption don't always have decent lives or humane deaths. I know he's only four, but I don't want to deceive him."

James didn't like the direction in which the conversation was headed. "We're not going to tell him boldfaced lies, but I'm not going to go into detail about slaughterhouse practices either. I think we should focus on the message he got from this Fay Sunray person. I'll search around on the Internet and see if someone posted a recording of her Nashville performance. She started this whole thing, so I want to know *exactly* what she said that upset Eliot so much."

"I wish my parents could remember. Of all the times for me to have dashed off to the restroom!" Jane lamented. "I feel like I've lost my mind since he made his announcement during dinner. I wouldn't be so worried if my friends at work hadn't freaked me out by recommending family therapy and links to a dozen parenting websites." She grew quiet for a moment. "I've never second-guessed my maternal instincts until now. I don't like feeling so uncertain, James. Like I'm going to emotionally scar this kid if I don't handle this situation perfectly."

Though James knew precisely how Jane felt, he also suspected they were both overreacting. "First of all, we won't be perfect parents and that's fine. Eliot doesn't need perfection. He needs the love and guidance you've been giving him since birth. Secondly, I've been perusing quite a few parenting books in my spare time. If these people had their way, the three of us would be in therapy until Eliot has a family of his own! Don't buy into this insanity. Stick to your instincts — you, *we* will figure out what's best for our son."

"There's something else you should know," Jane added reluctantly. "Eliot's been having nightmares about dead animals. Someone played a really cruel practical joke on us before we left for Nashville and it's affected him more than I'd realized."

James brushed aside the pile of job applications and sat forward in his chair. "What kind of joke?"

Clearly, Jane was reluctant to speak of it, but after some coaxing she gave in. "Someone put a dead robin in our mailbox. Probably a disgruntled student. You remember what it was like during midterm exams. Between all the overnight cram sessions and cans of Red Bull, the kids can lose their heads. Didn't a freshman student vandalize your car with shaving cream?"

Recalling the words, "Professor Puff Sucks!" written across his windshield as though it were yesterday, James muttered something unintelligible.

"Unfortunately, Eliot was expecting his *Big Backyards* magazine and so he ended up opening the mailbox," Jane continued. "The bird was way in the back, but when he pulled out the magazine and the usual stack of junk mail, the body fell right on his chest. I've never heard such a scream."

James shook his head in dismay. "Poor little guy. That would have spooked most adults."

"I know, but after Fay Sunray's comments about animals, whatever they were, I think Eliot now has this illogical fear that they'll come after him if he eats them." She made a growling noise. "You know, if I had a backstage pass to the next Fay Sunray Show I'd choke her with her own guitar strings. Child entertainers should leave their personal platforms out of their performances. I don't care how noble the cause!"

The parents discussed their son's meal selections for the weekend and then said their goodbyes. James stuck the sheaf of job applications into a folder, dropped it into his desk drawer, and sighed.

Change is never easy, he thought.

That night, he had his own frightening dream about birds. These were not robins, like the stiff red and blue body Eliot pulled from the mailbox, but black crows with malicious eyes and sharp, hooked beaks. Gathered on a leafless tree at the far end of the front yard, they suddenly flew at him en masse, forming an ominous cloud of shadows and feathers. Their caws grew louder and more aggressive as they raced toward him through the purple night sky. James' dream self darted inside his house and slammed the front door. Terrified, he scuttled down the hallway to his bedroom, hoping to draw the curtains before the crows could reach his window, but just as his fingers closed on the cotton drapes, the impact of a dozen beaks smashing into the glass made him cry out in terror.

James bolted awake in his bed, his heart drumming in his chest. He glanced nervously at the window, but exhaled in relief as he realized the rapping on the glass was merely raindrops and not a murder of hostile crows.

The spring storm persisted for most of Friday, but by Saturday morning, the sun was bathing the Shenandoah Valley in warmth. The flowers James had planted the week before had produced new buds and were inviting the attentions of honeybees, monarch butterflies, and hummingbirds. Squirrels chattered at him from their nests in the dogwood tree while he swept the front walk and raked stray leaves and pine needles from the lush grass.

After his outdoor chores were done, James took a shower and settled in front of the computer with a large glass of iced tea. He went to YouTube's homepage and searched for Fay Sunray, clicked on one of her videos entitled, "We Love Our Earth," and sat back to watch. Fay had golden hair styled in pigtail braids and large, bright blue eyes.

She was in her late twenties, but sang with a very high and girlish voice. She wore a navy dress covered with sunflower designs and a pair of green galoshes. As she sang about recycling and water conservation, a group of flower puppets with smiling faces provided background vocals.

"Nothing offensive there," James mused. "She seems pretty and sweet. The little boys probably all have crushes on her." He scrolled farther down the page. "I've got to find a link to that Nashville show."

James sat through several videos but heard nothing untoward in the verses or in the silly knock-knock jokes her sidekick, Dew Drop, liked to tell.

Finally, he clicked on a video for the song, "Animals Are Our Friends (Nashville Version)" and listened closely as people dressed in a variety of farm animal costumes sang along with Fay. The song was clearly one of the children's favorites and whenever the entertainer pointed the microphone at the audience, the kids shouted the appropriate animal noises at the top of their lungs. As another chorus reached a crescendo, the flower puppets James had seen on previous clips of Fay's television show popped up on stage.

"This has got to be the finale," James

tapped the mouse impatiently. He preferred shows like Sesame Street or Mr. Rogers and wished Eliot could watch old episodes of Captain Kangaroo or the Muppet Show instead of the bizarre contemporary cartoons he enjoyed. Fay Sunray was certainly a welcome throwback to the good old days of television, especially when compared to shows like SpongeBob or the Backyardigans.

As James waited, the computer screen filled with blinking lights. Rainbow-hued confetti came raining down on the Nashville stage. The animals and flowers bowed and most of them waved and wiggled off the stage to a roar of applause. However, the actors dressed in the cow, chicken, and pig costumes remained. Fay carefully laid her guitar on her stool and put an arm around the cow and the pig. The chicken snuggled up to her legs and gazed up at her with adoration.

"And remember boys and girls," she spoke melodically into her headset microphone. "Animals are our friends. We need to protect them. That's why I don't eat meat, because I don't EAT my *friends! I* am proud to be a ve-ge-ta-ri-an." Fay sang the word as she squeezed the cow, who hugged her fiercely in return as the pig nodded in agreement.

"Good night, children! Thank you for coming and remember to be kind to our planet! It's the only one we have!"

The video clip ended and James shook his head in disgust. " 'I don't eat my friends!' What kind of thing is that to say to a bunch of little kids? No wonder Eliot was influenced by this woman. He probably idolizes her and would never want to disappoint her."

For the most part, James agreed with Fay's pro-environmental messages, even though he was certain that kids between three and six-years-old had no idea what she meant by "eco-friendly measures." He'd have no issue with the pretty entertainer had she stuck to her usual montage, but he was aggrieved by how she chose to close her Nashville show and was sorely tempted to write her a letter.

He'd just begun composing an opening line in his mind when Jane and Eliot arrived.

"We had chocolate chip pancakes for breakfast! At my favorite truck stop!" Eliot shouted as he launched himself into his father's open arms. "With a strawberry mouth and bananas for eyes. And guess what the nose was?"

James scrunched up his face and pretended to be giving the matter serious consideration. "A grape?" he guessed.

"Nope!" Eliot shouted, delighted to have stumped an adult. "A cherry! Like the kind they put in Shirley Temples."

"Your mom is awfully good to you, buddy." James winked at Jane over Eliot's head. "Do you think you'll be hungry enough for lunch at the food festival?"

Eliot nodded. "Will there be cotton candy?"

Jane ruffled Eliot's hair. "Not for you, young man. You had plenty of sugar at breakfast. I'm sure there'll be some delicious, *healthy* foods for you to eat at the fair." She took James by the arm. "I only had a bowl of oatmeal, so let's head downtown. We could walk around for a bit and then grab some lunch. I could eat a hor —" she stopped herself just in time. "A humongous sandwich!"

The three of them climbed into the Bronco and drove south into town. James told Jane about the lack of suitable candidates for the part-time library position while she shared her concern about the sense of entitlement her students had begun to express during the final marking period. The former spouses reminisced on how work ethics and family values were the norms of their childhoods while Eliot amused himself by counting all the red cars he could spot.

As they approached the pink and purple cottages of the Wellness Village, James could see that the food festival had already drawn a huge crowd.

"I don't think we're going to find a parking space close by," James informed Jane. "We'll find a spot behind the ABC Store. Danny won't mind, especially if I pick up some Cutty Sark for my father before we leave."

James wasn't the only one with that idea. A mix of pickup trucks and hybrid sedans filled up most of the lot. After running into the liquor store to make a purchase and have a quick chat with Danny Leary, the proprietor, James lifted Eliot onto his shoulders, cherishing the burden of his son's weight. Jane took a picture of the pair with her cell phone camera and then the threesome jogged across the street.

The courtyard of the Wellness Village was covered by a large tent. Enticing aromas drifted into the parking lot where vendors had set up tables in order to distribute information on their health-conscious businesses or to sell wares such as reusable shopping bags, beaded jewelry, yoga equipment, or inspirational CDs. Skye waved at him from the Better State of Mind table and then focused her attention on putting a brochure into the hands of an interested passerby.

In the cool shade of the tent, James and Jane scrutinized the menus of the food vendors and debated what to select for lunch.

"All the food here is good for vegetarians," Jane told Eliot. "How does a chickpea burger and sliced peaches sound?"

Eliot curled his lip a little. "A pea burger? That's gonna taste funny."

James couldn't have said it better himself, but decided that Eliot needed to know that he couldn't subsist on French fries, pasta, and pizza as a non meat eater. "Son, being a vegetarian usually means eating lots of fruits and vegetables."

"I know," Eliot answered solemnly. "Are you going to get one, Daddy?"

Stepping closer to the sizzling patties, James thought they smelled quite good. "Yes, I am. We'll take three chickpea burgers," he informed the vendor.

"With cheese?" the man asked.

"Yes, please," James answered as Jane took Eliot to the next booth to order fruit smoothies made from locally grown produce.

The family found a free picnic table and James made several trips back and forth to the condiment counter in order to collect packets of ketchup, mustard, relish, and salt. After grabbing a few napkins and three straws, he picked up his chickpea burger and took a large bite, knowing Eliot was watching closely for an adverse reaction. But the burger was very tasty.

"Yum!" James declared honestly. "Go ahead, buddy. You'll like it."

Eliot took a tentative nibble. He chewed several times and then reached into his mouth with his thumb and index finger and pulled something out. "What's this?" he inquired.

"Eliot, don't take food out of your mouth," Jane reprimanded and then peered at the object on his plate. "That's a piece of tomato."

"Oh." Eliot examined the interior of his burger. "There's corn in here too." He squirted on another dollop of ketchup. "Doesn't taste like McDonald's, but it's okay."

The three of them ate their lunches and watched the thickening crowd. James noticed Roslyn Rhodes working her way through a knot of people. She looked utterly frazzled. Her long hair was tangled, her face was shining with perspiration, and her eyes darted around wildly.

"That's the woman who came to the library with the event posters," James told Jane.

Jane followed his gaze. "She looks a little freaked out."

In a few minutes, the reason behind her anxiety became clear. A group of grim-faced farmers barreled past, clearly following in Roslyn's wake. Concerned that Roslyn might need assistance, James darted after them.

Just outside the tent, James found Roslyn, Harmony, Skye, and two men standing on one side of a folding table while five farmers shouted at them from the other side.

"We're locals too!" one of them hollered with a clenched fist. "You only kept us out because we're livestock farmers!"

A second one slammed his hand on the table. "Your fruit-loopy friends are gonna make us lose business! It's bad enough you didn't invite us to this damned fair, but now you're tryin' to ruin our livelihood too!"

Roslyn held out her hands in supplication. "I did *not* invite those demonstrators and I do not have the authority to make them leave! They're on public property."

The man standing next to Harmony put

his arm around her in a protective gesture. James assumed he was her husband. "Gentlemen, the Wellness Village merchants decided to promote vegan and vegetarian lifestyles during this festival. It was their prerogative to make that call. No one involved with the Village is speaking against your farms, so please stop yelling at us."

The young man next to Skye who wore a tie-dye Grateful Dead shirt, frayed denim shorts, and an armful of beaded hemp bracelets, flicked a sandy-colored dreadlock off his shoulder. "Yeah. Chill out, dudes," he added.

Skye smiled at him and took his hand.

Temporarily derailed, one of the farmers glanced around as though in search of support from members of the public. He called out someone's name and a man in a purple polo shirt and tan chinos halted mid-stride and turned to face them. James recognized him. He was Ned Woodman, one of the town councilmen.

Seeing the standoff in progress, Ned pivoted away as though he hadn't heard his name shouted above the din of festival goers. More enraged than ever, the farmers darted after him and before James could offer his assistance to either group, the situation had been diffused. At least for the moment, he thought.

"Everything okay?" he asked, stepping up to the table.

Roslyn sank into a metal chair, wrapping her long hair around her hand as though her locks could offer her protection. "For now, but I'm afraid those men are too upset to behave rationally. The picketers out front . . . well, they really taunted those men."

James didn't like the sound of that. "Who are they? Animal rights demonstrators?"

Harmony nodded. "Yes. They often congregate at fairs like ours, as they are able to recruit volunteers and solicit donations from a receptive public. But it's a shame the day couldn't have been more peaceful." To change the subject, she introduced her husband Mike, and pointed at the young man standing next to Skye. "And this is Skye's boyfriend, Lennon Snyder. He's in charge of the maintenance here at the Village."

James shook hands with the men and then focused on Roslyn once again. "I'm going to give my friend Lucy a call. She's a sheriff's deputy and will know how to restore peace and order."

Roslyn and Harmony readily agreed to the suggestion and James went off to find a quiet corner behind a budding Crepe Myrtle tree. He dialed Lucy's number and was relieved when she answered on the first ring.

"I'm on my way!" she exclaimed when he'd finished relaying his concerns. "I've got Lindy with me so I'm not in uniform. We'd planned on a girls' day out, but I've got my badge and my gun, so I'll handle the situation, James. Just hold the fort until I get there."

Returning to the picnic table where Jane and Eliot waited, James hastily told his ex-wife what was going on.

"We didn't see any protestors on the way in," she stated, perplexed.

James put a hand on his son's shoulder. "They're here now. I think you two should stay put until I check things out."

Perfectly composed, Jane nodded. "No problem. We'll work on the 'Healthy Kids' activity book the smoothie lady gave us."

Thankful for her composure, James marched toward the entrance. The closer he got to the map of the Wellness Village, the more the sounds of loud chanting assaulted his ears. When the protestors came into view, James was unsurprised to find Gillian among them. She was busily writing a check while Bennett shifted uncomfortably beside her.

James took a brief glance at the posters being brandished by the picketers. They read, "Meat Is Murder," "Be Human, Not Inhumane," "Help Animals. Don't Be One," and "Live and Let Live."

"ANIMALS HAVE SOULS TOO!" A young woman screamed, her face red with exertion. "DOMINION DOES NOT MEAN DOMINATION!" She pointed a finger at an old man trying to scuttle past her toward the parking lot.

None of the other demonstrators seemed to possess this woman's fervor. With brown, spiky hair, and ears pierced by rows of silver hoops in ascending sizes, she appeared to be the group's leader. James took in her shapeless beige dress and gaunt arms and then his eyes were drawn from her person to her poster. It portrayed a headless chicken spouting blood from its neck as it ran around in an aimless, pathetic circle.

James felt anger rise within him. "That's a bit graphic for little kids to look at, don't you think?" he asked the woman when she paused to draw in a fresh breath.

Her dark eyes crackled with intensity. "And what about the *graphic murders* humans commit every second? Of helpless animals! It happens right here in Shenandoah County!"

Before James could reply, a cluster of teen-age boys materialized in front of the protest-ors. They carried takeout bags from Dolly's Diner and wore smug grins. Sitting on the ground, they unwrapped bacon double cheeseburgers with deliberate slowness, waved the food around, and shouted, "Car-nivores Rock! Carnivores Rock!" before sinking their teeth into the thick burgers.

Spurred by the teenagers, other members of the community now felt free to trade insults with the protestors. Both sides were egged on by the female leader and emotions were fraying. The young woman was un-daunted. She got right in people's faces, shouting and spitting as she described slaughterhouse practices in the most explicit terms. At one point, a pregnant woman who had paused to gawk suddenly dashed off, her hand on her swelled stomach. Con-cerned, James followed her and saw her doubled-over behind the bushes lining the parking lot. Afterward, she straightened, wiped her mouth with a tissue, and fled.

Bennett, who had joined James as he moved to watch over the pregnant woman, shook his head. "Hope she's all right."

"Where is Lucy?" James looked around for his friend's Jeep.

"I don't know, but she needs to fire a gun

in the air when she gets here." Bennett looked miserable. "Gillian used to be one of these people. Man, I know where they're comin' from, but this is not the way to change things. And how am I going to get Gillian outta here before folks start throwin' punches?"

James didn't have an answer. Gillian was as passionate about animal rights as the rest of the demonstrators, but she preferred to champion the cause in a more behind-the-scenes manner.

At that moment, Ned Woodman emerged from the crowd heading into the Village. He looked as frantic as Roslyn had earlier, but James blocked the councilman's exit. Pointing at the increasingly hostile throng, he said, "Ned! Can you do something to disperse these people? Don't the protestors need some sort of a permit? This is going to get out of hand if someone in a position of authority doesn't act quickly!"

Ned shot a panicked look over his shoulder. He seemed fearful. Not of the protestors, but of something or someone in the direction of the main tent. Suddenly, James' attention was drawn by the wail of a sheriff's cruiser siren. Deputy Keith Donovan pulled his sedan within inches of the demonstrators and jumped out of the car, his face set in a fierce scowl. When James turned to speak to Ned again, he only saw a glimpse of purple shirt as the councilman slipped back toward the heart of the Village.

Lucy parked her Jeep right behind the surly deputy and though Donovan strutted up to the protestors and began to order them around in his typical mulish manner, Lucy and Lindy were able to gently pull the female leader aside and speak to her calmly and quietly. Donovan, who had become obsessed with weight lifting over the past few months, now had such a thick neck that he looked more like a redheaded bulldog than ever. He had long been Lucy's nemesis and the supper club members did their best to avoid him whenever possible.

While Donovan mildly scolded the burger-eating teenagers, James lured Gillian away from the protestors. He captured her attention by telling her about Eliot's recent conversion to vegetarianism.

"What an *honorable* decision to make at such a tender age!" Gillian was delighted. "Where is he? I'd love to congratulate him and offer my *full* support."

Bennett shot James a grateful look as the three friends headed back into the Village and rejoined Jane and Eliot at the picnic table. Bennett and Gillian had barely said their hellos when Eliot tugged on James' hand. "Daddy! I need to go to the bathroom."

James noted that his son was doing little hops from side-to-side. "It was a pretty big smoothie, huh? Come on, we'll ask Harmony if we can use the restroom in her office. You and I aren't going near those port-a-potties by the entrance."

The Better State of Mind booth was unmanned, but Roslyn was more than happy to lend James the keys to her office. James and Eliot trotted to her blue door, but didn't need the keys as the door was not only unlocked, but left slightly ajar.

"Hello?" James called out, but the office was silent. "I guess Roslyn really *is* absent-minded."

He gave a quick glance around a reception area similar to Harmony's. Judging by the number of closed doors off the hallway, Roslyn's office unit contained a few more rooms than the hypnotherapist's. Luckily, the restroom was clearly marked. James quickly opened the door and turned the lights on for his son.

"I can go by myself," Eliot stated. Despite his son's declaration, James listened at the door as Eliot conducted his business and then washed his hands. When he didn't come back out after turning off the water, James opened the door by an inch.

"All done in there?"

Eliot reappeared, wearing a befuddled frown. "Daddy? Why is that man sleeping on the ground?"

"What?" James frowned and entered the bathroom.

There on the floor of the handicapped stall was a man's body. James recognized the figure in the purple polo shirt and tan pants right away.

"Ned?" he called out and stooped over the prone form. Even in the shadowy restroom stall, James could see that Ned Woodman's eyes were open. They were glassy and unblinking, their still gaze fixed on the peach and green tiled wall.

James checked for a pulse but didn't find one. Pulling his phone out of his pocket, he ushered Eliot into the reception room and began dialing Lucy's number. He wondered if she'd hear the phone over the noise of the crowd. When she didn't answer, he punchedin Bennett's number next.

"Bennett!" James whispered urgently into the speaker. "Tell Jane to come get Eliot from the Health House. It's two doors down from Harmony's. And call 9-1-1. Councilman Ned Woodman is in a bathroom stall back here." He lowered his voice even further. "And he's dead."

"Damn," Bennett whistled. "When it's my turn to pass on, that is *not* how I wanna go!"

FIVE:
BLUEBERRY DREAM PIE

Grams of
Sugar
26

It took less than five minutes for Jane to enter the office and collect Eliot. James gave her the Bronco keys and insisted she drive back to his house while he waited for the authorities.

Those authorities turned out to be Donovan, since he was already at the festival, and Lucy. The two deputies were in the midst of a full-scale argument when they walked across the threshold.

"You're not even in uniform, Hanover," Deputy Donovan sneered and hitched up his utility belt to emphasize her lack of nightstick, handcuffs, or firearm. "Leave this to the *men*."

Lucy rolled her eyes. "I would if there was one here. All I see is the same know-it-all jerk I knew in high school. When are you ever going to grow up, Keith? Didn't you just turn forty a few months ago?" She jerked her thumb at his thinning red hair as she brushed past him. "It's too bad you don't lose your bad habits the way you seem to be losing your hair."

Donovan snorted. "Go on, then. Be your aggressive, sarcastic self. That's why you can't hold onto a man, Hanover. Guys don't like pushy women."

The last comment struck home, especially because Lucy's fellow deputy knew full well that she still mourned her former relationship with James. To spare Lucy any further embarrassment, James avoided meeting her wounded eyes as he led the pair of squabbling deputies to the bathroom.

"He's inside," he said as Lucy opened the door. "I checked for vital signs but found nothing."

Donovan shook his head in disgust. "I'm glad that's not me in there. Would it have killed you to try a little CPR before pronouncing the man dead? Or is M.D. one of your dozens of degrees?"

"It didn't take a degree in higher education to see that Ned was gone," James answered, doing his best not to rise to Donovan's bait. "He didn't even feel warm. There was no trace of life left in him."

Before Donovan could continue berating James, his radio crackled with the announcement that Sheriff Huckabee was on his way. Donovan snapped to attention and, ignoring James, ducked into the bathroom. He and Lucy reappeared a few minutes later, just as the paramedics walked into the office. They eased a gurney into the reception room and after exchanging professional greetings with the deputies, the pair of young men went into the restroom to examine Ned Woodman's body.

Lucy dug a notebook out of her cluttered purse and then began searching for a pen among the gum wrappers, wadded tissues, and crumpled receipts. She finally found one, but it had come uncapped in her bag and had dried out. James smiled at her customary untidiness and handed her a pen from a cup holder on the coffee table. The pens were mauve and bore the name, phone number, and address of Roslyn's business.

While Lucy asked James for details regarding his discovery of the body, the EMTs carried Ned out of the handicapped stall and carefully lifted him onto the gurney. Donovan held the bathroom door open for the younger men and then stood behind them, hands on hips, as they strapped the inert form onto their wheeled cart.

"So what do you boys make of this?" he asked, his voice conversational.

Without pausing in his work, the man cinching the belt around Ned's legs replied, "Nothing official, of course, but it looks like your standard heart attack."

James listened with interest. He recalled how Ned's left hand had been balled into a tight fist and how his right arm had been stretched across his chest, as though he had held onto his left side before falling onto the floor.

"It's a shame," the second paramedic murmured. "Guy can't be more than sixty."

"Yeah, it sucks to be him," Donovan responded without an iota of genuine sympathy.

The paramedic's exit was blocked by the arrival of Sheriff Huckabee. Huckabee, who was stocky and wide-shouldered like Donovan, but weighed fifty pounds more than his deputy, strode into the room. Twirling the ends of his splendid mustache, which had turned dark pewter over the years, Huckabee had never looked more like a walrus than he did now. His meaty hand scratched the stubble sprouting on his second chin while his small eyes carefully surveyed the scene. He approached the gurney. "What's the verdict, gentleman?"

"Looks like a heart attack, Sheriff," Donovan answered before anyone else could. "At least it was quick, sir. I know he was a friend of yours."

"Thank you, Keith," the sheriff replied and then placed a palm on the side of the gurney. "Ned was a good man. I'm gonna go over to his place and tell Donna myself." He turned to the closest paramedic. "Where you boys taking him? I'll drive his wife over as soon as she's ready."

As the men reviewed the procedural details concerning the care of the councilman's body, James found that he couldn't take his eyes off Ned's face. Less than an hour ago, he'd seen this man walking around the festival. Now he was dead. It happened without warning, without witnesses, and without the presence of a single loved one. James hadn't known Ned well, but he'd spoken to him minutes before the man had taken his last breath.

Feeling frail in the face of such a sudden death, James glanced around, wanting to look at something else besides the body on the gurney. Leaning toward Lucy, who was still seated on the sofa, he whispered, "What happened with the protestors?"

"Relocated," she responded with a ghost of a smile. "I figured if we tried to shoo them away, they'd call us fascists or something and get even more riled up. I told them they were harassing the folks trying to enter the fair and that they were free to continue with their demonstration, but they'd have to move farther down the street. There's no shade in that spot and half of them had called it quits before Donovan got the call about Mr. Woodman."

The pair fell silent for a few moments and James reflected that he and Lucy had been in this position several times before. There'd been an unexpected death and the two friends had done their best to remain composed despite their feelings of shock or sorrow. Lucy had always handled such situations with professional aplomb, even before she'd become a deputy. James wondered if her ability to detach herself so adeptly prevented her from ever experiencing a genuine romantic relationship.

Selfishly, James wished she would find a suitable partner. If she could be as happy as he was, he could let go of the guilt he occasionally felt for having had to tell her that they could never be a couple again. James never expected his wish to be granted so quickly, but when Huckabee plodded over to the sofa and indicated that he'd like to speak to Lucy privately, the sheriff did just that.

As Huckabee and Lucy moved down the hall to talk, James waited to be told he was free to leave. The paramedics wheeled Ned's corpse from the room and Donovan tagged along, undoubtedly hoping to shout at anyone foolish enough to get too close to the waiting ambulance. In the silence, it dawned on James that he'd neglected to inform Lucy about Roslyn's office being unlocked. Yet when she returned, her face was filled with such joy that he forgot all about the omitted detail.

"Good news?" he asked.

Lucy waited until Huckabee also went outside and then allowed herself a jubilant smile. "Yes! You remember Sullie, right?"

Naturally James remembered the hunky deputy. He'd been the reason James and Lucy's relationship had failed the first time around. Lucy had become obsessed with Sullie and had turned her back on James. As a result, James had sought comfort in the arms of the reporter, Murphy Alistair. Thinking about the two women who'd caused him such heartache, James became cross.

"Who could forget Sullie the Magnificent?" His tone was petulant.

Too happy to notice James' peevishness, Lucy went right on talking. "He's transferring to our station! The sheriff wants me to arrange a welcome party. Oh, isn't this wonderful news?"

Recalling that only moments before he'd hoped for this very thing to happen, James nodded and forced his mouth into a smile. "It's great, Lucy." He paused and then churlishly asked, "Do you think he's still single?"

Lucy was unfazed by the question. "I know he is. I became friends with one of the female deputies in Sullie's station during the last tri-county department bowling tournament. *She* said that Sullie talks about me all the time."

James rose. He was ready to go home. "I hope everything works out for you, Lucy."

"Me too. I feel like it's finally my turn," she said and walked out of the office with James.

I hope Sullie doesn't want to have a child, because Lucy certainly doesn't, James thought as he caught a ride home with Bennett to check on his own kid.

117

■ ■ ■ ■

By the time Monday rolled around, James had recovered from the unsettling experience of Ned Woodman's death. Fortunately, Eliot continued to believe the man had simply chosen to take a nap on the bathroom floor. His four-year-old brain reasoned that the grown-up must have been really hot and had found relief on the cool tile floor. James and Jane said nothing to correct this notion.

The workday was refreshingly uneventful. James discarded another pair of thoroughly unpromising job applications, manned both the circulation and information desks as the Fitzgerald twins put on a Dr. Seuss puppet show for a group of kindergartners, and made it through eight hours without a single sugar craving. That afternoon, he nearly hugged Harmony when she invited him into her office for their second session.

"I've lost two pounds!" he boasted happily. "I know that isn't much, but I feel like this treatment is exactly what I needed!"

Harmony smiled in encouragement. "Kicking your sugar addiction is a great start, but remember that you still need to eat balanced meals and exercise regularly if you want to be truly healthy."

James didn't want to admit that he hadn't been to the gym once over the past week so he merely nodded in agreement.

After gesturing for her client to be seated in the recliner, Harmony took her place on the sofa and gazed at him with friendly concern. "I heard your son discovered Mr. Woodman's body on Saturday. Is he okay?"

James wiggled around in the chair until his body weight felt evenly distributed. "Eliot thinks Ned was just resting. He's forgotten all about it by now." He opened the folded blanket Harmony handed him and spread it over his legs and belly. "Did you know Ned?"

"No," Harmony answered. "Not personally, I mean. I knew that he was a councilman and I've seen his wife around the Village. She's a regular at Knead Your Cares Away. That poor woman. Her husband's death must have been a terrible shock."

Staring at one of the soft watercolors above Harmony's head, James nodded. "I hope he didn't die because of stress. The last time I saw him alive, he was standing near the protestors. He looked utterly panic-stricken. I asked him to help keep the crowd calm, but he disappeared as soon as Deputy Donovan showed up."

Harmony didn't seem surprised that Ned dodged what James considered to be his responsibility as a town official. "Not everyone is comfortable handling a volatile situation. The noise, the escalating emotions, the possibility of violence. I'm sure several people were upset by the protest, but I'm still grateful to live in a country where our expressions can be voiced, no matter how disagreeable to some."

Wanting to avoid a political discussion, James decided to change the subject. "Tomorrow night is the first meeting of our supper club in which we're all sugar-free."

"Well, let's make certain you stay that way," Harmony said. "Are you comfortable?"

"Very."

Harmony turned on her CD player and the tranquil mixture of birdsong, running water, and wind chimes drifted into the room. James closed his eyes. The session was similar to the first one, but instead of visiting his brain's control room, Harmony asked James to picture the sugary treats he loved during childhood.

One at a time, he called the images to mind. Charleston Chews, chocolate chip cookies, ice cream sandwiches, Twinkies, his mother's homemade doughnuts, and hordes of Halloween candy floated across his vision, and he couldn't help but grin over the variety of sweets his memory had been able to bring forth. One by one, James laid out the delicacies he'd succumbed to for nearly forty years and then turned his back on the entire display. When he awoke, he felt a sense of freedom, as though he'd reprogrammed his long-term memory and it would no longer have the power to make him believe he wanted to submit to the culinary temptations of his boyhood.

Once again, James collected his reinforcement CD from Skye and then headed out of the office. Skye's boyfriend, Lennon, was raking a swath of white pebbles in the Japanese rock garden in between Harmony's office and her neighbor on the left, the massage therapist. James watched the young man's steady and deliberate movements and then realized he must be raking in time to music, as a pair of white wires dangled from his ears and disappeared into the neck of another tie-dyed T-shirt.

James glanced around the tidy garden, the spotless cement walkways, and the carefully trimmed bushes. Bluebirds flitted about the treetops and the sun fell through the leaves, dappling the ground with patterns of light and shadow. The Village was incredibly serene this Monday compared to the boisterous scene on Saturday.

The feeling of relaxed empowerment fled the moment James returned home and hit the play button on his answering machine.

"It's me," Jane's voice trembled slightly. "I was really hoping you'd be home. I . . . I need to know how worried to be about what happened today. Someone left another dead bird at my house, James, but this one wasn't in the mailbox." She paused to collect herself. "It was nailed to the front door."

James called her back immediately. "Honey, are you okay?" He didn't notice the use of the endearment; it had rolled off his tongue naturally.

"I actually had a shot of whiskey to settle my nerves. Really, I'm better now. Luckily, Eliot didn't see it since we always come inside through the garage." Jane sounded exhausted.

"You've had quite a shock," he told her. "I can hear it in your voice. But sweetheart, you've got to call the police. This has moved beyond the realm of practical joke to vandalism. A person sick enough to nail a dead bird to your door could be capable of much worse."

Jane sighed. "I'll do it in the morning. I promise. Right now, I just wish . . . well, I wish you were here."

It was all the invitation James needed. "Give me an hour," he said and hung up.

By the time he reached Harrisonburg, Eliot was already asleep. Jane was clad in a pair of blue cotton pajamas covered with designs of bacon and eggs. After hugging her, James pointed at her nighttime ensemble and smiled.

"Do you like my 'breakfast in bed' PJs?" She laughed and then her face grew serious. "Thank you, James. It's not like me to feel insecure in the house by myself, but I knew with you here I'd feel much safer."

James pointed at the sofa. "Should I make this up?"

"No," Jane said with a flirtatious grin. She stepped closer, her eyes shining with invitation. "You'd be a much more efficient bodyguard in my bed."

Without the slightest hesitation, James scooped her into his arms and planted a kiss on the exposed skin of her neck. "Why do I hear Whitney Houston music playing in my head?"

Jane's lips found his. Huskily, she murmured, "Get that other woman out of your mind. Tonight, you're mine."

Whispering into her hair, James answered, "I think I always have been."

The next morning, Eliot was delighted to find his father standing over the stove, fixing scrambled eggs with cheese with one hand and drinking coffee from one of Jane's purple JMU coffee mugs with the other. However, his initial pleasure quickly turned into a sulk as he realized he'd missed James' arrival the night before.

"I didn't know there was gonna be a sleepover!" Eliot whined. "I missed the fun!"

At that moment, Jane entered the kitchen and distributed good morning kisses to both males. "It was grown-up fun," she said and winked at James. Taking a drink from his mug, she pointed at the stovetop clock. "You'd better get going or you'll be late for work."

James cast an anxious look toward the front door. "Are you sure you're fine dealing with this by yourself? I can take a sick day."

Jane nodded and lowered her voice. "I'll do it after I drop Eliot off at day care. Having cops at our house might freak him out. Then again, he might love it. Either way, he won't be here."

"Call me later, okay? I've got an interview

scheduled for two this afternoon but otherwise I should be available to talk." He hugged his ex-wife and then presented his son with his breakfast. "An egg-monster for the coolest kid in the room."

Eliot examined the lumpy pile of eggs forming an oval face, the apple-slice mouth, the baby carrot nose, and the four eyes made out of cheese cubes and laughed. "Hey! I'm the only kid. You and mom are *old!*"

James pretended to pull an invisible knife from his chest as he gathered his overnight bag and waved goodbye. Before leaving, he snuck around to the front door in order to get a firsthand look at the dead bird.

This was no pathetic robin resting on a pile of mail, but a big black crow, like the ones in James' nightmare. Both wings had been spread and a nail had been driven through each wing bone into the wooden door. The bird's head and neck sagged sideways and its feet were curled inward as though it had died in agony.

Repulsed, James took a step backward. He glanced around the stoop, looking for a note or any indication that would explain the gruesome display of vandalism. His eyes swept the property and then he walked slowly to his truck, thinking that it would be a challenge to have staged the macabre display in Jane's neighborhood. The houses were relatively close to one another and there were very few mature trees dividing the yards. Most of the neighbors were two-parent families and though many of the mothers worked outside the home, the women living on either side of Jane did not.

"Who walks up to the front door of someone's house, nails a dead bird on it, and then drives away unseen?" he asked the quiet street. "And just as important as the 'who' is the 'why.' Why do this to Jane?"

James put his hands on his hips and glared in every direction as though he could frighten away the perpetrator with the sheer force of his presence. Putting his faith in the abilities of the local police, James backed out of the driveway and headed south to Quincy's Gap.

The Fitzgerald twins were in a buoyant mood when they met James on the library steps at a quarter to nine. In fact, both of the young men, who had taken to riding their mountain bikes to work, were so impatient to share their news that they dismounted hurriedly and let their bikes drop unceremoniously onto the grass.

"Guess what, Professor?" Francis was

flushed from exercise and excitement.

Hoping the announcement would distract him from the image of the dead crow, James paused in the act of unlocking the front door. "You won the Mega Million jackpot?"

Scott shook his head. "It's way better than that! We entered a contest for people who have ideas for groundbreaking new video games and —"

"We won!" Francis shouted and the brothers exchanged celebratory chest bumps.

James shook each of their hands. "That's terrific. What was your idea?"

Francis beamed. "This is why you're awesome, Professor. Everybody else asked us about the prize, but *you* want to know what we dreamed up."

"Our proposal stemmed from our experiences working here, at the library," Scott added.

Suddenly, James had a visual of Murphy's book cover. This time, however, it had been shrunk to fit the box of a PC game. Pudgy sleuths made of megapixels scrambled around the screen, picking up clues while simultaneously taking bites of junk food. "Did your proposal have anything to do with the mystery genre?" he asked woodenly.

"Nope! It's a game where you can travel between fantasy worlds. For example, you start as Alice and play in Wonderland, but as Alice advances in levels, she can travel to Tolkien's world," Francis explained.

"And there she can add an ally to her group, like Legolas, the elf, or a wizard like Gandalf," Scott continued.

"So with each new world, the group grows by another character," Francis finished.

Relieved, James smiled at the twins. "It sounds brilliant and complex and really fun. I assume there would be a final battle scene once your group of characters has leveled out." When the brothers nodded, James asked, "In what setting would this epic fight occur?"

"Back in Wonderland," they answered together. "Against the Queen of Hearts, of course."

James praised the two young men until they blushed with embarrassment. "Don't you two quit on me! I still haven't found a replacement for Mrs. Waxman."

"Don't worry, Professor. The prize is that we're being hired as consultants during the two years it'll take to produce the game." Scott exchanged a look with Francis. "We'd never leave the library, but for once, we won't have to skimp on some of the things we've wanted to buy. Our bachelor pad is about to be totally transformed!"

"That should entertain your landlady," James remarked with a chuckle.

"Mrs. Lamb is one feisty old lady," Francis said. "She said the first thing we should buy is a disco ball!"

The librarians laughed and went inside to begin their workday. All three of them had an industrious morning. Between the two book club meetings (James led the fiction club's discussion at ten while Scott led the biography club's at eleven), lunchtime arrived quickly.

Watching Francis rush to the refrigerator with glee, James realized that he had no lunch of his own. There'd been no time to stop on the drive from Jane's house to the library. He waited for the twins to finish theirs and when he finally ventured into town, he was starving. Only Dolly's Diner would do. It was Tuesday and that meant Clint's perfect meatloaf sandwich and a side of garlic mashed potatoes.

Dolly's was always packed on Tuesdays. The locals adored the meatloaf special and as summer approached, Dolly began serving her famous Blueberry Dream Pie. For a mere ninety-nine cents, her patrons could feast on a generous wedge of pie with the purchase of any entree. Most of Quincy's Gap took advantage of the offer.

"Professor Henry!" Dolly shouted from behind the hostess station. "Such a pleasure to see you!"

To most, this type of greeting was spoken out of politeness, but Dolly meant every word. She'd known James and his family for years and was now as fond of Milla and Eliot as she was of her own kin. Dolly loved Clint, food, and gossip, and not always in that order. Somehow, her customers shared their problems with her despite the knowledge that their secrets would be circulated the minute they left the diner.

"Not even a seat at the counter," James mourned and his stomach rumbled in protest.

"Lemme see if anybody's about finished up. If they are, I'll give 'em a gentle shove out the door. I know you've got to get back to the library." Dolly hustled off, her sharp eyes in search of dawdlers.

As James waited, a pretty young woman with shoulder-length auburn hair, fair skin, and a dash of freckles across her nose got up from her chair at a table for two. She squinted in his direction and then slipped on a pair of tortoise-shell glasses. Leaving a paperback on her seat, she walked over to James.

"Did she say that you worked at the

library?" she inquired in a pleasant alto.

James nodded. "I'm the head librarian."

The woman gave him a bright smile. "I'm Fern Dickenson. I'm supposed to have an interview with you at two." She gestured toward her table. "I just ordered and since there aren't any open seats, would you like to join me?"

"That would be great," James answered, feeling well disposed toward the thoughtful young woman already.

Over lunch, James proceeded to ask Fern all the questions he'd been saving for the afternoon's interview. Fern told him that she worked as a freelance photographer for a dozen Virginia publications but was having a hard time making ends meet without a steady paycheck. She loved all areas of the Humanities, was well read, and extremely personable. She'd had experience serving the public during her two years working part-time for the Virginia State Parks Department and while she enjoyed the job, she was ready for a change.

From what James could tell, Fern had a great sense of humor, a solid work ethic, and a deep love of reading. She was perfect for the job.

When Dolly arrived to clear their lunch

plates, Fern excused herself to use the restroom.

"Isn't she a little young for you, Professor?" Dolly wiggled her eyebrows and then laughed, her whole body shaking in mirth.

James waved her off. "She's going to be my new part-time librarian. This meal became an impromptu interview."

Dolly was beside herself over being the first to hear such interesting news. "You all need to celebrate. Be back in a flash!"

Before James could protest, she was gone. By the time Fern returned from the restroom, two dessert plates containing slices of Blueberry Dream Pie had been placed on the table by the diner's exuberant proprietor.

"On the house!" Dolly told Fern. "And welcome to Quincy's Gap. We're mighty glad to have you. Are you movin' to our town? Are you on your own or do you have a *significant* other?"

Fern accepted Dolly's welcome and took her questions in stride. "Thank you. I'm glad to be here. As for my living situation . . . I'm apartment hunting and I'm single. I'm an only child and my astrological sign is Libra. Blood type is O Negative." She looked quizzically at James. "Wait, does this mean I got the job?"

"It's yours if you want it," James declared. When Fern nodded enthusiastically, James gestured at his plate. "Shall we toast with a forkful of pie?"

Dolly hadn't budged during this exchange and James didn't dare offend her by turning down her gift of pie, so he loaded up his fork, clinked it against Fern's, and popped it in his mouth.

A blend of cream cheese, fresh blueberries, and sugar coated his tongue. Sighing as the fresh berries popped between his teeth, he waited for the feeling of intense pleasure to overpower him, to create that high he was accustomed to experiencing when eating a sweet food, but it didn't happen. He enjoyed the treat, but wasn't so focused on it that he couldn't pause between bites to converse with his new employee.

"When should I start, Mr. Henry?" Fern inquired once she'd cleaned her plate. "I'm available whenever you need me."

James wiped a blueberry smear from his cheek. "How about tomorrow? I'll have Scott show you the ropes. I believe you two are going to get along very well."

Six:
Cucumber & Feta Salad

Grams of
Sugar
1

After spontaneously hiring Fern over lunch, James returned to the library with a light step. He hummed quietly all the way into his office, stopping only to listen to his voicemail. Jane had left a message saying she'd filed a police report earlier that morning and the officer she'd spoken to promised to have a car assigned to patrol her neighborhood for the rest of the week. The helpful lawman had also removed the dead crow from her front door and buried the sad creature in the far reaches of the back yard.

"I feel so much better today," she said and

James could hear the relief in her voice. "And I want to thank you again for last night." She paused and he could easily picture the blood rushing to her cheeks as the double meaning of her words became apparent. "Um, about last night . . . I don't want to jump to any conclusions, but what we did felt really natural and, well, pretty damned wonderful! I've been acting like a pre-teen girl with a serious crush all day — wearing this goofy smile and writing your name all over my desk calendar . . ." she chuckled. "Okay, I'm trying not to make you blush or anything. I just wanted to say that you make me happy. Bye!"

James smiled. He felt buoyant, as though everything in his life was neatly falling into place. His reconnection with Jane had been a unique experience. After all, they *had* been married, but she had been a self-centered lover when they'd been together and had often seemed dissatisfied with their sex life. Last night, she was a different woman in bed. Playful and giving, she'd quickly put aside her shyness and allowed him to explore her voluptuous body. In return, she'd loved him with a mixture of tenderness and passion she'd never shown during their marriage.

James could feel his pulse racing as he

replayed the night over and over, but then doubts began to worm their way into his mind, disturbing his reminisces and causing him to question the wisdom of being led by his libido.

We can't mess around like teenagers, he thought. *No matter how good it feels. There's Eliot to consider. If Jane and I are going to be together, it must be for all the right reasons. I've got to be one hundred percent sure she and I are the real deal this time.*

And therein lay the rub, James thought. He believed they'd been the genuine article the first time around. He'd been so certain of their future the night he'd knelt down and proposed. After he and Jane divorced, he thought Lucy might be the love he'd waited for. And then there was Murphy.

He'd been wrong about all of them.

"Let's face it," he remarked glumly to the photo of Jackson and Milla on his desk. "I don't have clear judgment when it comes to women. Yet *you!*" he pointed at his father. "You got it right — not once but *twice!* And you're a cantankerous old man! How'd you win the hearts of such wonderful women, Pop?"

"Talking to yourself again?" A teasing voice inquired.

James looked up to see Murphy Alistair

standing in the threshold, her arms crossed as she leaned against the doorframe, mouth upturned in amusement. If not for that expression, he might not have recognized her right away, for she no longer looked like the small-town reporter he'd once dated. Her hair had been dyed to a rich, molasses-brown, chic Chanel frames had replaced her academic-looking glasses, and she'd grown shockingly thin. Her angular body was encased in a black sheath dress and she wore a multi-strand red coral necklace. To James, she resembled a younger version of Sarah Palin.

Out of politeness, he rose from his seat. "You look very cosmopolitan."

Murphy laughed. "Everyone really *does* wear black in New York. I'd forgotten how all the Quincy's Gap ladies wear Pepto-Bismol suits and Beatrix Potter hats."

"The whole Valley is more colorful than your concrete jungle." James felt defensive of his beloved berg. "And there's a great pizza place in town now, so I don't think The Big Apple's got much on us."

"Right. Except for Broadway, the Met, unparalleled architecture, dozens of fabulous restaurants, and the latest trends in fashion, I guess Manhattan can't hold a candle to this place." She gestured out the window with a mocking smile.

James frowned. "If New York is such a utopia, why come back to the sticks?"

Murphy smoothed her glossy hair. "In all honesty, it wasn't easy to make friends there. I couldn't enjoy my success in a sea of anonymity. My family is here in Shenandoah and frankly, I missed the hustle and bustle of putting out *The Star.* Now, I own the paper and a house that I've always admired but could never have afforded."

"You've got nerves of steel, to move back after insulting half the town in your infamous *book.*" He'd never before infused such a beloved noun with that much spite. "Now, how may a humble librarian be of service today?"

Putting both hands on her angular hips, Murphy sighed in exasperation. "My novels are works of *fiction!* When are you ever going to accept that fact? And I'm here on a professional basis, especially if the rumor about your having a kid with your ex-wife is true."

"Your sources are correct. I have a son. His name is Eliot Henry." James felt such pleasure in imparting this information to his former flame.

Murphy took a step deeper into his office, her posture akin to that of a stalking panther. "So are you all living together in your sweet yellow house on Hickory Hill Lane?"

There was no cynicism in her tone; she was genuinely interested in his current circumstances, and it gave him a juvenile satisfaction to leave her thirst for information unquenched. As though she hadn't spoken, he came around to the front of his desk and indicated she should accompany him out of the library's inner sanctum. "How can I help you today, Ms. Alistair?"

"I'd like to interview you for a piece I'm writing on Ned Woodman," she answered after studying him for a moment. Murphy knew that his formal tone meant he was through discussing his personal life.

James shrugged in resignation. "I can't help you there. I only knew him because he was a councilman and his name and photo appeared in the paper a few times."

"But you found his body!" Murphy protested. "Surely you must have some reaction. Do you think his death could be linked to the presence of the animal rights demonstrators at the festival?"

It wouldn't do for James to be misquoted regarding the demonstrators or the Wellness Village. "What do you mean? He had a heart attack. It's not like he was murdered by one of the protestors."

"Maybe he was, though we'll never know because his wife refused an autopsy," Murphy replied breezily. "He's had two previous surgeries for blocked arteries, so Donna Woodman didn't seem too surprised by the diagnosis."

Studying her face and the glint in her eyes, James knew Murphy was chasing a tantalizing lead. "You don't think his death was an accident?"

"He was a councilman, James. When guys like him die young I always take a second look at their lives. According to my sources, Ned was acting odd the day he kicked the bucket." Her mouth curved in a predatory grin. "Those two facts are enough to make me want to dig deeper. Once you tell me how he looked when you found him, I plan to investigate his recent political activities."

Apparently, Murphy's success as a novelist hadn't cooled her interest in dragging skeletons out of the townsfolk's closets. "Sorry, I have no comment. I don't want Ned's family to read a detailed report of the man they loved lying facedown in a bathroom stall."

"Even though you're not going to help me, I'd like to assure you that my article will be a tasteful memorial piece," Murphy promised and then turned away. Over her shoulder she added, "Unless the councilman did something improper. If so, the community deserves to know the whole truth."

Again, he spotted that glimmer in her eye. It was a hunger, a lust for bringing secrets to light and for the briefest of moments, he wondered how far Murphy Alistair would go to get what she wanted. Was it possible that she'd moved back to Quincy's Gap in order to reignite their relationship? Why was she so interested in his living arrangements? Was she capable of nailing a dead crow to Jane's front door?

A patron requiring assistance in the audio book section interrupted his brief but disturbing musings. After discussing the merits of the new Baldacci release versus the latest offerings from Douglas Preston and Lincoln Child, the thriller fan checked out both titles and left the library with a jaunty stride. James envied the man an afternoon spent in a deck chair, listening to a book with his eyes closed and a cold drink in his hand.

"I see your old girlfriend's back, Professor," Scott whispered as both men completed organizational tasks behind the circulation desk. "She wouldn't listen when I asked her to wait out here so I could warn you she was on the prowl." The younger man ran his hands through his hair, his forehead creased in concern. "That's the perfect phrase for her, Professor. Especially now. She's got that look about her — like she's caught the scent of wounded prey and is just waiting for the right opportunity to pounce."

Francis had appeared from the break room in time to hear his brother's metaphor. "Are you the prey?" he asked James.

"Lord, I hope not!" James answered glumly.

When James left work at five, he stepped out beneath a blue sky filled with sunshine. Inhaling the scent of fresh-cut grass, he stretched out his arms as if he could embrace the beauty of the spring afternoon. Then and there, he decided he would not allow Murphy's return to affect the good things happening in his life.

In the meantime, he had important issues to consider, such as what to bring to Gillian's house for dinner. It was her turn to host the Supper Club meeting and she'd sent a dictatorial email the day before announcing that dinner was to be comprised of all vegetarian dishes.

"No pizza either!" She'd written. "If Eliot

Henry can eat balanced meals at four-years-of-age, then the rest of us can come up with something *creative* and *colorful* to grace our plates. I'll be preparing a *sumptuous* sushi platter."

James wasn't overly fond of sushi. He liked a few of the identifiable selections, such as California or Philly rolls, but in general, he preferred not to subject his digestive tract to uncooked fish. Bennett had replied to Gillian's email by saying there was an afternoon staff meeting at the post office so he'd make it to her place by six o'clock sharp. With no time to cook, he planned to show up with a bagged salad. Lucy had quickly volunteered to bring a sugar-free dessert from the town's bakery, The Sweet Tooth. Like James, she was a bonafide carnivore and probably didn't want to bear the responsibility for a vegetarian entrée. Luckily, Lindy offered to make a meatless moussaka casserole, leaving James with the responsibility of preparing what Gillian called, "a healthy side dish to bring *finesse* to the meal."

Wanting his contribution to echo the Greek food theme of Lindy's dish, James checked out two cookbooks from the library. Sitting in Food Lion's parking lot, he flipped through the books until he found a quick and easy recipe for Cucumber and Feta Salad.

At home, he changed into shorts and a T-shirt, tuned his radio to the local country station, and sang along to Brad Paisley's latest hit as he cut two cucumbers lengthwise and removed the seeds with a spoon. After chopping the cucumbers into cubes, he put them in a bowl, sprinkled them with salt and then added chopped green onions to the mixture. The next ingredient was a container of feta cheese — the brand that came packaged with a blend of black pepper, basil, oregano, garlic, and sun-dried tomato. Lastly, James drizzled lemon juice and olive oil onto the salad with panache while pretending that he was being filmed for The Food Network.

"Delicious and nutritious!" he declared to an imaginary cameraman.

Covering the bowl with plastic wrap, James grabbed the bouquet of sunflowers he'd purchased for the hostess and drove off. As he pulled up in front of the colorful Victorian, he saw Gillian and Bennett on the porch swing. Clearly, his friends hadn't heard the sound of his truck engine. In fact, he didn't think they were aware of much, being far too busy kissing. James smiled as he spotted Bennett's bagged salad on the welcome mat. It seemed that the mailman had only arrived a few minutes before James, dumped his salad to the floor, and dragged his girlfriend over to the porch swing where he could greet her properly.

James cleared his throat as he walked up the path and then quickly dropped to one knee and feigned the need to tie his shoe lace. Out of the corner of his eye, he saw his friends leap apart.

"The whole country knows you two are an item." James stood up and grinned. "Bennett, you announced your feelings for Gillian on live television! A million people know your story. Why do you still try to keep your relationship under wraps?"

Gillian's face was nearly as red as her hair. Looping her arm through Bennett's she said, "We don't want our friendship with you and Lindy and Lucy to change. When the five of us are together, Bennett and I want to continue being our *individual* personas."

"So the moment we're not around, you turn all lovey-dovey?" James teased.

Bennett squirmed. "Look, my man. We live in a small town. Plenty of folks have a hard time acceptin' a mixed-race couple. I figure it's best not to shove it in their faces, you know?"

He picked up his bagged salad and walked into the house, James following closely on his heels, surprised that Gillian hadn't contradicted Bennett by declaring that the two of them could change the world by changing the point of view of a select few. He'd certainly heard her make similar pronouncements about dozens of other subjects.

James placed his salad bowl on Gillian's wooden farm table and studied his friends. "You *can't* act as if nothing is different. You're in love. To hell with what people think. Look how long it took you to find each other. Don't let any more time get away from you!"

Gillian paused in the act of setting the table. She put a hand on James' forearm. "Are you sure you're still talking about *us?* I can sense a *struggle* going on within you. Has your relationship with Jane entered into a *new* phase?"

Flummoxed over the tables turning as well as the accuracy of Gillian's statements, James was saved from having to answer by Lucy's arrival. The moment she stepped into the kitchen, Gillian's rotund tabby, the Dalai Lama, immediately stopped bathing his hindquarters and growled. Lucy looked down at the bristling feline and hissed in

146

return. "You've smelled my dogs for years now. Get over yourself, cat."

"You should try to approach the Dalai with respect and gentleness," Gillian suggested. "Animals know when a human dislikes them and it's hard to change their minds once they view you as a hostile invader."

"Hrmph. Hostile invader. What am I, an eighties video game?" Lucy grunted.

Lindy appeared in time to elbow her friend in the side. "You sound cranky, Deputy." She smiled and then bent down to scratch the Dalai on the neck. "What's up?"

"I am not cranky, I'm nervous," Lucy answered honestly. "Sullie starts tomorrow and we're going to be working a shift together. I don't want to act so smitten that I forget to put the car in park or put my flashlight in my holster instead of my firearm or —"

"Leave the bakery box open so the Dalai can lick the topping off the pie?" Lindy asked and pointed at the counter. The tabby's pink tongue was delicately scraping the whipped cream from the surface of the pie, his feline mouth curved into a mischievous smirk.

"Hey! I thought you were gettin' somethin' we could eat without cheatin'!" Bennett protested as Lucy chased the Dalai off the counter.

Lindy slid her casserole into the oven and set the temperature. "That's right, *chica!* We're supposed to be giving up sugar." She pointed a finger at Lucy. "This guy is already making you crazy!"

Lucy scowled. "I bought one of The Sweet Tooth's new sugar-free desserts. This is a *sugarless* key lime pie. I figured a fruit pie would tie in nicely with our vegetarian theme."

James was delighted to hear about the bakery's new offerings. Though part of him felt the need to abstain from ingesting sugar whenever possible, the other part argued that if guilt-free treats were available, why shouldn't he enjoy them?

Gillian wasn't pleased. "Perhaps it's a *sign* that the Dalai tainted the pie. Without real sugar, it may be full of chemicals. Why don't we have a *naturally* sweet, organically grown dessert? I have some raspberries and boy-senberries in the fridge."

Shrugging, Lucy settled down at the table. "Whatever you all think is best. I can always take the pie to the station tomorrow. I'll cut off the piece your cat licked and give it to Donovan!"

The five friends laughed at this splendid idea.

"I've got some news," Lindy said as she poured iced tea for the ladies and distributed bottles of cold beer to James and Bennett. "I don't have to fly down to Mexico to meet Luis' mama. Do you know why?" She widened her eyes but didn't give anyone a chance to guess. "Because she's coming *here!*"

Bennett snorted. "What for? To interview you for the position of future daughter-in-law? See what kind of cook and housekeeper you are?"

Lindy looked miserable. "Pretty much. She probably wants to get an eyeful of my breeding hips too."

"Don't worry, Lindy. We'll come over and help you prep for the visit," Lucy assured her. "When does she arrive?"

"Sunday afternoon. And thank you, Lucy, but I can hardly ask my dearest friends to spend a precious Saturday cleaning my toilets." Lindy put on a brave smile, but they could all see the anxiety in her eyes.

James knew that Lindy desperately wanted to win the approval of Luis' mother, but hoped Luis would propose regardless of what his dear mama thought of Lindy's potential as a homemaker.

Ruminating over parental blessings caused James to wonder if Jackson would be able to accept Jane into their family for a second time. His father tended to hold grudges for eons and though he was polite to Jane (probably because Milla forced him to be) he didn't speak to her unless it was necessary.

Relationships are never easy, he thought. Aloud, he said, "If we have to scrub your toilets and dust the blades of your ceiling fans to impress this woman we will. But she'll see what a treasure you are, Lindy, and it won't matter if you serve her fried Alpo, because she is going to love you."

Lindy sniffed back grateful tears. "Thank you, James. And I refuse to allow you to take part in the cleaning brigade. You need to spend time with your precious Eliot. I'm sure Bennett looks very sexy in rubber gloves and an apron!"

Bennett spluttered as his friends laughed.

The oven clock beeped and Gillian retrieved the moussaka and served steaming spoonfuls of it to the group. When it was cool enough to eat, they all did so hungrily, praising Lindy for her ingenuity in replacing the traditional ground beef used in the dish with diced zucchini. The friends then compared notes on their hypnotherapy sessions and rehashed the events at the food festival. Naturally, this subject led to a discourse on Ned Woodman's death.

"Rumor has it Ned may have been a bit crooked," Lucy stated and then paused. She always enjoyed having insider information and her friends could see that she was dying to tell them the latest bit of department gossip.

While everyone else waited patiently for her to continue, James said, "Let me guess. He was skimming from the town treasury."

Lucy trained a pair of startled cornflower blue eyes on him. "How'd you know?"

Now it was James' turn to be surprised. "I was just joking. Honestly!"

"Well, you're right on target. Not all of the evidence has been gathered yet, but it looks as though Mr. Woodman overcharged the town for his landscaping services."

"Is that really serious?" Gillian sounded doubtful. "Gas prices are *so* high these days. Maybe he needed to charge more because of increased costs?"

Lucy finished chewing a mouthful of moussaka before answering. "We're not talking about the kind of money to buy oil for the weed whackers or a few tanks of lawn mower gas, Gillian. He took a lot of money! Not only was he billing three times

151

the actual for his services, but apparently, whenever it was his turn to pay the town's bills, he'd pay himself for work his company didn't even perform!"

"What's the bottom line?" Bennett asked.

"I can't say anything officially," Lucy warned. "It's not my investigation, but we're talking somewhere in the neighborhood of thirty thousand dollars. And his wife claims to know nothing about it."

"Whoa! Thirty grand for cutting lawns and trimmin' a few bushes!" Bennett shook his fork in indignation. "I am in the wrong line of work!"

The friends ate silently for a moment. James became aware that he was picking at his entrée like a child forced to eat distasteful vegetables. The moussaka tasted fine, but he didn't care for the texture. The entire dish felt like mush in his mouth. Even chewing the crisp cucumbers of his own salad didn't quite match the satisfaction of grinding a nice piece of steak between his molars.

Don't be so close-minded! he chided himself, and forced down another bite of Lindy's dish.

"Wonder what he did with that extra money?" Lindy ruminated quietly. "Ned, I mean. If his wife didn't know, where'd he hide it? In a safety deposit box?"

"In his girlfriend's house?" Bennett quipped.

The supper club members exchanged inquisitive glances.

"Are you thinking what I'm thinking?" Gillian whispered theatrically and fixed her gaze on Lucy.

Lucy wiped her mouth with her napkin, folded her hands on the table, and nodded. "That someone else might know the location of Ned's money?"

"And has already helped themselves to it!" Lindy cried.

"Time out, folks." James rose and returned to the table with a bakery box from The Sweet Tooth. "The money could be buried under a tree for all we know, but if we're going to bat around wild theories for the rest of the evening, then we're going to need this pie after all."

SEVEN:
BACON, EGG, & CHEESE MELT

Grams of
Sugar
2

By the time the weekend rolled around, Murphy had successfully ferreted out every detail involving Ned Woodman's transgressions. The deceased councilman had overcharged the town for his services for years, but not by enough to draw attention. It was only within the last few months he'd turned truly greedy.

According to Murphy's explanation in *The Star,* council members took turns paying the town's bills. This rotation was put in place to protect the town's coffers, but it was only effective when each council member kept a close eye on the books. Because there hadn't been a penny unaccounted for in years, the council members didn't go over the numbers with a fine-tooth comb. Unfortunately, Ned took advantage of his trusting colleagues and during his bill-paying rotation made large payments to his own company. The bills included exorbitant fees for simple services such as pruning and laying mulch.

Eventually, someone else on the council would have noticed the depletion of town funds, so it was "as though Woodman was attempting to quickly stockpile ready cash," Murphy wrote. "His widow, Donna Woodman, claims to have no knowledge of her husband's illicit activities. Mrs. Woodman said there was no trace of the stolen money in their joint bank account and added that her husband had made no big-ticket purchases. Authorities are currently investigating Mr. Woodman's finances, but it appears that the councilman cashed a series of town checks over a twelve-week period. With no clues as to the whereabouts of the stolen money, the former councilman may have taken the cash and his reasons for embezzling from his friends and neighbors to the grave."

To the left of Murphy's article on Ned

Woodman's criminal acts was a shorter piece covering his memorial service. A large photo of Donna Woodman served as a divider between the two stories and James found himself repeatedly returning his gaze to the black and white shot. Ned's widow was an athletic blond. Her sleeveless black tank dress showed off muscular arms and a stomach as flat as an ironing board. It was difficult to see her face as the photograph was a profile shot and Donna's eyes were obscured by a pair of enormous sunglasses. It was her lips, set in a thin line of grief, and the way she clutched a single rose, that made the photo leap from the page. The emotion depicted in those clenched hands looked like something Jackson would have captured in one of his paintings.

"Poor woman," James murmured and passed the paper to Jane. "I wish this stuff about Ned had come out after the funeral. At least Donna Woodman could have buried her husband without the press circling the cemetery like a bunch of hungry hawks."

Jane studied the photograph and made a sympathetic noise. "Can you imagine how she feels? She must doubt every moment she shared with that man, wondering if she ever really knew him. Why did he take the money? Did he have an addiction? A mistress? A desperate friend in need?" She shook her head. "His secrets will taint all of her good memories. She won't truly be able to grieve until she knows the truth."

James tapped the photo. "Judging from this shot I'd say she's definitely begun the grieving process."

"That's not grief, it's anger," Jane answered with certainty. "Look at her mouth, her hands. This woman is filled with rage and has no way to let it out. The source of her anger is dead, and yet, she's got to stand at the edge of his grave and be composed in front of the cameras, when what she'd like to do is jump up and down on his coffin and scream at him." Seeing James' stunned expression, Jane gave a self-effacing shrug. "Maybe I'm reading too much into the photo, but that's how it strikes me."

"Let me look at that again." Scooting his chair closer to hers, James inhaled the clean scents of Jane's aloe body lotion and eucalyptus shampoo. As she leaned over to pour him more coffee, he caught a trace of lilac perfume and smiled.

His mother had also loved lilacs and he'd always associated the aroma with her warm embraces, easy laughter, and goodnight kisses. He thought of all the evenings she'd snuggled with him on his twin bed, reading him story after story until he finally fell asleep. Every night of his boyhood, he'd drifted off to tales of bravery and adventure, dark plots and ruthless villains, enchantment and beauty. James' mother had gifted him with his love of books. It was a gift he wanted to pass on to his own son and he was glad to know that Jane had been reading to Eliot since he was an infant.

"What are you thinking about?" Jane asked, nudging him with her elbow. "You've got on a very dreamy expression."

James gazed at his ex-wife, at how pretty she looked in her denim skirt and white blouse, her hair tucked into a headband and her face free of makeup. Had she known that lilac was his mother's trademark scent? Was she wearing it deliberately, to more easily earn his trust and affection? James folded *The Star* in half with a snap.

No, he thought. Jane doesn't need to manipulate me. She has her own money, a successful career, a supportive circle of family and friends. I've seen the way men look at her, too. Jane could have her pick of several male colleagues. It's not like she's desperate to find a man. Stop second-guessing her, his inner voice scolded.

"I was remembering how my mom loved the smell of lilacs," he replied to Jane after a long pause. "Your perfume reminds me of her. Actually, *you* remind me of her more and more now that we're spending so much time together."

"What a lovely compliment!" Jane squeezed his hand gratefully. "Your mother was an incredible woman. Kind, generous, funny . . . and boy, did she know her way around the kitchen! You're never going to find her equal in me when it comes to cooking. You know that, right?" She pretended to look alarmed. "You're not expecting me to start making soufflés and coq au vin, are you?"

"Forget haute cuisine, my dear. I'm very interested in your *other* assets," he searched for her lips with his own.

All too soon, Eliot's voice interrupted their kiss. "Are you two going to make a baby?"

Jane let her arms slide from James' shoulders, but she let her hand linger on his. She laughed. "Where'd you get *that* idea?"

"Lesley-Anne says that when a grown-up boy and a grown-up girl kiss, they make a baby." Eliot was clearly pleased to be able to share this bit of knowledge with his parents.

James cocked his head. "What else does Lesley-Anne say?"

Eliot focused on pouring himself a bowl of Honey Nut Cheerios before answering. "She says that the lady gets really fat and then the stork picks up the baby from the lady and brings it to the daddy. The baby cries a lot because it has bad dreams about storks until it can talk. Then it's not scared anymore." When Jane rose to pour milk on Eliot's cereal, he put his arms around her neck. "Did I have bad dreams about storks?"

The mention of birds put a damper on Jane's lightheartedness. "No, darling. But your friend, Lesley-Anne, sounds like quite an imaginative little girl."

Unsure of whether his friend had just been praised or slighted, Eliot shrugged. "She can be mean sometimes. She said Fay Sunray is for babies, but I don't care. Fay's pretty and I like her songs."

James carried his breakfast dishes to the sink. Jane wiped off the counter and whispered to him over the sound of the running water. "Lesley-Anne is going to be *that* kid. You know, the one who spoils the idea of the Tooth Fairy, the Easter Bunny, and Santa Claus for the rest of them. Mark my words!"

"Sad. Some mysteries were never meant be solved — the locations of the North Pole or the pot of gold at the end of the rainbow, for example," James said wistfully. "And then there are the ones we'd love to unravel, like the reason Murphy Alistair moved back to Quincy's Gap, what prompted the vandalism cases against you, or what Ned did with the stolen money. Those might elude us forever."

Jane paused in the act of loading the dishwasher. "Oh, you and your supper club will decipher all three of those riddles before the Fourth of July. I'm certain of that." Wiping her hands on a tea towel, she glanced around the tidy kitchen. "Now let's get going. If we miss the Firefighters' Parade Eliot's going to ask Miss Know-It-All Lesley-Anne how a kid can be granted a legal dispensation to live with his grandparents!"

Hours later, the Henry family were worn out from a memorable day of sunshine, music, and entertainment. At the annual Shenandoah Apple Blossom Festival, they'd listened to live bluegrass music, heard the energetic strains of marching bands, and watched a parade of fire department vehicles and floats bearing the Apple Blossom queen and her court. While Jane took Eliot to get a closer look at one of the rescue vehicles, James bought her an apple blossom necklace made of sterling silver from one of the many local craftsmen. After they'd dined on a meal of grilled cheese and tomato sandwiches he slipped it around her neck.

"Oh, it's beautiful!" Jane exclaimed with delight. Observing her radiant face, James realized that he'd never surprised her with unexpected gifts when they were married. He couldn't even remember if he'd ever bought her a bouquet of flowers or a box of chocolates during their time together. Watching her examine how the necklace lay on the soft skin where her collarbones met using the compact from her purse, James made a silent vow to be more spontaneous with his displays of affection in the future.

After their picnic lunch, the Henrys lost a handful of dollar bills playing games on the midway, rode a few of the tamer carnival rides, and then wove through the festival crowd toward the parking lot, content but thoroughly weary. Eliot was dragging his feet by the time they reached the outer rim of the festival and James knelt down so the boy could climb on his back for the remainder of the trek. Eliot immediately placed his cheek against his father's shoulder, sighed with contentment, and closed his eyes.

As they passed several vendors selling funnel cakes, soft-serve ice cream, and hot dogs, James heard the sounds of raised voices ahead. Pausing, he listened to the shrill shouts and frowned. "It's those protestors again. The ones from the food festival last weekend. I recognize the shrieks of their ringleader."

"We'll just walk past them as quickly as we can," Jane calmly responded.

Despite the increased noise level, Eliot didn't so much as lift his head, and when James spied the latest series of graphic posters held by the demonstrators, he sincerely hoped his son would keep his eyes shut until they were safely away.

Unfortunately, the Henry family had chosen the worst moment to leave. The group's zealous leader, the young woman with the spiked hair and the rows of hoop earrings, nearly collided with James and she stepped forward to hurl a cute plush pig at the hog dog vendor.

"BRUTE!" she screamed at the middle-aged man in the green apron as James leapt backward. "You're serving people ground-up pig! You're making money from bits and parts of an intelligent animal!"

The vendor stared at the place where the plush pig had landed and so did his line of customers. The man was obviously startled and a little intimidated by the group of protestors.

Seeking a quick escape, James tried to skirt around those waiting for food and the encroaching throng of demonstrators, but the crowd bunched together, effectively cutting off any chance of him finding a way through. James felt sorry for the hot dog vendor, for the young leader's eyes blazed with a righteous fury as she directed one of her companions to toss another pig at his booth. However, James' main concern was for his family's welfare and the possibility of violence erupting seemed high. He looked around for help, but everyone seemed frozen by the unfolding scene.

"You're contributing to the MURDER of the INNOCENT!" The spiky-haired leader yelled and then pointed at the stunned customers. "And YOU people! You're about to pay four dollars for a bunch of pulverized brains, bone, intestines, skin, and pink dye stuffed into a casing of edible *plastic!* How can you put that stuff into your body? Become a vegetarian! Save animals from being bred to become *your* food! Preserve your body from *disgusting,* ground-up refuse like this man's hot dogs!"

One of the male protestors handed her a sign. "Tia! *Now!*"

Together, Tia and her friend unrolled a

large banner. Several members of the shell-shocked crowd gasped in horror. Under the text, MEAT IS MURDER! were two pictures. The first showed a pig being shot in the head with some kind of gun and the second showed his body hovering over a stainless steel trough as blood poured from the slit in the creature's throat.

"This is how it happens, Carnivores! The pig is stunned by a bolt pistol. Not killed, *stunned!* It's *alive* when its throat is cut! ALIVE!" She pointed at a man in the crowd. "Just like your best-buddy, Fido, and your darling kitty, Snowball," she said as she directed her index finger at a woman wearing a T-shirt reading, "Beware: Crazy Cat Lady."

A small girl in the funnel cake line began to cry. She was quickly joined by the sobs of several other children.

A frightened and angry mother stepped out of the line. "Shame on you! Showin' stuff like this to a bunch of little kids!" The woman tried to tear the banner from Tia's hands and when that failed, she pushed by the other demonstrators with a snarl, her two tearful children in tow.

Her chastisement suddenly animated the crowd and the surge of hostility on both sides swelled. Peering over Jane's shoulder,

James saw a group of grim-faced security guards and burly firefighters moving in their direction.

"Help is on the way," he told her with relief as Eliot stirred on his back.

Tia saw the cavalry coming as well. She whispered something to the man holding the other end of the banner and then glanced briefly in James' direction. Her expression abruptly changed. In one moment, the young woman's face had been aglow with passion and determination. Now her jaw was slack and her eyes wide with fear. Dropping her end of the banner, she turned and ran off.

With their leader gone, the rest of the demonstrators rapidly dispersed and by the time the first security guard arrived, the commotion was over.

"Guess Tia didn't want to tangle with those firemen," Jane said as she pulled James to the far left, finally getting away from the excitement by using the volunteer's entrance gate as an exit. "Can't say I blame her. They don't look too happy. Did you happen to notice that the hot dog vendor is wearing a Volunteer Firefighter T-shirt under his apron?"

James hadn't, but didn't want to linger another second. Eliot woke up for a few brief seconds while being strapped into his car seat, but the moment James started the engine and eased out of the parking lot the fatigued little boy fell right back to sleep.

"You know, I agree with the protestors about the majority of their platform," Jane whispered once they'd reached the highway. "But they go too far."

"In these days of media sensationalism, they probably believe that that's the only way they can gain attention," James said. "Believe me, I think it's awful to expose folks to some of those posters, but at the same time, I admire their passion. They weren't out there today or last week for personal gain, but to help creatures that have no voice. I respect them for that." He slowed down as the Bronco hugged a sharp curve in the road. "Perhaps there's another, less offensive method to get their point across."

Jane raised her eyebrows. "I recognize that look. You're hatching a plan."

He laughed. "Oh, I was just thinking that the new owner of *The Shenandoah Star Ledger* might enjoy interviewing Tia. If I mention what happened today, Murphy will be here before the sun goes down, sniffing the ground for traces of the Apple Blossom conflict."

"I can see the headline now: 'Firemen and Fugitives'." Jane chuckled. "Still, an article would grant the activists the exposure they need." She reached over and squeezed James' arm. "You're a good man, Professor Henry."

"And you are the smartest, best-looking woman to have ever graced that passenger seat."

Jane ran her fingertips up his bicep and over the ridge of his shoulder so she could caress the nape of his neck. He sighed in contentment as she worked the kinks from his muscles.

"Despite the theatrics back there, today was perfect," she said. "It was one of those days I wish I could pack away in a box — save it like a treasure and then take it out again whenever I needed cheering." She blushed. "Boy, am I a sap or what?"

"You don't sound like a sap, but a woman who knows exactly what she wants," James replied.

"That's true," Jane said with a smile. "And what makes me happiest in the world is right here in this dear old truck. My two Henry men. What more could a girl ask for?"

An answer surfaced in James' mind and he was shocked to suddenly visualize an

168

item that he never thought he'd think of in connection to his ex-wife ever again. But here he was, glancing at her left hand and wondering if the "more" Jane might secretly desire was a wedding ring.

Jane and Eliot left for their house in Harrisonburg after church on Sunday. Mother and son wanted to plant a small vegetable garden and surprise James with their efforts the following weekend.

"I'll see you on Saturday unless you need me to drive up during the week again?" James asked suggestively as he kissed Jane goodbye.

"Oh, I will *definitely* need you," she answered with a playful wink.

After Jane's car had disappeared from sight, James checked his watch. If he drove hastily, he could reach his father's place in time for Milla's Sunday brunch. She often issued spontaneous invitations to her acquaintances from the First Baptist Church and prepared extra dishes ahead of time in the event her friends accepted. Luckily for James, the Methodist service ended thirty minutes before Milla's church let out so he stood a fair chance of pulling into the driveway as his stepmother was serving up hot food.

As the Bronco maneuvered the winding roads leading to his boyhood home, James visualized frying pans filled with bacon and sausage, a tray covered by buttery biscuits, and a platter of Milla's plump cinnamon buns, warm from the oven and covered with drizzles of sweet, buttery icing.

"Uh oh," he spoke to his reflection in the rearview mirror. "With Jane sleeping over, I forgot to listen to my reinforcement CD. I've missed two nights in a row! No wonder I feel the old cravings coming to life." He parked the truck next to Milla's lavender minivan, relieved that he'd be the only guest. "It's a good thing I'm seeing Harmony for another session tomorrow."

The renovated kitchen in his former home was filled with delicious aromas. Milla was just pulling a coffee cake from the oven when James tapped on the back door and let himself in.

"Oh! I am *so* glad you showed up!" Milla placed the cake on the stovetop and gave James a hug. The warmth from her oven mitts seeped through his shirt, sending a soothing feeling across the width of his back. "I asked Willow to join us this morning, but she couldn't make it. She and Francis are off to catch a matinee — some killer robot movie Francis has been waiting to see for months."

"Looks like you cooked enough to fill them to the point of exploding!" James exclaimed, eying a platter of crisp bacon and sausage links. "But I'd be delighted to eat Willow's share. In fact, I came over hoping you'd want to feed me."

Milla beamed. "Nothin' would please me more. And you know I have to make piles of bacon for your daddy. That man loves his meat!" She sprinkled pepper over a frying pan filled with scrambled eggs and gestured at the coffeemaker. "That's a fresh pot. Get yourself a cup and tell me how my grandson is doin' with his new diet."

James selected a mug from the cupboard, noting the chip on the rim. The majority of the coffee cups were damaged in some way and the dinner plates weren't much better. Jackson might have given the kitchen and upstairs bedrooms and baths a makeover, but those major cosmetic changes were enough to last him for decades.

Milla had brought her own cookware to the marriage, but she appeared to be perfectly content with the chipped crockery, the twenty-year-old curtains, and the ancient television in the den. She merely filled a closet with her clothes, added some pots and pans to the cabinets, and hung a few pictures on the wall. Most of these were of her beloved Corgi, Price Charles, who had passed away in his sleep shortly after Jackson and Milla were married, but there were photographs from her childhood as well. The end result was a house simultaneously marked by both of Jackson's two wives and no one entered the structure without feeling immediately and inexplicably at home.

"Eliot is still committed to his decision to be a vegetarian," James answered Milla's question as he fixed his coffee. "He complains about all the extra fruit and vegetables that show up in his lunchbox, but he eats them."

"Stickin' by his guns, just like his daddy and granddaddy." Milla used a spatula to lift a scalding bacon, egg, and cheese sandwich from her griddle onto a plate. James stopped her before she could add a piece of coffee cake, though the cinnamon crumble topping sorely tempted him. "You still trying to avoid sugar?" she asked.

"I am. I don't know that it's done any good, but I'll weigh myself tomorrow and hope for the best." James put his plate down on the kitchen table. "Where's Pop? Out in the shed?"

"Yes. He's doing a new series of paintings showing women at work." Milla set a loaded dish in front of Jackson's place. " 'Course he won't let me look at them until they're done, but perhaps you'd be willing to risk your neck and tell him his lunch is ready and already getting cold."

Jackson shouted his usual, "Go away!" when James knocked on the shed door.

"Come on, Pop. Milla's made you a meal fit for a king!"

"I don't doubt that," Jackson mumbled, but his voice betrayed his anticipation. "I gotta finish this one thing, but it just ain't comin' out right." There was a pause and then Jackson shouted, "Damnation!"

James smiled. "Let me in, Pop. Or I'll huff and I'll puff . . ."

After a long hesitation, Jackson shuffled over to the door and slid a key into the padlock. His face appeared in the doorway, but he made no move to allow James inside. "That big, bad wolf thing never gets any funnier, no matter how often you say it." Finally, he sighed and backed away, letting his son enter his private haven. "Go ahead. Never mind my food's gettin' cold as ice."

Jackson had begun his artistic career by painting birds. He then focused on the rendering of people's hands as they performed various tasks. After that, he produced a large number of paintings of little boys (all of whom bore a close resemblance to Eliot) until the D.C. gallery owner (who also happened to be Lindy's mother) asked him to find a fresh subject.

Taking her advice, Jackson had worked feverishly for the past few months. He'd started at Dolly's Diner, watching the waitresses and of course, Dolly herself. After painting a woman bearing a heavy serving tray, he'd selected a cashier at Food Lion, a female construction worker, and a mother balancing a toddler on one hip and a bag of dog kibble on the other. The women were busy concentrating on their tasks, their faces aglow with purpose. Every captured movement held a trace of power, and the determination in each woman's plain face transformed them into radiant beauties.

"You've done it again," James whispered in awe as he stared at the canvases. "These are magical."

Suddenly, he had an idea. "Pop? I'd like to talk to you about a commission."

Jackson snorted. "You can't afford me, my boy."

Knowing his father was just giving him a hard time, James slung an arm over the older man's bony shoulders and squeezed. "Come on, Pop. I know how much you want me to drive you to Home Depot this afternoon."

"All right, son. We'll talk in the kitchen. Can't make sense of anythin' without a big plate of bacon."

Later that afternoon, James returned home with the parts he needed to replace the leaking faucets in the master bath and the kitchen sink. He'd never had reason to perform home repairs before as Jackson had handled all the maintenance around the Henry home, but he was excited to learn. Armed with a Time Life book on basic plumbing, James felt confident that he possessed the smarts and the tools to complete the necessary repairs.

He began with the bathroom faucet. By the time he'd figured out how to turn off the water, replace the faucet, and clean the water spots from the countertop, mirror, and floor, the sky had begun turning the orchid-purple of twilight.

James decided to repair the kitchen sink before heating up a dinner of roast chicken marinated in white wine and rosemary with a side of butter beans. It was only when he laid out his tools on a dishcloth next to the cutting board that he happened to glance out the window facing the backyard.

Something was hanging from the yellow birdhouse he'd placed in the center of a ring of Knock Out rosebushes behind the deck. The birdhouse stood on a tall wooden post and a light breeze was wafting through the yard, causing what appeared to be a piece of paper taped to the base of the birdhouse to flutter up and down.

Laying his wrench on the dishtowel, James stepped outside and walked to the garden bed. After pulling the letter off the birdhouse, he swiveled so the waning sun would illuminate the plain white sheet. He read the single sentence printed there in plain block letters. Stunned, he read it again. It said:

STAY AWAY FROM HER

Taped to the bottom of the paper was a single black feather.

EIGHT:
JALAPEÑO POTATO CHIPS

Grams of
Sugar
50

James stood rooted to the spot for several minutes, his eyes moving from the letter to the deepening shadows in the trees and back to the letter again. His eyes fixed on the words and his body became unnaturally still, as though an invisible Gorgon had turned him into a piece of statuary. When something flew past his face, startling him, he looked up and saw a cluster of bats darting across the purplish sky. The rapid fluttering of their wings and their high-pitched squeaks awoke James from his immobility.

Rushing into the kitchen, he eased the letter into a gallon-sized freezer bag, grabbed his car keys from the counter, and dashed out to the Bronco. A combination of anger and fear caused him to take the winding mountain roads at a risky pace, but his dependable old truck gripped the pavement as though sensing James' need.

Once, as James paused at a stop sign, he glanced at the letter lying on the passenger seat. The words, printed in bold ink, seemed to be silently shouting at him and the black feather looked like the curve of a malicious smile at the bottom of the paper.

He did not look over again.

It took less than ten minutes to reach Lucy's house on the outskirts of town. As James pulled into her dirt driveway, stirring up billows of dust as he rammed his gear stick into park, her three German Shepherds bounded from the open gate in the backyard and swarmed the Bronco. Though the dogs had known James for years and were intelligent enough to recognize his truck on sight, they enjoyed the idea of intimidating any intruder and began a chorus of snarling and barking raucous enough to wake the entire valley.

James rolled his window down an inch. "Bono! Bon Jovi! Benatar! It's *me!*"

Clearly, the canines were not impressed

by the voice of their mistress' ex-boyfriend. In fact, they curled their lips, revealing more of their threatening fangs and their dark eyes glimmered with excitement.

"Come on, now." He pleaded with them through the window. "I've seen all of you act like oversized lap cats plenty of times! I know this is all a front. A few Milkbones and you're putty in anyone's hands. Are you going to let me out or what?"

Apparently, they weren't. Tails swishing with glee, the dogs circled the Bronco and carried on with their howling until Lucy opened her front door. James only saw her for a second, but he could have sworn that she was wearing a slinky nightie. She vanished from view, returning less than a minute later.

Attired in sweatpants and a tank top, Lucy trotted down her front steps and walked hurriedly toward the drive, shouting at the dogs to "stand down." James noticed her feet were bare and she didn't seem too pleased to see him.

That was when James noticed there were two vehicles parked along the fence line toward the rear of Lucy's house. Her dirt-covered Jeep and a mud-splattered Camaro.

"I'm sorry," he said after she'd secured the disappointed canines in the enclosed backyard. "If I known you had company . . ." he trailed off. "Actually, I would have come anyway. You're the first person I thought of to turn to . . ." He met her eyes and saw that the initial disapproval he'd seen there had been replaced by concern.

"What's wrong, James?" She stepped aside, beckoning for him to get out of his truck.

He handed her the letter and then explained about the dead birds left at Jane's house.

Lucy brought the plastic bag closer to her face. "Doesn't sound like a coincidence to me. A crow was nailed to her door and now there's a crow's feather taped to this letter." She shook her head. "I don't like this. Someone's trespassed on two properties and deliberately placed animal corpses or threatening letters in strategic locations. It's too invasive and far too sinister to be considered a practical joke."

"What should I do?" James hated the plaintive sound to his voice, but he couldn't help it. "I'm not worried about me, but I feel like Jane and Eliot are vulnerable. The cops have put her place on their drive-by list, but now that I've received this, it's clear that this person followed her to my house. Jane's got some kind of psycho stalker!"

Lucy studied the note a little longer. "You'd better come inside. I'd like to show this to Sullie and get his take."

So that's who owns the Camaro, James thought and was surprised at how quickly Sullie and Lucy had become intimate, as her previous attire strongly indicated.

Half expecting to see Sullie lounging on the sofa wearing silk boxers while Barry White's voice crooned from the stereo, James entered the house hesitantly. Instead, he found the hunky deputy seated at the kitchen table, sipping a bottle of Budweiser as he paged through a magazine. Like Lucy, he was clad in sweats and a T-shirt. Upon seeing James, he jumped up and smiled.

"Good to see you, man! You're lookin' well." He grasped James' hand and shook it heartily.

"You too," James answered, observing Sullie's manly jaw, mammoth shoulders, and tree trunk legs. The man looked like he'd been carved from a block of limestone. Though he didn't possess the sharpest of wits, he was handsome and extremely friendly. James had done his best to cultivate a dislike for the man in the past, but found he harbored no ill will toward the amiable deputy.

"Welcome back to Quincy's Gap, Sullie. I

truly apologize for disturbing your evening, but I'm feeling a little desperate." James gestured at Lucy. "She's always been the problem-solver of our group and I've got a major problem."

Lucy gave him a grateful smile and then placed the note in the center of the table. When she spoke, it was with the voice of an officer of the law. She reviewed the pertinent details for Sullie and then awaited his assessment.

"Your ex-wife believes the perp could be one of her students?" Sullie asked.

James shrugged. "It seemed like the most logical conclusion at the time, but now that I've gotten this note . . . well, it's just hard to imagine a disgruntled coed tracking me down and leaving me this letter because of a low exam grade."

"Do you and Jane share any common enemies?" Lucy's fingertips hovered just above the crow's feather. "Perhaps someone who likes birds or spends a lot of time outdoors?"

Sullie nodded, as though Lucy's question was a sound one. He then crossed the kitchen in three strides and retrieved two bottles of Bud from the refrigerator. Popping the caps off into the garbage can, he handed one to James and offered the second to Lucy. She declined, her attention fixed on the letter.

"Honestly, the only person who might have reason to dislike us both is Murphy." James felt his cheeks rush with heat. "I think she planned on rekindling our old flame upon her return to Quincy's Gap and wasn't too thrilled to hear that I had a son and was on great terms with my ex-wife."

Lucy's expression was masked and James hoped he hadn't offended her. In describing Murphy's hopes, he'd basically described the way Lucy had felt until very recently. She remained silent, but Sullie took a swig from his beer and said, "Makes sense. If Murphy wants you to stay away from your ex and is angry about you two spending time together, then she might have written this."

"Still, I can't see her driving to Harrison-burg and nailing a dead crow on Jane's front door," James protested. "You'd have to be pretty twisted to do that."

James had barely finished speaking when Lucy slapped her palms against the table, startling both men. "May I remind you that this woman was secretly writing a book about you, about *us,* the whole time you were dating? Don't underestimate what she's capable of!"

Chastised, James pretended to be very interested in the pattern of Lucy's linoleum floor.

She touched him briefly on the arm, as though to apologize for being harsh. "The least I can do is find out what Murphy was up to this evening. Not officially, of course, but I know she'll be at The Sweet Tooth tomorrow morning, picking up coffee and a croissant, and I can casually question her then." Lucy frowned. "That woman eats carbs every single day and is thinner than a tomato stake. It's just not fair."

"Men don't like women to be skin and bones." Sullie put a proprietary hand on Lucy's hip. "We want soft curves with just the right amount of steel underneath. Like you, baby. You're all woman."

Seeming embarrassed but pleased, Lucy removed Sullie's hand from her hip and kissed him on the palm. James resumed his interest in the diamond pattern on the floor as the pair of deputies exchanged murmured endearments. Finally, he cleared his throat and said, "Well, I'd better be on my way. Thanks for hearing me out — both of you." He gestured at the letter. "Should I leave this with you?"

Lucy nodded and accompanied him to the door. "If I think Murphy is lying to me about her whereabouts this evening, I'll whip this out and see if it creates a reaction." Her blue eyes flashed, reminding James of the aggressive glimmer he'd seen in her dogs' eyes when he'd first arrived.

"I know you'd like to bring Murphy down a peg," James said softly. "Lord knows she deserves some kind of comeuppance besides fame and fortune, but I still can't imagine her doing something like this."

The pair stood on the stoop for a moment, watching the moths flutter around the lamppost guarding the entrance of Lucy's path. James experienced a strong surge of déjà vu, for he and Lucy had lingered in this spot many times before, as good friends and later, as lovers. For months, a feeling of awkwardness had existed between them, but James wanted their relationship to return to what it had been when they'd first formed the supper club. Glancing at her, James wondered how to express this desire.

"This is good," he said, once the silence had stretched on too long. "You and Sullie. I know it's a relatively new thing, but you seem right for one another. There's an ease between you two that usually only develops after a couple has been together for a long time." He cleared his throat and continued. "You're one of my best friends, Lucy. I want you to be happy. Thanks again for being so gracious tonight."

Giving her a smile, he began to walk toward the Bronco.

"James!" Lucy called after him. "I'll also check in with the Harrisonburg police tomorrow. Let them know that the person bothering Jane is up to something down here too. That ought to ensure her house stays on their patrol list a little longer." She put her hands on her hips, doing her best to look fierce. "At least that'll give you some peace of mind. And I'll be driving by *your* place myself. After all, nobody messes with one of *my* dearest friends and gets away with it."

And just like that, their friendship was restored.

James drove home beneath the white light of the full moon. Hung high in the sky among a cluster of stars and a brighter orb that was likely a planet, the moon seemed to grin down upon the round hills of the Shenandoah Valley.

Back at home, James took a beer out to the deck and settled into a plastic lounge chair. He listened to a chorus of crickets and the buzzing of other insects until his grumbling stomach reminded him that he'd neglected to eat dinner. It was late and he was tired, so he settled for a generous snack of Jalapeño-flavored Pringles. He sat this way for a long time, his anxiety ebbing away as the night wore on. Sighing, he let his body sink into the chair and as his lids grew heavy, James realized he'd eaten the entire tube of potato chips.

This does not bode well for tomorrow's weigh-in, he thought and sluggishly climbed into bed. Still, he decided that a threatening note could force even the most disciplined eater into a junk food binge. Anyway, it's not like I had a bunch of sugar, he reasoned before drifting off to sleep.

The next morning, James shucked off his T-shirt and pajama bottoms and prepared to face off against the scale. It had nearly killed him to go through an entire week without weighing himself. He was, after all, a creature of habit and it was his habit to wake up, shuffle into the bathroom, turn on the shower, and shed his clothes. He'd then put his hands on his belly in front of his bathroom mirror, pivoting this way and that and squeezing his flesh, trying to determine whether his paunch felt bigger or smaller than the day before.

Pinching the flesh around his belly button, James' hand would then travel to his love handles. He'd grasp them between his hands, wiggling the flesh up and down. Finally, he'd suck in a deep breath and watch his stomach shrink by several inches.

Now, having gone through his usual routine, he murmured to the bathroom mirror, "Doesn't feel any different. Let's see what the numbers have to say."

As was customary, James inhaled a giant breath and then forcefully exhaled. When he felt as though every ounce of air had been expelled from his lungs, he stepped on the scale. Shifting until his feet were perfectly centered on the glass surface, he held himself as still as possible and waited for the digital numbers to surface in their silver window. He never breathed until they'd revealed themselves. Now, as his weight appeared, his inhalation was sharp with frustration and disappointment.

"I haven't lost a thing!" he shouted at the device. "Why bother giving up sugar when my weight stays *exactly* the same!"

In the shower, he angrily massaged shampoo into his hair and then scrubbed his skin roughly, using a washcloth, as though punishing his body for a less-than-desirable result during the daily weigh-in.

By the time James reached the library, his mood had improved slightly due to a large cup of creamy coffee and a nutritious breakfast of whole grain waffles and strawberries. When he saw Francis and Scott pedaling into the parking lot on their mountain bikes, racing to see who would reach the book drop first, he couldn't stop his mouth from curving into a grin.

"Whoa!" Francis shouted. "You're like a lightning bolt today, bro! You must really want to get busy *training* Fern over in the Tech Corner, huh?"

Scott's cheeks burned red and he punched his twin in the arm. "Shut up, dude!" Next, he chained his bike to the rack and jogged up the stairs, saluting James when he reached the top. "We're all set for Mrs. Waxman's retirement party, Professor."

"Milla and Willow told us they'd handle the food, so all we have to do is make the punch and decorate," Francis chimed in as the three men entered the library. "Um, should one of the punch bowls be spiked, Professor?"

"Absolutely. And I've got an amazing gift idea lined up, assuming my father can paint as fast as you two can ride those bikes," James said. "Ah, here comes Fern for her final day of training. She's a quick study, isn't she gentlemen?"

"Too quick. I wish I had more time with

her," Scott muttered and then beamed at Fern as she breezed through the security gate, the full skirt of her rose-colored sundress flowing behind her. Her eyes immediately sought Scott's and she gave him a special smile before greeting James and Francis.

The four librarians prepared for their first patrons of the day. When the clock struck nine, people trickled into the building and the library hummed softly with activity all morning long. Just before lunch, James heard an inappropriately loud and combative voice from the direction of the circulation desk. He'd been busy helping old Mrs. Withers navigate the computer. Having decided to sell her collection of Beanie Babies, she wanted to look up current market values on eBay. James had directed her to the online auction site and then paled when she produced a notebook filled with pages of Beanie Baby inventory.

"You'd like to check the value of each of these?" He asked, dreading her reply. "How many do you have, ma'am?"

"Oh, a thousand or so," Mrs. Withers replied merrily and patted the notebook. "I'm hopin' to raise enough money to take my daughter on a little trip. She hasn't been away since Roy Junior was born and *that* was five years ago. She won't leave the boy, but if I buy the tickets, she'll feel like she has to go." She pursed her lips. "Parents hover too much nowadays. When I was a mother I had my own life. I played bridge and tennis and was president of the gardening club. My girl needs to cut the damned cord and I'm gonna help her do it!"

Using his concern over the raised voice at the circulation desk as a reason to avoid several hours of eBay tutelage, James excused himself and hustled off.

He was most surprised to see Murphy and Tia in a standoff against Scott. Of course, Tia was the only one not speaking in hushed tones. Standing with one hand on her left hip, she gesticulated wildly with the other, clearly ignoring Scott's requests to lower her voice.

Murphy stood slightly apart from the younger woman, as though attempting to distance herself from the argument. Still, her face was alight with voyeuristic pleasure.

"Ladies!" James stepped beside Tia and forced his lips into a tight smile. In an exaggerated whisper he asked, "How can I help you?"

Tia turned her dark eyes on him and then she deliberately looked back at Murphy and hissed, "Forget about the library! Let's go to the grocery store!" And with that, she walked out through the lobby doors.

Murphy gazed at James with a mixture of wonder and befuddlement. "Boy oh boy, you sure have a way with women, Mr. Henry. She nearly lost a few of her piercings in her haste to get away from you. Why is that?"

James shrugged. "I have no idea." He glanced over at Scott, more interested in pacifying his distressed employee than satisfying Murphy's endless curiosity. "What did the young woman want?"

Scott pushed a small poster across the desk. "To hang *this* under the Community Happenings section of our bulletin board. I told her nicely that it was too scary for our younger patrons, but she wouldn't take no for an answer." His cheeks flushed. "I'm afraid I stopped being a polite public servant. I repeated myself several times, but when she called me a fascist and an accessory to murder I got a little mad." He raked his hands through his hair and sighed ruefully. "I should never have mentioned that I was having a meatball sub for lunch."

James gave his employee a sympathetic pat on the shoulder and then leaned over to scrutinize the poster. It portrayed the image of a cartoonish pig lying on its back with its legs sticking in the air. It had x's for eyes and a long tongue lolled from its mouth. Above the pig, a spider resembling Charlotte from the E. B. White novel had industriously written the following words in her web: *Don't Kill Wilbur. Become A Vegetarian.*

"Old Charlotte must have been all done in after spinning such a lengthy slogan," James remarked. "It's clever, but you're right, Scott. I think it would definitely upset the kids and quite a few adult patrons as well. You made the right call."

Murphy, who had made no move to accompany Tia, crossed her arms and studied James. "And yet, your own son has recently become a vegetarian, has he not?"

"Yes, but . . ." James was about to say that Eliot hadn't been shocked or emotionally traumatized into the decision, but he knew that wasn't the absolute truth. After all, his son had been so influenced by Fay Sunray's words that he'd had to flee the dinner table in the face of a slice of pepperoni pizza. "Is this your new way of conducting interviews?" he inquired airily. "I thought you preferred to gather material over one of Willie's frozen custards and a cappuccino?"

"I do," Murphy agreed. "But Tia is one sharp negotiator. She talked me into putting these posters all over town before she'd answer any of my more probing questions. I've been collecting background material on her as we work, but I'm her hired hand until the posters are all up." She glanced in the direction of the lobby doors. "And she's not going anywhere without me because we took my car." Murphy reclaimed the poster and wiggled an index finger at James. "And you can bet your Dewey Decimal system that I'm going to find out why she looked at you as though you were the Charles Manson of Quincy's Gap."

James scowled. "Perhaps she's read your *novel* too many times and is worried that hanging around me will spell certain death."

"You *do* have a certain magnetism when it comes to corpses." Murphy smiled and touched his cheek with an intimacy that made James uncomfortable. "I find that quality strangely sexy."

James didn't feel like skipping to A Better State of Mind as he had for his past two sessions. In fact, he'd been in a foul mood ever since Murphy's visit to the library and he hadn't been able to do anything to lift himself out of it. Pulling into a parking space next to a shiny new SUV, James paused to admire the moss-green paint, the tidy tan leather interior, and the vanity plate reading, VEG OUT.

"Hey man!" Lennon called out as he headed in James' direction. "You like my ride? It's a Ford Escape Hybrid. Gets thirty miles to the gallon and has super clean emissions. *Totally* earth-friendly."

"It's a beaut." James glanced at the frayed ends of Lennon's jeans, his washed-out Bob Marley T-shirt, and his worn sandals. Leaving all tact aside he said, "That must have cost a pretty penny."

"Dude, like, a generous relative gave me some dough and I spent it," Lennon smiled guilelessly. "I believe in living in the moment, ya know. I could totally get hit by a bus tomorrow, so why not party hard today?" He gestured at the rack affixed to the back of the SUV. "Do you bike, man? I could show you some of the awesome local trails I've discovered. My all-time fav is the Brandywine Lake Trail. Fifty-two miles of rock 'n roll." He flicked a frayed lock of hair away from his face. "Whenever I'm stressin', that place chills me right out. And I've got two bikes! I can put on the dual rack in a snap!" He gestured at the back of his truck. "Wanna let loose?"

James laughed at the image of himself barreling down a wooded path. "Think I'll stick to four wheels, but my coworkers, Scott and

Francis, ride their bikes to work. You should drop by the library sometime so I can introduce you. You guys are about the same age and I bet they'd love to explore a new trail." Checking his watch, James saw that he still had a few minutes until his appointment. James wanted to linger with the younger man a little longer, enjoying the influence of his winsome, buoyant presence. He pointed toward the pink and purple cottages. "How about Skye? Does she ride too?"

Lennon shook his head. "Nah, she's more into running. It's her time to center, ya know? Just her, an iPod, and a long stretch of road. That's cool, but sometimes a guy's gotta rip down a hill with the trees flying by like *whish, whish!*" He gesticulated with his well-calloused hands. "Anyhow, the work day is done, my man, so I am outta here. Gonna go suck in some fresh oxygen! Peace out!"

Feeling slightly silly, James returned the universal gesture for peace and walked through the Wellness Village to Harmony's office. Skye accepted his payment and offered him a glass of citrus-flavored water and a friendly smile.

"Harmony is running a little late," she apologized on behalf of her employer.

"Would you like to browse through our newest magazines while you wait?"

James took a few from Skye's graceful hands. "Thank you." He placed the magazines on the sofa and watched Skye water a potted ficus tree in the corner of the reception room. "I ran into Lennon outside. He's a very friendly young man. I can see why you two make such a good couple. You both exude such a positive . . ." He trailed off, unsure of the correct wording.

"Aura?" Skye finished for him. "That's sweet of you to say. Lennon and I haven't been dating long, but I admire how he puts his entire being into each and every task. The smallest details are important to him, from raking the rock garden to hosing out the trash cans to picking wildflowers for me." She colored prettily. "I've never known someone so gentle and yet so dedicated."

"Well, he's a lucky man to have captured your heart," James said as Harmony's door opened and Lindy walked slowly down the hall, still drowsy from her time of deep relaxation.

James was delighted to see his friend. "I didn't know you'd be here today!"

"I *had* to get help!" Lindy whispered loudly. "I never thought the three hours I spent with Luis' mama would throw me into

197

such a tailspin, but that woman is a Tasmanian devil — emphasis on 'devil'!"

Stifling a grin, James led Lindy to the sofa. "That bad, huh?"

"She ran her finger along the baseboard *underneath* my kitchen table and glanced at the dust as though it might eat away her hand! She held up each piece of silverware to the light, looking for spots. And then she polished them on her *own* handkerchief. She ate three bites of the meal I'd slaved over all day and then declared she'd suddenly lost her appetite." Lindy rubbed her tired eyes. "She never spoke directly to me. If she wanted to know something about my house, my family, or my job, she'd ask Luis as if I weren't sitting right there! It was awful!"

James gave his friend a hug. "Did Harmony make you feel better?"

Lindy nodded. "I asked her to help me keep a firm hold on my self-confidence, but this is going to be a mighty long week." She sighed lugubriously. "I'll be listening to my new reinforcement CD in all my spare time."

"Bring her along to Mrs. Waxman's retirement party," James suggested. "We'll pour champagne punch down her throat and stuff her full of Milla's cake."

"Can't I just drop her off at the local

taxidermist instead? That would get her out of my hair forever," Lindy joked and James was pleased to note that his friend's sense of humor was intact. "Are you going in for another sugar-busting session?"

"I don't know." It was James' turn to be downcast. "I haven't lost any weight and I feel like I'm at war with myself. Basically, I'm ticked off."

Harmony arrived at that moment and smiled at both of her clients. "Perhaps today's session should be about striking a balance between your mind and body," she advised gently. "Lindy, feel free to call me if you need to see me again this week. Just remember to listen to your CD and to believe in your value as a wonderful and unique individual."

Lindy nodded and shut her eyes for a moment. After opening them again, she said good-bye to James and then reached for the front door, repeating Harmony's phrase like a mantra. "I am a unique and wonderful individual. I am a unique and wonderful individual."

Harmony didn't interrupt Lindy but softly directed Skye to catch up to their client outside, as Lindy had departed without her reinforcement CD. Skye neatly labeled the CD before heading for the exit.

"Won't she be too late to catch Lindy?" James asked as he followed Harmony into her office.

"Skye was a track star in college. She doesn't run like the wind, she *vanquishes* the wind." Harmony gestured at the recliner and James sank heavily into the chair. "Tell me what's going on."

"I haven't lost a single ounce and I'm angry. At myself," James answered. "Like Lindy, I've had a stressful few days and I feel like I'll never make any progress in the weight loss department until, well, I can have some faith in myself. Right now, that's running a little low."

Harmony considered her client's problem for a moment and then wrote a few notes on a legal pad. "Considering these developments, let's change our direction slightly. Instead of focusing on sugar cravings, we're going to ask your mind and body to work together as a single unit — for your entire self to be one team, striving for health and a sense of well being. How does that sound?"

"Can you throw in a dose of stress relief too?" James implored. "I feel like if I don't dial down that part of my brain I'll be hijacking Little Debbie trucks before long!"

The sound of Harmony's musical laughter

filled the room. When her expression of calm concern returned she asked, "In addition to your frustration over not having lost any weight, are there other factors causing you to feel anxiety?"

James issued an unattractive snort. "It'll take more time than we've got to cover them all! Let's just take care of my inner war today. We can tackle maniacal ex-girlfriends, psychotic letter-writers, and crazy vegetarian activists next week." He cleared his throat. "No offense."

"None taken," Harmony replied and dimmed the lights.

Nine:
Milla's Chocolate Mocha Cake

Grams of
Sugar
4

In preparing for Mrs. Waxman's surprise party, James and his coworkers encountered Tia's pig poster everywhere. It hung from the bulletin board at Food Lion, the YMCA, and the post office, and had been taped to the windows of dozens of small businesses including the ABC store, Goodbee's Pharmacy, the Polar Pagoda, and not surprisingly, The Yuppie Puppy. It seemed as if Quincy's Whimsies and The Sweet Tooth were the only establishments in town that had refused to display the attention-grabbing poster.

By the time Wednesday evening rolled around, the talk among the library staff revolved around the prone piggy and Murphy's newspaper article on animal rights activist, Katrina "Tia" Royale.

"Bro, she didn't act like someone whose parents were mega rich," Scott commented to Francis. "When I think of tycoons' daughters, I picture mafia princesses like Meadow Soprano or airhead socialites like Paris Hilton."

His twin shrugged as he blew up an orange balloon. "Yeah, it's kinda cool that Tia isn't posing for the media or carrying around little dogs with diamond collars," he said while tying the balloon's stem into a knot. "Maybe, in order to be her own person, Tia decided to put all her time and money into protecting animals. From what I read in *The Star,* she could spend every day shopping and still not put a dent in her trust fund, yet she doesn't act like a spoiled brat."

Willow scowled and handed her boyfriend a yellow balloon. "Why don't you save your breath for the balloons, Francis?"

"What? Did I say something wrong?" Francis reached out to touch Willow's pale, blond hair, but she swatted his hand away.

"*Some* of us don't have trust funds or

uber-rich parents," she pointed out heatedly. "*Some* of us work at regular jobs *and* serve our causes in our spare time without screaming at senior citizens or making little kids cry!"

Scott passed Fern a roll of tape and a crepe paper streamer so she could affix the decoration to the exit sign. Peering down at Willow from the top of the small ladder, Fern said, "I haven't been your roommate for long, but *I'm* impressed by how many hours you volunteer at the animal shelter."

"I just love being there," Willow replied, pleased to receive recognition for her efforts. "Don't get me wrong, I love my work at Quincy's Whimsies, but it's *so* rewarding to watch a family pick out a dog or cat." Willa sighed happily. "Did you know that our shelter doesn't euthanize? It's wonderful, but it also means our cages are always full." She pointed at James, who was busy pouring chilled champagne into one of the punch bowls. "I keep trying to persuade Mr. Henry to adopt a pet for Eliot. Every kid needs a furry friend." She lowered her voice. "Especially an only child. It's nice for them to have someone to talk to. Can't you just see Eliot and a frisky little puppy rolling around in that big backyard of Mr. Henry's?"

Fern smiled at Willow. "I'd like to volunteer at the shelter too, but I'm afraid I'd end up filling our apartment with animals. How do you keep from bringing them all home?"

"Easy — our landlord would toss us out on our butts!" Willow laughed. "But maybe when our lease runs out in the fall we could rent a small house instead? That way, we can at least provide foster care for some of the shelter animals until they find permanent homes."

"I'd love that," Fern readily agreed. "And I'm one of those crazy people who actually enjoys yard work, so you'll never have to cut the grass."

As the two young women exchanged excited chatter, James smiled at how rapidly they'd become friends. He finished arranging the plastic punch cups on a card table and then dropped a pile of napkins in the center. Standing back, he examined his handiwork with a frown.

"Doesn't look too good," he murmured.

"It was a nice try, dear, but this calls for a woman's touch." Milla gently pushed him aside. "Why don't you carry in the food from my van and leave the decorating to me?" She patted him lovingly on the back. "You need to keep your daddy away from the spiked punch," she ordered, her eyes twinkling. "He's been grumbling all day over having to be here and if he drinks too much on an empty stomach, he's gonna ride that wheeled book cart home before the party even gets started!"

Laughing, James went out to Milla's lavender van and carried in trays of hors d'oeuvres, a platter of ham biscuits, and a stunning cake made to resemble a stack of library books. Easing the cake carefully onto a side table, James paused in order to admire Milla's artistry. The frosted book on the top was entitled, *Quincy's Gap Loves Mrs. Waxman.* Below that line was a chocolate fudge subtitle listing the years she'd worked at the library. In place of the author's name were the words, *From Your Grateful Patrons.* James inhaled the delectable scents of chocolate and coffee and sighed.

"Chocolate mocha cake with coffee icing. It's Mrs. Waxman's favorite," Milla told him as he admired the confection. "Why don't you take a picture of the food before the festivities start? Fern told me she'd like to assemble a scrapbook of the party for our retiree." She glanced over at James' newest employee. "She's a lovely girl. You know how to pick 'em, honey." Milla's mouth crinkled into a smile. "I do believe she's sweet on our Scott, too. How do you feel about inter-office love affairs?"

James rubbed his chin. "Their shifts don't overlap much, so I'm not worried about things getting awkward if they start dating and then break up. What perplexes me is Scott's reluctance to ask the young lady out." He lowered his voice. "You see, he's become close to someone via the computer and feels that he can't pursue a relationship with Fern until he meets this other girl in the flesh."

Milla put her hands over her chest. "So they need to see if the sparks will really fly — how exciting! Where and when is this face-to-face going to happen?"

"It's hard to say," James removed the plastic wrap from a platter of sliced strawberries and baked brie. "She canceled their original meeting time at the last minute, so Scott is now filled with doubts. Poor kid."

Clucking her tongue disapprovingly, Milla said, "Computer dating sounds awful sticky to me. Call me old fashioned, but I don't think it's wise to fall in love with a person when you can't look into their eyes or listen to the sound of their laughter." She placed a silver ladle next to the punch bowl. "Folks just don't come off the same in black and white. You can make yourself into anybody you want by typing a few words, but then someone might fall in love with a 'you' who doesn't really exist."

"It's how our world works now, Milla. People do most of their communication through the computer."

Puckering her lips, Milla waved her hand around the room. "A machine will never be able to replace *this*."

James had been so busy placing the food trays where Milla wanted that he hadn't taken notice of the library's transformation. Bright balloons and paper streamers hung from the ceiling and floral cloths covered the study tables in the main room. Fern and Willow were setting small vases filled with Gerbera daises in the center of each table, while Scott laid out a guest book for the party goers to sign and Francis programmed one of the computers to play three hours' worth of smooth jazz and then strummed an air guitar to amuse Willow.

Several guests had shown up early intending to lend a hand. One placed garbage cans in strategic positions, another wheeled the cart of sale books in from the lobby, and a third helped Jackson lift his latest painting, covered by a white cloth, onto an easel on the counter of the Information Desk.

As the sound of saxophones, trumpets, and clarinets floated through the room, the supper club members began to trickle in as though lured from outside by the enticing strains of music.

Gillian and Bennett entered first and James was pleased to note that they were holding hands. Lucy was the next to arrive. James had told her to bring Sullie along and she'd been delighted by the suggestion. Lucy introduced her handsome boyfriend to the other guests as a fellow deputy, but her face, glowing with happiness, betrayed her deeper feelings. Sullie kept glancing at her from the corner of his eye and occasionally he'd whisper something into her ear, causing her to laugh or blush with pleasure. James had never seen Lucy look so beautiful.

When Lindy appeared, running ten minutes late, she sped right over to James and clutched his arm as if he could save her from slipping through a thin patch of ice. "Look out, James, she's here! The Dragon Lady of Mexico! Is there *anyone* you can find to entertain Luis' mama for five minutes?"

"Only five minutes?" James teased.

Lindy nodded. "That's all it'll take for me to chug down three cups of champagne punch. I don't want her to see me drinking or that'll be yet another strike against me. It's bad enough that I'm a 'half-blood'."

James frowned. "She called you that?" He watched as Luis and a small, plump woman with wiry black hair and walnut-brown eyes entered the room, surveying the surroundings with a curled lip as though she was standing in a landfill and not in James' beloved library. Luis walked with rounded shoulders, darting apologetic glances in Lindy's direction as his mother pulled on his sleeve, forcing him to bend to her height so she might more easily release a stream of complaints (all in Spanish, of course) into his left ear.

At that moment, Luigi joined the party. Mrs. Waxman had spent countless hours giving the restaurateur advice on the education of his six children and he had become one of her adoring fans. He'd even offered to cater the event, but Milla and Willow wouldn't hear of it.

"PROFESSOR HENRY!" He shouted from across the room. "THE LIBRARY — CHE BELLO!"

Waving Luigi closer, James offered him a glass of punch. The restaurateur accepted the beverage with a booming "GRAZIE" and then left James to mingle with the older widows and divorcees. By the time the other guests arrived, along with Mrs. Waxman and her closest family members, Luigi had made his way to the side of Luis' mother.

"ALMA? SUCH A *LOVELY* NAME! YOU ARE THIRSTY? COME! LUIGI WILL GET YOU A DRINK!"

James held his breath, expecting Alma to reject Luigi's vociferous offer, but to his surprise, she seemed to forget all about her son and, smiling, took Luigi's proffered arm. Luis stared after them in amazement.

The noise level escalated as Mrs. Waxman made her rounds. James felt a pang of sadness as he watched his former middle school teacher and coworker accept handshakes and warm embraces from everyone in the room.

"I still don't think I should be here," Fern whispered to James. "It doesn't feel right."

"Mrs. Waxman specifically asked that you attend," James reminded her. "And I'm thrilled that you're here. After all, you're part of our team now and you're capturing the event on film." He pointed at her camera. "Whenever Mrs. Waxman misses us, she'll only need to open the scrapbook you're creating in order to feel like she's with her friends in Quincy's Gap. See? You're an asset already."

"Your father's painting will help her remember too. I can't wait to see it." Fern glanced around the room. "Have you ever thought of using all that great wall space to display the work of local artists?"

James followed her gaze. The three walls surrounding the tech corner were well lit, yet rather bare. A few posters featuring celebrities holding their favorite books were the only adornment.

"That's a terrific idea, Fern. Maybe my father would let me hang his next series before the paintings are shipped off to D.C."

As Fern navigated the room snapping candids, Scott acted as her assistant. He carried her punch glass, replenished her empty dinner plate, and directed the guests to stand this way and that so Fern could take their photographs.

The noise level rose as the punch bowls and platters of food grew empty. Francis had to turn up the music more than once in order for the guests to be able to hear the songs over Luigi's thunderous chatter.

Finally, it was time for Mrs. Waxman to cut the cake. She accepted a knife from Milla and then positioned herself behind the cake, dabbing under her glasses with a tissue. "Please don't force me to make a speech," she sniffed. "I know I've talked most of your ears off between my tenure as teacher and librarian, but there aren't enough words in the English language to express how grateful I am to have been a member of this wonderful community. To say that I will miss you all is the greatest understatement of my life. Thank you so much."

She slid the knife into the cake to a round of raucous applause. Afterward, she personally distributed a generous wedge to everyone in the room. Even Alma's stony expression softened when Mrs. Waxman welcomed her to town and praised Luis for being the most progressive and talented principal she'd ever known.

"You are too kind," Alma responded, and then turned to chat with Luigi once again.

Once all the guests had eaten their cake (including each and every one of the supper club members — this was one sugary treat they weren't going to pass up), Scott and Francis directed every-one's attention to the Information Desk. Standing on either side of the shrouded easel, their boyish faces flushed with anticipation, the twins waited for James to say a few words about Mrs. Waxman's farewell gift.

"Thank you for coming tonight," James began. "I always suspected that Mrs. Waxman was friends with half of Quincy's Gap, but it wasn't until this evening I realized it was true. We have all benefited from her wise, patient, and generous spirit. She's treated every student and every patron in this library with respect, dignity, and equality."

Mrs. Waxman honked into her tissue, allowing several members of the audience to wipe their own moist eyes and exchange nods of agreement with their fellow townsfolk.

Turning to Mrs. Waxman, James concluded his brief speech. "Teacher. Librarian. Friend. You have left your mark on many, many people. Now thanks to my father, Jackson Henry, you can at least take a moment of your life in Quincy's Gap with you when you join your sister in sunny Arizona. Godspeed, dear Mrs. Waxman. You will be sorely missed."

The Fitzgerald twins reacted immediately to their boss' signal — a slight dip of the chin after uttering the last word. In perfect synchronization, they whisked the white cloth off the surface of the painting, beaming as they witnessed Mrs. Waxman's reaction to her gift.

The guests broke into spontaneous applause as they gazed at the work of art. A portrait of Mrs. Waxman, it depicted the older woman in her familiar place behind the information desk. For years she had reigned over that small territory, squared in by four equal countertops displaying the monthly staff picks and the latest book club reads.

Every evening, she'd put her dinner in the break room and then organize the stacks of bookmarks, recommended reading flyers, and piles of free magazines and community newsletters located on her countertops.

Jackson had included her regular workspace in his painting, but what he'd captured best was the joy Mrs. Waxman felt in helping another person. He had positioned her standing at a slight angle and her face, gently etched with wrinkles and laugh lines, was focused on a young girl of about ten years of age. The girl had been painted in profile with her hands held out in order to receive the book Mrs. Waxman was presenting. Her young face was filled with gratitude, as if she understood that the librarian was offering so much more than a simple book. The painting showed Mrs. Waxman in her element — every fiber of her being was invested in opening up new worlds to her young patron. Passion shone from her eyes like a beacon.

"It's wonderful!" Mrs. Waxman cried, her lips trembling. She allowed James to put an arm around her and squeeze while she struggled to keep her emotions in check. "Your father is a maestro! How can I ever thank him?"

Knowing that Jackson was bound to be hiding in James' office, James promised to lead Mrs. Waxman to him before he grabbed Milla and made an escape. "Now that the food portion of the evening is done, there's a good chance he's hanging out in the van. He likes to sit in the den and watch game show reruns before he goes to bed. He says they settle his stomach."

Mrs. Waxman laughed. "His habits must have served him well. Look at the man! He's fit as a fiddle. Not only is he thin, but it must take a great deal of energy and concentration to produce paintings like his, so he's strong as well. James, your father is as sharp in the mind as he is in the body." She patted his hand. "You've got some good genes going for you, my boy."

James tried not to frown. "I think I take after my mother. As you can see, the only thin part of my body is my hairline and as far as possessing any artistic ability, I can't even draw a stick figure." He smiled, not wanting to spoil a second of the Guest of

Honor's special night. "There's just more of me to love," he joked and excused himself to go off in search of Jackson.

Tracking down his father took longer than expected. Everyone wanted to comment on how much they admired Jackson's work and James found himself conversing briefly with several guests about their own art. Before he knew it, he'd received commitments from three artists willing to display their watercolors, engravings, and textile pieces on the walls in the Tech Corner.

When he finally reached the circulation desk, he stopped again in order to praise Fern for her wonderful idea. "Our library gallery is going to be a hit! Well done."

"I'd like to be included as a local artist too," Fern added with a trace of shyness. "I think I told you that I was a freelance photographer, but my passion is nature photography. I have a whole series of color photos that I took in the Great Smoky Mountains National Park. I framed them myself."

James put a hand on Fern's shoulder. "Your work will be displayed first. This was your idea and it would be a wonderful way to introduce you to our community. We could post a short bio and, if you have a website or an email where folks can buy prints from you, that might help you with your long-term goal of renting a house."

"I don't have a website yet," Fern answered, her entire being sparkling with enthusiasm. "But maybe I could build a simple one over the weekend."

"If you need any help, Scott's quite adept at that sort of thing." James suggested slyly and headed for his office. The moment he stepped inside, he knew something was wrong.

Jackson was seated in one of the office chairs facing the desk. His shoulders were slumped and he didn't look up when James approached. Milla was squatting on her heels, a hand on each of Jackson's knees as she spoke to her husband in a voice riddled with worry. When James entered the room, she shot him a fearful glance and then turned back to her husband.

"Your left side? Does it hurt?" She asked Jackson.

"What is it?" James' eyes darted back and forth from Milla to his father. "Pop?"

Jackson tried to wave him off. "It's nothin'. My leg's gone to sleep — probably from sittin' around this damned place all night."

James looked closely at this father's face. "But you're not experiencing any pain or discomfort?"

"Nah," Jackson answered, but suddenly his gaze seemed to lose focus.

Brushing aside the apprehension blooming in his mind, James gently lifted his father's left hand. "Can you squeeze my fingers, Pop?"

"James!" Jackson's voice seemed to come from a long way off. He reached out with his right hand, clumsily feeling for his son's shoulder. "I can't see you!"

"Call 911!" James urged Milla and then captured his father's panicked hand in his own. "It'll be all right, Pop. Hold on. We're going to get you help."

James listened as Milla spoke to the emergency operator. He knew the call would be routed to the fire station across the street and that an EMT could be in the room in less than five minutes.

Those minutes were the longest of his life. As James held onto his father, trying not to concentrate on the frailty of his weathered hand, the left side of Jackson's face slowly drooped downward and a line of spittle leaked from his open mouth.

"Pop?" James tenderly shook his father. "POP!"

A black pulse of fear throbbed in James' chest. Milla had left the room to wait for the paramedics in the lobby and, alone in his office with his unresponsive father, James struggled to keep his voice calm and even. "Don't leave me, Pop. Hang on. I'm right here with you. I won't let go." James had to stop speaking because his throat swelled tight with emotion. He refused to give way to despair, so he inhaled a deep breath, choked back the terror, and continued to repeat the words, "It's okay, I'm right here," over and over and over again.

He barely noticed when one of the EMTs placed a firm hand on his shoulder and eased him away from his father's unresponsive form. James stepped back, listening to a blur of muted speech, a blood pressure cuff inflating, a stethoscope shimmering on the pale flesh of Jackson's chest, a light darting across a pair of unblinking blue eyes.

With infinite care, the paramedics lifted Jackson onto a stretcher. They placed an oxygen mask over his nose and mouth, and James couldn't tear his gaze from the device, for it seemed to rob his father of a future that spoke of strength and independence.

James followed the uniformed men as they wheeled his father through the lobby past rows of silent and sympathetic faces. When the Fitzgerald brothers detached themselves from the rest of the group, asking if they could help, James realized that he couldn't just race off after the ambulance. It was one of the hardest things he'd ever had to do, but he paused and took a moment to think.

"Francis, can you and Scott tidy up the library and handle all the opening duties in the morning?" He removed a set of keys from his key ring and handed them to Scott. The twin gazed at them wide-eyed and then closed his fist around the brass keys with reverence.

"Don't worry about the library, Professor. We'll run this place just like you would." Francis promised.

James clenched his lips together so they wouldn't tremble and gave each brother a pat on the arm. "Please ask Willow to do the same at Quincy's Whimsies. And give Mrs. Waxman a hand loading her painting into the car. Tell her I'm sorry I couldn't say goodbye," he added as he turned toward the doors leading outside.

Tormented by the unwelcome thought that the portrait of Mrs. Waxman might be Jackson's final painting, James jogged toward his truck. He tried to hide his misery beneath a façade of resolve and hope as he opened the passenger door for his step-mother.

"He's strong," Milla stated firmly as James got in beside her and sped off behind the ambulance, the strobe of red lights bathing the white hood of his Bronco in an eerie glow.

No one spoke on the way to the hospital. Milla's hands were clasped and her eyes were shut, and James suspected she was deep in prayer. He also made silent appeals to the Almighty until they reached the hospital complex.

In the emergency room waiting area, James completed the stacks of paperwork given him by the triage nurse, and then asked Milla to buy two cups of coffee from the vending machine down the hall. He knew that they were likely to spend most of the night in the waiting room and hoped that the hot brew might take an edge off the shock.

They hadn't spent long in the bucket-like chairs when another nurse asked them to follow her deeper inside the hospital. Within another smaller waiting area, this one offering padded chairs, an attractive female physician in royal blue scrubs met them with a kind smile. She introduced herself as Dr. Frey and after shaking hands with James and Milla, gestured for them to take a seat.

"It appears that Mr. Henry has suffered a

stroke," she stated and James appreciated that she broke the news with gentle directness. "He's been stabilized and we're sending him for an MRI. We should know more after those results come back." The doctor went on to ask Milla questions about Jackson's health history and then left to check on Jackson and her other patients.

Time crawled. Doctors, nurses, and family members passed through the waiting room in an endless parade. James looked at every person dressed in blue scrubs with hopeful eyes, keenly watching their faces in case they had something to impart, but they all walked by, focused on other patients and tasks. It took over an hour for Dr. Frey to return with the MRI results.

She carefully reviewed what the test had shown and then advised them to go home and get some sleep and return during visiting hours in the morning.

When James started to protest, Dr. Frey touched his hand. "Your father is currently sedated. It would be best if he weren't stimulated. I know it's hard, but you'll do him the most good by being here fresh and bright-eyed first thing tomorrow."

The doctor's words were delivered with such sincerity and concern that James and Milla felt compelled to heed them. James led his weary stepmother back to the Bronco.

"I'm going to stay with you tonight," James assured her as he pulled into his driveway. It felt like midnight although it was only half past ten. "Just give me a minute to grab a few things."

Inside the house, the darkness seemed to close in on him. James turned on every light he passed, grabbing the portable phone off its cradle as he headed down the hall to his bedroom. As he shoved his toothbrush and some clothes in a duffle bag, he dialed his ex-wife's number.

"Jane," he croaked when she answered. "Oh, Jane." And then he let the tears come.

TEN:
JANE'S BLACK BEAN CHILI

Grams of
Sugar
19

James made sure Milla was settled before trudging down the hall to his boyhood bedroom. Jackson had done little to change the small room since his son had moved to his own house on Hickory Hill Lane. The only alteration James noticed was that Milla was now using his aged, kneehole desk to organize her business accounts. The corner of the desk once occupied by James' tin rocket ship bank now featured a pair of framed photographs taken during Milla and Jackson's winter wedding. Another photo showed Eliot making a snowman in the

Henry's backyard. Eliot had tried his best to create a snowman resembling his grandpa. To accomplish this, the little boy had taped a paintbrush to the end of one of the stick arms and wrapped Jackson's favorite plaid scarf around the snowman's wide neck. Milla had captured him planting a kiss on Snow Jackson's icy cheek.

Eliot's smiling, playful face was a balm to James. Cradling the photograph, he carried it to the nightstand and stared at his son while he wondered what news tomorrow would bring regarding Jackson's condition.

At first, James resisted sleep, feeling guilty that he would be resting in comfort when his father was alone in a hospital bed miles away. As the night wore on, however, his tired body and weary mind were no longer able to dwell on the dozens of "what if" questions that had been steadily amassing inside James' head. Eventually he surrendered to slumber.

The next morning he awoke to the pleasant sound of Milla moving about downstairs in the kitchen. These ordinary domestic noises — water whooshing through the pipes and the clanging of bowls and pans allowed James to believe that it was possible for life to return to normal. He jumped out of bed, showered, and got dressed in record time, worried that his father was already awake and frightened.

"Don't fret," Milla said as he rushed into the kitchen. "I called and asked about your daddy. He's still resting quietly, so come fill your belly with a hearty breakfast. You know there won't be anything decent at that hospital. Lord knows I cannot take another swallow of the slop that vending machine calls coffee."

Nodding in agreement, James accepted a plate of eggs and bacon, but he found himself forcing down the food. For once in his life, he didn't feel like eating. He cleaned his plate, however, because he knew it would please Milla, but it took every ounce of patience he possessed to watch her tidy the kitchen before finally turning toward the door.

"I know you want to race to his side, dear." Milla patted James on the cheek. "But we're still going to get there well before visiting hours start as it is."

James frowned. "I don't care about the rules. If they refuse to let us see him, the least I can do is try to track down Dr. Frey and gather more details about Pop's condition. Why did he have a stroke in the first place? Is he going to need surgery? Rehab? Will he eventually be . . . okay?" The word came out sounding strangled.

Milla slid her arm around him and leaned her head against his shoulder. "We'll make it through, honey. And if I don't get a chance to tell you today, then let me say it now: I sure am grateful you're with me, James. I couldn't have asked for a better son had I raised you myself."

Hugging her tightly, James carried their travel coffee mugs to the Bronco and, after watching Milla load a basket of baked goods into the back seat, drove north toward the hospital.

"What time *did* you get up this morning?" he asked her, gesturing at the basket.

"About four," she answered brightly. "I figured it couldn't hurt to whip up some cinnamon scones for the nurses. Jackson isn't going to be the easiest patient they've ever had and I figured I'd best start bribing them right off the bat."

James chuckled. "Nicely put."

The volunteer at the hospital's reception desk directed them to Jackson's room. As they approached the door, last night's knot of fear reformed in James' chest. Taking Milla's hand, he moved into the room and then stopped, inhaling sharply.

Jackson lay on the bed, attached to a multitude of tubes and wires. His arms and face were almost as white as the sheets covering his body and he looked shrunken, diminished. After all, to James, Jackson was the epitome of manliness. He was willful and fearless, his unapologetic personality rendering him taller and more powerful than his wiry physique suggested.

"Pop," he whispered.

A nurse bustled into the room and James turned to her in anxious appeal. "Miss? Can you tell us how he's doing?"

The woman smiled at him. "He had a peaceful night," she replied brightly while checking Jackson's IV and making notes on a chart. "Woke up once during my shift and tried to talk, but he couldn't get the words out. I told him where he was and that you all would be here to see him in the morning. He grunted and went right back to sleep." She glanced at her watch. "We change shifts at seven, so I'll introduce you to the nurse on duty before I leave."

"What about Dr. Frey?" James persisted. "Is she available to see us?"

The nurse paused to think. "Dr. Frey was on call last night, so one of her partners will be seeing Mr. Henry today. His name is Dr. Scrimpshire and he's a neurologist. He's on rounds at the moment, but should be swinging through here any second now." She gave them a comforting smile on the way out. "Your daddy's in good hands, I promise you."

Not knowing what else to do, James and Milla pulled chairs up to the side of Jackson's bed and waited. They chatted to Jackson about last night's party in hopes that he could hear them, but he remained unresponsive. The only comfort his family could garner was the steady rise and fall of his chest.

Dr. Scrimpshire entered the room fifteen minutes later and upon seeing a white lab coat, James jumped to his feet. The physician had encountered countless family members desperate for information about a loved one's condition, so he wasted no time in explaining the situation. He placed a thin stack of folders on the nearest table and shook hands with Milla and James.

"Mr. Henry has suffered a cerebral embolism," he began in a deep, no-nonsense voice. "This occurs when a clot, usually originating from the heart, travels through the bloodstream and lodges in an artery in the brain. This blocks the blood flow to the brain."

Milla was wringing her hands. "That sounds pretty serious."

The doctor turned a pair of sympathetic

eyes on her. "Your husband has sustained damage to his brain, Mrs. Henry. He will have to relearn many of the simple tasks we take for granted. But with the help of occupational therapy, there's no reason he can't live a long and fulfilling life."

Relief washed over James. "So he doesn't need surgery?"

"No." Dr. Scrimpshire shook his head and uncapped his pen. He began to examine Jackson and made several notes in one of his files. James and Milla remained silent, watching the doctor with expressions of dread and awe. "We'll start him on blood thinners to prevent those clots from reforming, but he doesn't require surgery. That doesn't mean that his road to recovery is going to be quick or easy. Fortunately, patients with supportive families tend to show the most marked improvement in rehab."

"Is he going to wake up soon?" Milla ventured.

The doctor nodded. "It won't be long now. He may be disoriented at first and I suspect he will have difficulty speaking. He may also express signs of fear, anger, or both. He's basically waking up to a body that won't do what he wants it to do." He capped his pen and closed the file. "Just so you're prepared . . ."

James glanced at his father. "Before the paramedics came, he seemed to have lost feeling in the left side of his face. Is there any way to tell the extent of the . . ." James had to push the word out, "damage?"

"I have the results of Mr. Henry's initial imaging tests on my office computer. As soon as I've finished seeing the rest of my patients, I'll come get you and we'll look at them together." The doctor rose and gathered up his paperwork. "The nurse will page me once your father is awake." After giving them another compassionate smile, he left the room.

James and Milla were silent for a moment.

"I'm not sure I understood all of that," Milla finally said, "but I'm holding fast to the part about Jackson living a long and full life!"

Reaching out to cradle his father's limp hand in his own, James said, "Me too."

Less than an hour later, James noticed his father's eyelids fluttering and dashed from the room in search of a nurse. He knew he could have hit the call button on Jackson's bed frame, but he trusted his own actions more. As he rounded the corner of the hallway, he nearly knocked Jane right off her feet.

"I'm *so* glad to see you!" he cried. She gave him a fierce hug in return but James abruptly broke free and pulled her toward the nurses' station. "Pop's waking up!" he simultaneously told Jane and the pair of nurses behind the counter.

By the time Jackson opened his eyes, a small crowd had gathered around his bed. A nurse bent over him, fussing with this and that while Milla squeezed Jackson's hand to alert him that she was near.

"Good morning, darlin'," Milla spoke tenderly, keeping her voice calm and even. Her husband looked in her direction and she exhaled loudly relief. "You can see me, can't you?"

A strangled sound came from Jackson's mouth.

"Don't try to talk, sweetheart," Milla coaxed. "You're in the hospital. You had a stroke last night. Can you nod your head if you understand me?"

Jackson dipped his chin, his gaze never leaving Milla's face. Milla's and James' eyes met across the bed. The fact that Jackson could see, move, and respond to other people gave him a surge of optimism.

From that point onward, the medical team took over. They ran tests and checked vital signs and machine readings and Jackson's fluid bag while James tried to find something useful to do. It was only later when he met with Dr. Scrimpshire and stared at images of his father's brain on the computer screen that he began to fully understand what had happened to Jackson.

The doctor swiveled his computer screen toward James and pointed out the shaded areas indicating damage. When James responded by blanching and gripping the arms of his chair, the neurologist put a firm hand on his shoulder. "The brain is a wonderful and mysterious organ, Mr. Henry. Damaged tissue does have the ability to recover."

"But not dead tissue?" James asked after he'd collected himself.

"No," the doctor admitted. "It will take many more tests to see what kind of rehabilitation your father will need. The good news is that our Rehab facility is one of the best in the state."

James looked away from the computer screen. "Sorry. I'm trying to digest everything. This hit us out of the blue. One moment, he was my typical, cranky, feisty father and the next . . ." He stood and thanked the doctor. "Let me tell my stepmother about the results. I'd rather she didn't see this image unless it's absolutely necessary. She's already having a hard time taking all of this in, and I think it would be best if she and I focus our energies on his recovery." His eyes strayed back to the color-coded screen. "That's the present. Now I'd like to turn to the future."

Dr. Scrimpshire nodded in agreement. "That sounds like a very wise plan."

Later, after hospital visiting hours were over, Jane and James shared a quiet dinner at his house. Jane had arranged for Eliot to be picked up from preschool by his best friend's mother. To the little boy's delight, he was to experience his first sleepover that night.

"It's a good thing my parents were already planning a visit this month," Jane said as she dropped a dollop of sour cream followed by a sprinkle of Monterey-Jack cheese over a bowl of black bean chili. "I told them to fly in this weekend. As for me, I just need to turn in grades this week, tidy up the office, and then I'll be available."

James absently picked up the spoon she handed him. "Available?"

"To take care of you, silly." She smiled at him. "I know you, James. You'll work eight hours a day, help Jackson with his rehab, continue to be the World's Best Father, and go to church every Sunday." She sat across from him with her own bowl of chili. "And that's too much for any mere mortal to handle. With that kind of schedule, you won't be able to do laundry or clean the house or stock your fridge. Whatever energy you have left will be spent driving up to see us, so I think Eliot and I should live here over the summer, if that's okay with you."

The fear and worry that had been holding James hostage for the last twenty-four hours eased their grip. He stared across the table at his ex-wife in wonder. "I thought you were teaching two courses this summer."

"They're online courses. My summer students are actually working adults and with their busy schedules, courses via computer are what they want. This way, they can work toward their degree without having to appear physically on a college campus." She took a bite of chili and gestured for James to do the same. "So all I need is my laptop and a few hours of quiet in order to post lectures and do my grading. It's perfect really. I get to spend more time with my favorite men. Three months of bliss."

James took a bite of his dinner and groaned. "This *chili* is bliss! No wonder Eliot has converted to vegetarianism so easily. Shoot, *I* could give up meat if you cooked for me like this." He spent a moment savoring the taste of black beans, garlic, onions, and fresh cilantro in a tomato base. Then, he scooted back his chair, walked around to Jane's side of the table, and leaned over to kiss her.

"I love you," he whispered into her hair. "For the chili, for being willing to upend your life to be near me, and for the way you make me believe everything will turn out okay."

Jane wrapped her arms around his neck and returned his kiss with passionate tenderness. "I love you too. So very much."

Later, after they'd cleaned up the kitchen, James took Jane's hand and led her down the hall to the master bedroom.

"I can rub your back until you fall asleep," Jane offered as she pulled back the covers. "You must be exhausted."

James flopped on the bed as though he was too weary to move, but at her words, he sat up, grabbed her around the waist and pulled her on top of him. "I'd have to be half-dead to fall right asleep with you here, lying next to me." He slid his palms over the soft curves of her hips and murmured, "Besides, I want to show you just how grateful I am to have you here. Tonight and for many nights to come."

"That sounds like a good deal to me," Jane replied huskily, stretched out her arm, and switched off the lamp.

James went back to work the next day and did his best to concentrate on his usual tasks. He phoned Milla every few hours to ask after his father, but there hadn't been much of a change since the previous day. Jackson could barely speak and had lost the use of his left arm and leg. The medical staff told Milla that it was too early to tell how permanent those disabilities were, and added that they were unlikely to ever voluntarily discharge him if she continued to bring them such succulent baked goods.

"His vision is fine, so that's a blessing," she told him. "And we're able to talk in our own way. Your daddy's never really had a flapping tongue, so I blab away and he grunts and nods. It's not too different from our regular conversations," she added lightly.

Pleased that Milla sounded both rested and hopeful, James asked if she wanted him to check in on Willow.

"She can handle Quincy's Whimsies as well as I can," Milla answered. "In fact, she'd been hinting for weeks that I should take a vacation, so now I'm taking one! I'm planning to read *The Jungle Book* to your father. He's never heard the story and it's been more years than I care to recall since I have, so we'll take a sort of literary safari. One of the nurses told me reading aloud is good for stroke patients."

"A well-written tale is as curative as homemade chicken soup," James agreed. "I'll be in after work to see Pop. And Milla, don't you worry about mowing the lawn or taking the trash to the street. I'll do all of that this weekend."

Milla clucked her tongue. "And *I* plan to stockpile your freezer, so don't you fret about your meals."

"Just keep on baking for the nurses. I've got my own personal chef these days." James told Milla about Jane and Eliot moving down for the summer. Milla squealed in delight. "It'll do your daddy a world of good to have Eliot filling the house with energy and chatter. Jackson'll want to get better just so he can play with him again. Oh, I've gotta run. Dr. Scrimpshire's here to check on our favorite patient."

After hanging up, James spent the rest of his lunch hour helping Fern hang a collection of photographs on the walls surrounding the tech corner. Once the last framed print was in place, James stood back and admired the results.

"These are fantastic, Fern. You're really talented." He pointed at a photograph of a carpet of multicolored autumn leaves. "This one's my favorite." Turning to look at the four photos mounted on the wall behind him, he added, "But the close-up of the purple rhododendron, I've got to have that one for Jane. She'd love to hang that in her office."

Fern blushed. "Scott made me a website already. It's beautiful. He used that photo as the frame for the home page. You were right when you said that he was good with computers."

James studied Fern's bio, which had been fastened with thumbtacks alongside a series of photographs showing the Blue Ridge Mountains during each season. Taken from one of the scenic lookouts on the Blue Ridge Parkway, the photographs captured the beauty of the wilderness. The pine trees in the valley that were draped in capes of snow in the winter scene were just as lovely as the towers of dried brown needles serving as a contrast to the brilliant gold, orange, and crimson leaves of the hardwoods in the fall. Taking advantage of his time alone with the young woman, James said breezily, "I think Scott has a bit of a crush on you."

Fern sighed. "I like him too. It's just, well, I have feelings for another guy, a fellow artist. Until I can sort out exactly what those feelings are, I'm trying really hard to just be a friend and coworker to Scott. Still, the more time I spend with him . . ."

The young woman's expression was anguished. "These things are rarely easy. Take it from me," James told her. "I've made two or three lifetime's worth of romantic gaffes."

The relationship theme had him thinking of how wonderful it had been to wake up to the sound of his alarm that morning and to find Jane lying beside him, her hair fanned out over the pillow and her arm splayed out over the edge of the bed. He'd stared at her lovely face as long as he could and then showered as quietly as possible so as not to wake her. He hadn't succeeded however, for when he stepped out of the bathroom to get dressed, her side of the bed was vacant. She was waiting for him in the kitchen with breakfast, a steaming cup of coffee, and a warm kiss.

"It's hard to imagine your making a serious mistake. You seem like someone who has it all figured out," Fern remarked shyly.

James nodded and smiled. "Maybe I

finally do. You see, after all this time, I'm still in love with the first girl I ever loved. It's exhilarating, because she feels the same way, but it can be a little scary too. Once you've figured out what's important in life, you want to do anything in your power to hold onto what you've got." He glanced back at the seasonal photographs of the mountains. "But your work has given me a terrific idea. Go ahead and put me down for that entire series. Those photographs are going to help me secure my future."

"All four of them? Thanks!" Fern beamed. "I've got to tell Scott I've made my first sale from this exhibit!"

Grabbing her gently by the elbow before she rushed off, James said, "If he's the one you run to when you've got big news, then you really care about him. Just don't leave him hanging too long, okay? He's not like one of these prints, Fern. That young man is an original."

At five o'clock, James trotted down the library steps, intending to hop in the Bronco and speed north to the hospital. Lucy was waiting for him by his truck, holding a cardboard box filled with food with one hand and her cell phone in the other. When she saw James, she pocketed the phone.

"Your fellow supper club members have made enough food to see you through at least six meals. We didn't know what else to do." She pushed her sunglasses onto the crown of her head and gazed at him with concern. "How is Jackson?"

James thanked her and gave an abbreviated version of his father's condition as he loaded the goodies into his truck.

"I haven't had a chance to tell you about my little chat with Murphy," Lucy rubbed at a grease spot on her uniform shirt and then gave James a crooked smile. "She was pretty cagey when we chatted in The Sweet Tooth. Even Megan Flowers said she's never seen Murphy grab her croissant and run like she did when I asked her what she'd been up to Sunday evening."

Rubbing his temples, James frowned. "If Murphy is the note's author, what could she expect to gain? She's smart enough to know that I'd do anything to keep Jane and Eliot safe. This whole thing has only brought us closer."

Lucy looked thoughtful. "Maybe she wants to create stress between you and Jane. It's hard for you to protect your family when you live in separate towns, so Murphy might be using the fear and anxiety created by the threatening notes and creepy dead birds as a way to drive a wedge between you."

"Lord knows I'm stressed," James admitted. "But if she thought this crazy behavior would cause a rift between Jane and me, she's dead wrong. In fact, Jane and Eliot will be living with me this summer." An angry flare ignited in his brown eyes. "And no one will hurt my family. They'll have to get past me first!"

Lucy touched James on the arm. "Sullie and I will continue to do drive-bys until this weirdness is nothing but a distant memory. Let's just hope that when Murphy sees the three of you around town over the next few weeks, she'll realize there is nothing she can do to keep you apart."

She opened her mouth to say something further, but Francis came bounding down the library steps as though the building were on fire. Spotting James in the parking lot, he raised his hand. "Professor! Wait!"

James stiffened, bracing himself for bad news. Francis was rarely rattled, but now the young man's face was drawn and his pupils were tiny black dots of shock. "It's your wife . . . I mean, your ex-wife. It's Jane!" he blurted all in one breath. "She said something about the crazy note writer and that he went after Eliot. She's really upset and wants to speak to you right away!"

Francis hadn't even finished his sentence when James began to run. Lucy was only a second behind. "Where is Eliot?" she shouted.

"In Harrisonburg," James answered, taking the stairs two at a time.

"Then it's not Murphy," Lucy said, holding open the lobby door. She raced behind James into his office. "I saw her at Dolly's Diner during lunch and again a few minutes ago at the Wellness Village."

"Whoever it is — if they've hurt my son . . ." James grabbed the receiver and lifted it to his ear. He barely recognized his own voice; it sounded as though a stranger spoke Jane's name.

ELEVEN: FROZEN MAC & CHEESE

Grams of
Sugar
54

Lucy insisted on driving the Bronco.

"Your hands are shaking. You're a danger to yourself and to others," she pointed out as she urged the old truck to accelerate around a tractor-trailer. "Besides, at a time like this you need a friend, especially one in uniform. Even if said uniform *is* a little wrinkled and there's a grease stain on the left boob pocket." Lucy smiled briefly. "When we get to Harrisonburg, I'll fill the police in on the note you received. If we all put our heads together, we can figure out who's messing with your family. Tell me again exactly what happened today."

James was aware that Lucy was only trying to keep his mind occupied until they reached Jane's house, but he recounted the details for the second time. "Eliot was on the playground at school when a man wearing sunglasses tossed him a paper airplane. Eliot ran over to fetch it and by the time he'd looked up again, the man was gone. Nothing about the man was familiar. The plane had been made from one of those paper airplane books sold in a number of stores across the country. A teacher in Eliot's school had bought a similar book for his son, so he recognized the World War Two bomber pattern, but not the black Sharpie writing on the sides of the plane."

Lucy frowned. "What bird did the man try to fashion the plane into?"

"That's unclear," James answered and clenched his fists. "A hawk? A vulture? Who knows? He drew some feathers on the wings and made a sharp beak on the nose of the plane. It's the writing that makes me so damned angry. How dare this whacko call my son —"

"He called the *plane* 'The Little Bastard.' Let's not jump to conclusions." Lucy said in an attempt to mollify her friend, but her words had the opposite reaction.

"Come on, Lucy!" James shouted. "He was obviously referring to Eliot. My son was born out of wedlock. Even now, he only has a part-time father. I just wish . . ." He trailed off, too upset to continue.

Lucy reached over and grabbed James by the hand. "Forget about how some lowlife defines him! You're a wonderful father and he's a happy little boy. He doesn't know what these words mean. What he knows is that he has two parents who love him more than anything in the world."

James nodded and squeezed Lucy's hand in gratitude. "You're right. And I need to get a grip before I see Eliot. I don't want him to be frightened even though *I* am." He rubbed his temples and tried to focus on the scenery. "I hope he didn't get upset when the police questioned him."

"Jane may not have allowed them to talk to Eliot directly," Lucy said. "Cops can be pretty intimidating to little kids."

"Not to Eliot," James replied. "He thinks policemen and firemen are the coolest people ever."

"Hey, the kid's got good taste." Lucy grinned. "Okay, you'll have to give me directions from here. I don't know where Jane lives."

Lucy had to park the Bronco in the street

as a police car had already claimed the remaining space in Jane's driveway. James hustled up the front path and burst into the house, relieved to discover Jane and a female officer calmly sharing a cup of coffee in the kitchen. He kissed his ex-wife and then turned back toward the living room. "Where is he?"

"In his room listening to an audio book," she answered in a steady voice. James noted the red and blotched skin under her eyes and wished he'd been here to comfort her while she'd cried. "He's got his headphones on and is perfectly fine. He really doesn't realize that anything out of the ordinary has happened. I think we should talk to Officer Beatty together before you see Eliot."

At that moment, Lucy entered the kitchen. "James was in no shape to drive," she quickly explained to Jane and then introduced herself to Officer Beatty. "I'm here to offer whatever help I can."

Jane gave her a warm smile. "Thank you, Lucy. James told me you've been trying to find out who left that note on his birdhouse. I was pretty freaked out by the bird carcass, but now that this guy has targeted our son, I won't feel safe until he's been apprehended. Hopefully, he'll get thrown in a jail cell with a serial killer as his roommate!"

She glanced at her fingers. "Even without the serial killer part, I just want this guy to get caught."

"May I see the paper airplane?" James directed his question to Officer Beatty.

The young officer, who looked to be in her mid-twenties and had guileless blue eyes and ash-blond hair secured in a tidy bun, reached under her chair and retrieved the plane. Stored inside a plastic freezer bag, the object seemed innocuous at first glance, but as James pivoted it under the light and examined the crudely drawn feathers and block lettering, a fresh wave of rage rolled over him. "No one at Eliot's school got a look at this guy?"

Jane shook her head. "No. The school's playground borders a fairly busy street. People walk by it all the time."

"The only description we have is that he was an adult male wearing sunglasses?" Lucy asked Officer Beatty.

The pretty policewoman tapped on the open page of her pocket notebook. "Eliot also told his mom that the man wore a purple baseball cap. He said it looked like the purple shirt his mom wears when she works in the yard, so we're assuming he's referring to her JMU sweatshirt."

James groaned in frustration. "This is a

college town! Those hats are for sale all over the place!" He turned to Jane. "Did he notice hair color? Height? What clothes the guy wore?"

"Eliot's a little boy, honey," Jane answered softly. "Not Poirot. He was following a trail of ants close to the fence and this guy in a purple hat and sunglasses tossed him the plane and then disappeared. End of story."

"Thank God he can't read," James muttered.

Jane covered his hand with hers. "He's really okay, James. He thinks Officer Beatty is here because she's my new friend and we wanted to hang out in the kitchen and talk about girl stuff. Plus, he's so excited about moving to Quincy's Gap this summer that I don't think anything can bring him down."

"Thank goodness for that." James sighed.

The four adults exchanged ideas and theories, but since Murphy was no longer on the suspect list, none of them could come up with a possible replacement for her.

"Could it be another former romantic partner?" Officer Beatty asked, looking back and forth between James and Jane. Lucy shifted uncomfortably in her seat and then jumped up, offering the other women a coffee refill.

"Oh, you're a guest, Lucy. Let me get it," Jane insisted. She set clean mugs on the table and collected the coffee carafe. "My list of ex-boyfriends isn't very long and all of those relationships ended amicably. The only exception was Kenneth Cooper. He's a lawyer living in Williamsburg and is my most recent ex. He'd never do these crazy things though. That man is totally obsessed with his image."

Lucy eyed Jane with interest. "Then it must have been quite a blow to his ego when you left him."

Jane shrugged. "I doubt that. He was dating a Barbie lookalike behind my back months before we broke up and he certainly wanted no part in raising Eliot. He —" she stopped suddenly and then picked up the bag containing the paper airplane. "Kenneth used that word once, in reference to Eliot. He called him a bastard." She gave James an apologetic glance. "I threw a vase at his head. It smashed inches away from his face and I'm still sorry I missed. He packed his bags and moved out later that day."

"Have you seen Kenneth since then?" Officer Beatty had her notebook out.

"No." Jane sank into a chair and wrapped her hands around her mug. "But why would he do this? He didn't want to be with me

252

and he didn't want anything to do with Eliot. He was relieved to be free." She looked at James. "He wasn't a kind man and he didn't like kids, so I was glad to see the last of him, especially since it gave me a chance to start over with you."

Lucy and Officer Beatty exchanged a quick glance and then the younger woman closed her notebook and rose. "I'm going to make some inquiries about Mr. Cooper. To do so, I'll need his date of birth, place of business, and last known address."

After Jane supplied the necessary information, the two law enforcement officials went outside to converse in private. A few moments later, Lucy announced that she planned to grab a bite to eat with her fellow officer.

"We'll leave for Quincy's Gap at seven-thirty," James told her. "I want to give Jane time to pack what she and Eliot will need for the rest of the summer and then we're gone."

"Got it." With a wave, Lucy followed Officer Beatty to her squad car.

Back in the kitchen Jane stood in front of the refrigerator, frowning as she peered inside. She ran her hands through her wavy brown hair and then opened the freezer door.

"I didn't get a chance to shop for groceries today," she apologized. "I'm afraid we'll be dining on frozen mac and cheese and a side of canned green beans. I can melt fresh grated Parmesan over the noodles, but that's as close to gourmet as we're going to get."

"I've never met a bowl of macaroni and cheese I didn't like." James pulled her to him and held her close. "Everything's going to be okay. I promise."

Jane wiped her face and smiled bravely at him. "Go ask your son which toys he can't live without this summer while I fire up the oven. I'll keep the wine corked until we get to your house. I'm already imagining myself drinking several glasses tonight."

"Me too," James answered as he headed out of the kitchen. Pausing, he added, "And it's not 'my' house anymore, it's 'ours.' "

Night was falling in a curtain of deep blue by the time Officer Beatty dropped Lucy off at the curb. James, who was placing two suitcases in the Bronco, swiveled around and searched her face. "Did you find out anything about Kenneth?"

"Other than he's got a squeaky clean record, no." She was clearly disappointed. "Not even a speeding ticket within the last three years."

James dropped his arms to his sides, deflated. "So that's it?"

"There's still the question of his whereabouts," Lucy said. "We called his office and were told by his secretary that he's on medical leave. She referred us to one of his partners, but that guy wasn't exactly forthcoming with information. Since we have no evidence against Kenneth, we had no choice but to back off when the partner refused to answer our questions." She tossed her purse into the back seat. "Don't worry. I'm not giving up. I have a feeling about this guy."

"Thank you, Lucy." James hastened inside to collect the rest of Eliot's things. He finished loading the truck as Lucy and Jane spoke in hushed tones in the kitchen.

"We're all done, bud." James carried his son fireman-style, already dressed in his dinosaur pajamas, and loaded him into his car seat. "Last call for Quincy's Gap!" he yelled in the direction of the house.

Jane shouldered her purse, turned off the lights, and locked the front door. "I can't begin to guess why Kenneth would be on medical leave," she whispered to Lucy as they walked across the lawn. "He didn't have any health issues when we were together. And I don't like the idea of him not having to show up for work for several days in a row. It means that he was free to come here." Her voice was strained. "I cannot understand why he'd want to scare me like this. Assuming he's the bad guy."

Lucy put an arm around Jane. "Don't let him get to you." She gestured at the truck. "He doesn't have the power to break the three of you apart, right?"

Anger flared in Jane's eyes. "No, he does not."

"Hold onto that truth and he loses, no matter how he tries to upset you." Lucy opened the back door and pretended to be nervous. "Oh! I don't know if it's safe to sit next to a T-Rex," she said with a shiver. "His teeth look *very* sharp."

Eliot raised his plush dinosaur and laughed. "He's not a T-Rex! He's an Allosaurus. He only bites mean people."

"Then I might need to borrow him sometime," Lucy stated solemnly. "We could make him an honorary deputy."

All the way back to Quincy's Gap, Eliot questioned Lucy about being an officer of the law. He was especially interested in how she got assigned to work with the K-9 units and wanted to hear about Lucy's dogs even though he had never heard of the rock stars

Bono, Benatar, or Bon Jovi were named after.

When James pulled into his driveway, Lucy insisted on doing a sweep of the house before anyone else went inside. After receiving an all-clear signal, James walked Eliot to his room and kissed his son goodnight. He still had to run Lucy back to the library so she could retrieve her Jeep.

"I really think you should get a dog," Lucy counseled as they drove through the sleepy town. "Did you know that the sound of a barking dog is the number one theft deterrent. A big canine with a mouthful of teeth and a deep growl is much better than some electronic alarm. No one's going to stick around long enough to tack notes to your birdhouse if they know they risk the chance of being bitten."

James envisioned a wolfish-looking dog sinking a row of razor-sharp teeth into Kenneth's leg. It was a supremely satisfying image. Back when Jane had left him for Kenneth, James had looked up his rival on his law firm's website and had been sickened to see that not only was Kenneth the youngest partner in the firm's history, but he also looked like a Calvin Klein model.

"I'd want a kid-friendly dog breed, not Cujo." James said as he shook off the memory of Kenneth's headshot. "I know your German Shepherds aren't child-eaters, but they *are* enormous and can be rather intimidating." He grew thoughtful. "I could ask Willow. She volunteers at the local shelter and I bet she could recommend the perfect pooch for our family."

The ringing of a cell phone interrupted Lucy's reply. "It's Sullie," she mouthed and then cooed, "Hey, Sugar" into the phone. Whatever Sullie said in return wiped the smile from her face, replacing it with a tightening of the lips and a quick glance out the window. "We're coming up on the turnoff now," she told him, her voice tinged with urgency. "I'm with James. I'll explain later."

James wondered why Lucy was now sitting ramrod straight in her seat, every muscle tensed.

"Turn here!" Lucy directed before he had a chance to ask. The Bronco's tires screeched on the asphalt as James obeyed. He sped down a gently curved road leading to a thoroughbred farm and a development of upscale houses built at the feet of one of the Shenandoah Valley's beautiful blue hills. The residences of Bridle Path Road were some of the wealthiest in the county, and James couldn't imagine why Lucy suddenly needed to take a detour in this direction.

"Lucy?" he asked, slightly put out. "Would you like to tell me where we're going?"

She was clearly trying to read the brass numbers secured to the mailbox posts. "Sorry. I don't want to blow by the house. It's number two-fourteen." She tapped on the window. "That was one-eighty, so we're getting close."

"To what? It's been a long day and though I am so incredibly grateful to you for —"

"Sullie's found a body!" Lucy interrupted hotly. "He hasn't even had time to identify the victim but there's obviously been a struggle and he needs back-up ASAP so he can secure the house." She took a shallow breath and continued. "He was responding to a neighbor's 9-1-1 call and has only been inside for about five minutes. The EMT guys are already en route, but I couldn't drive by without stopping to help. What if the perp is still around?" Even in the dark, James could see the glimmer of excitement in her eyes. "Here it is!"

James drove up a long driveway illuminated by solar lights. Sullie's cruiser was parked in front of a detached two-car garage. When James pulled in behind the brown sedan Lucy said, "You'd better stay here."

James hesitated for a moment, but then he followed her up a brick path lined with miniature boxwoods to the double entrance doors of a stately white Colonial. A faint strip of light escaped from between the front doors, one of which was slightly ajar.

"Sullie?" Lucy shouted into the foyer.

James heard the thuds of a heavy tread on the floorboards above their heads. "Upstairs!"

Lucy shot a warning glance at James. "Don't touch anything."

Though he was tempted to remind her that this was hardly his first crime scene, James kept his mouth shut and followed her up the carpeted staircase. A strange odor hung in the air.

"Do you smell that?" he whispered. "It's familiar . . ."

Lucy sniffed. "Reminds me of that nasty incense Gillian likes to burn during her home meditation sessions."

"Yes, that Patchouli stuff." He looked at the rich wood of the banister and the expensive chandelier hanging from the center of the ceiling. "Seems out of place in this environment."

They'd reached the top of the stairs by then and James was glad to see that the hall lights had been turned on. Sullie popped out from a room at the end of the corridor and glared at James. "What's he doing here?"

Lucy looked over her shoulder as though she'd forgotten she wasn't alone. "I drove him up to Harrisonburg because the Birdman made contact with his son. He was bringing me back to my Jeep when I got your call, so I had him make a detour."

Sullie stared at James for a moment longer, as a range of emotions flitted over his face. Trust won out over suspicion, however, for his blazing eyes softened and he nodded at James in apology. "Is your kid okay?"

"He's fine, thanks." James gave the other man's hand a hearty shake. "My whole family is going to need your protection until this guy is caught."

"Don't worry, we've got your back." Sullie straightened his shoulders, looking like a linebacker prepared to drill an unsuspecting receiver deep into the turf. He then snapped back into professional mode. "E.T.A. for the paramedics is five minutes. The vic's in here."

Sullie handed Lucy a pair of gloves. As she put them on, she turned to James. "You need to stay in the hall. This is a crime scene now."

"How can you tell?" he asked, but as he moved to the threshold of the spacious bedroom, he realized that it was a dumb question.

The first thing he noticed was the pair of legs sticking out from behind the bed. It was hard not to fixate on them for they were encased in a pair of purple and green striped socks. James had a flash of the Wicked Witch's feet protruding from beneath Dorothy's farmhouse. However, while the witch's corpse was pinned under a home, this corpse was positioned between the wall and the bed, creating the illusion that the rest of the woman's body was hidden from view beneath an ivory dust ruffle.

James' gaze traveled around the room, taking in the rumpled bed, the overturned bedside table and the lamp lying askew on the carpet. The bare bulb threw circular shadows onto the back wall, creating the mirage of an eclipse in the center of the floral wallpaper. Books and picture frames were scattered at the base of a cherry dresser, leaving only the incense holder containing a single stick of fragrance on its polished top. A poster tacked to the wall next to the dresser caught his attention. He recognized it as one of Tia Royale's animal rights posters. Looking around the room again, James counted ten different posters, some of which appeared much older than those he'd seen during Tia's recent demonstrations.

Lucy spent a moment absorbing the scene before she stepped carefully across the carpet to kneel down next to the body. James could only see the top of her head as the four-poster bed blocked his view. "Do you know her?"

"Yes. So do you." She peered at him over the coverlet. "It's Tia Royale."

James was flabbergasted. "Is this her house?" He'd pictured her living in a dimly lit apartment decorated with futons, beaded curtains, lava lamps, and shag rugs.

Sullie opened a door leading to the walk-in closet. "Lots of plain dresses, jeans, and T-shirts in here. Some rolled-up banners with pictures of dead pigs and cows and chickens."

"This is her room then," Lucy said with a sigh. "I know the girl rubbed folks the wrong way, but who would want to kill her?"

Standing anxiously in the doorway, James stuck his head into the room. "How did it happen?"

"She might have been strangled. There are bruises on her neck." Lucy suddenly seemed to realize that James was out of place at a crime scene. "You'd better go. Sheriff Huckabee won't be happy if he knows I brought you here."

James wanted to be of assistance, but he knew he would only impede both the paramedics and deputies if he stayed. Thanking Lucy again, he solemnly wished both her and Sullie good luck and then headed downstairs.

Just as he was about to leave, he heard a noise coming from one of the rooms toward the back of the house. Fearing the killer might still be inside, James raced up the stairs two at a time and frantically asked Lucy and Sullie to investigate the rooms on the bottom floor.

"I did a preliminary sweep after I found the body," Sullie told Lucy as they responded to James' plea. "No sign of disturbance except in the victim's room."

Sullie took the lead, turning on lights with one hand while holding his gun out in front with the other. Lucy had also drawn her weapon and was walking slightly behind Sullie, training her gun to the side while also checking to make sure no one was sneaking up from behind. The couples' movements were so synchronized and graceful that they seemed more like dancers in a Russian ballet troupe than two sheriff's deputies on the hunt for a murderer. James followed in their wake, every muscle tensed as his blood surged through his body and his heart pumped at a frenzied pace.

Upon entering the kitchen Sullie immediately lowered his weapon. "Here are our intruders." He relaxed and pointed toward a side door facing the detached garage.

"Awww." Lucy holstered her gun and grinned.

James pushed past her and saw the pet flap built into the door. Alongside the door was a bowl of water and an empty ceramic dinner plate. Two animals gazed up at the three humans with hungry eyes. Lucy squatted down and stroked the head of a little schnauzer and then reached out to pet a tortoise-shell tabby. The animals responded eagerly to her attention and soon, a chorus of barks and meows echoed in the kitchen.

At that moment, a pair of male voices shouted, "EMTs!" and entered the house. Sullie dashed out of the kitchen and as Lucy turned to go, James held her by the elbow. "What about these two? What will happen to them?"

"I'll have to call animal control in the morning." She glanced at the dog and cat and then jerked her eyes back to James' face. "Unless someone else takes them now."

James didn't even hesitate. "I'm bringing them home with me. If I have to sign papers or something later on, I will. But I won't leave them here with their caregiver lying dead upstairs. These two need food and a quiet place to sleep."

Lucy nodded and hustled out of the kitchen while James rummaged around in the cabinets until he found a stack of Alpo cans and another of Fancy Feast. He gave a can to each animal, surprised that they were so good-natured over having to share the same plate. By the time they were finished, the noise level had increased within the house. James loaded a grocery bag with canned and dry food and was relieved to discover a pair of pet carriers in the far reaches of the pantry.

He placed the carriers on the floor, got down on his knees, and reached out to the animals. They both came right to him, snuggling against his leg.

"I'm James Henry," he told the friendly pair as he examined their collars. "Nice to meet you, Snickers," he said to the smiling schnauzer. And with a laugh, he spoke to the cat. "And you too, Miss Pickles." He pointed at the carriers. "I know it's late, but I'm going to take you someplace safe. Come on," he gently pushed each animal into a crate. "We're going home."

Twelve:
Vegetarian Pizzadillas

Grams of
Sugar
33

When James returned home carrying two animal crates, a bagful of dog and cat food, and a litter box, Jane was speechless. As he quietly explained what happened on the way to drop Lucy off at the library, James unlatched the metal doors of the crates and coaxed Snickers and Miss Pickles out. Both animals took their time exiting their carriers. They each put their front paws on the floor and then paused, sniffing nervously. When James mentioned Tia's name, Snickers released a soft whine and James pulled the small dog against his chest.

Jane listened, horrified, as he described Tia's thin legs, clad in those silly striped socks, sticking out from behind the bed.

"I'm relieved not to have seen more than that," James declared with feeling. He set out a water bowl and two dishes of kibble for the animals. "She was just a girl, really, and so infused with vitality. She had a whole life to lead yet. I didn't like her, Jane, but when I saw her pets, I couldn't just leave them there to be collected by animal control in the morning. I felt like I owed her something for having been there, for having seen what I shouldn't have seen."

Nodding, Jane reached out and scratched Miss Pickles under the chin. "What if Tia's family wants to reclaim these guys? I know you were acting out of kindness, James, but Eliot is going to go berserk when he discovers these two tomorrow. He will love them instantly. How can we let him become attached to these sweet creatures when they might be taken away in a day or so?"

"I hadn't thought that far," James confessed. "When I saw the faces of her pets and thought of how passionately she fought for animals . . ." He broke off, smiling as Miss Pickles began to bat about a rubber band across the kitchen floor. "I'm sorry. I didn't mean to create any more drama for us."

Snickers licked Jane's hand and she giggled. "You did the right thing, honey. We'll simply explain to Eliot that we're acting as a foster family and that these animals might not be staying with us permanently." She kissed the mini schnauzer on the crown of his head and smiled. "I always wanted a dog when I was a little girl, but my father was allergic to anything with fur. I had goldfish instead. Not very exciting pets, let me tell you." Snickers rolled on his back, put his paws in the air, and gazed at Jane with a look of pure adoration. "Oh, I hope we *do* get to keep you both! Come here, Miss Pickles. Let Mama get a look at you!"

Jane played with the animals for a little longer, but ultimately decided she was too exhausted to keep James company while he watched mindless television. James was tired as well. It had been a trying day, but he found he couldn't go to sleep. He sat on the sofa while images flickered on the screen and blue light danced across the dark living room, but his mind refused to focus on a particular show. Instead, his thoughts kept returning to the events of the past week. He replayed the night of Jackson's stroke and called forth every physical detail of the sinister paper airplane delivered to Eliot. He then closed his eyes and traveled back into Tia's room, seeing the overturned lamp, the posters on the wall, and the dead girl's legs.

As the hours passed, James was incredibly grateful to have the animals beside him. Both of them had explored their new environment and had a snack. Now, as weary from the emotional evening as James, they curled up against his legs and placed their heads in his lap. He stroked each animal, feeling comforted by the warmth of their bodies and the soft sounds of their breathing. It was well past midnight when James finally drifted off to sleep.

He didn't recall waking during the small hours of the morning and making his way to the bedroom. Yet he was right beside his digital clock when the alarm went off at a quarter to seven. Jane let out a groggy groan and Snickers jumped up from where he'd been sleeping between James' feet and began to yip in excitement.

Within seconds, Eliot was in the room and on top of the bed too, squealing with happiness as he hugged Snickers, Jane, and James again and again until Miss Pickles meowed from the doorway.

"Holy moley! A cat too!" he cried in

ecstasy. "This is the best day ever!"

Jane wasted no time in explaining the situation to Eliot and the boy seemed satisfied to live in the moment. As James sat down for breakfast at the kitchen table, listening to the new range of noises filling his house, he felt a surge of renewed hope.

"Is the coffee really that good?" Jane glanced his way and then popped open a can of Fancy Feast. Miss Pickles stood on her back feet and stretched her front paws out toward the cat food.

"I was just thinking that I am one lucky man to be able to wake up to this happy hubbub all summer long." He waved his hand around the room. "Our little nest — it's almost as if no one can touch us in here."

Jane pointed at her chest. "Or in here."

Later, she sent him out the door with a kiss and a brown bag lunch.

From that point on, James' day only grew brighter. The library was busy and nearly every patron stopped by the reference desk to ask after Jackson's health. By midmorning, he was able to share the wonderful news that his father was being released from the hospital.

"I just got off the phone with Milla!" James shouted in the break room. "Pop's going home this evening!"

Francis, whose mouth was stuffed with an Italian hoagie, gave his boss a hearty thumbs-up.

"He'll still need to go to rehab every day, but I know he'll get better faster once he's sleeping in his own bed again." James spoke mostly to himself.

"And to be eating Milla's cooking instead of hospital food." Francis grimaced at the thought. "But Professor, how is Mr. Henry going to get up and down the stairs? Didn't you tell me his left side is super weak?"

James hadn't considered the extent of his father's disability until that moment. He stood in the center of the room, awash with guilt. "There's been so much going on. I hadn't even thought about how different things will be for him now."

"Don't worry, Scott and I will meet you at their place after work." Francis gave him a reassuring smile. "We can just move his bed into the den."

"Brilliant!" James clapped Francis on the back so hard that the younger man nearly choked on an enormous bite of his salami, ham, and provolone on rye sandwich.

Once the twins were done with their break, James laid out the lunch Jane had prepared, noting that he was enjoying his vegetarian diet more and more. He gobbled up an egg-salad sandwich made with a hint of Dijon and lots of salt and pepper, and savored a bowl of fresh strawberries with a side of Crème Fraiche. When he unfolded a Post-it note from the bottom of his brown bag at the end of his meal, he smiled to see that Jane had drawn a heart with their initials inside with a purple crayon.

In the remaining minutes of his lunch break, James called Milla to discuss the relocation of the master bedroom. She made several jokes about how Jackson would never go to therapy if he could spend all his time watching reruns of *The Price Is Right* instead, but was grateful to the Fitzgeralds for both the idea and the willingness to move furniture.

"And James," she whispered conspiratorially. "If your daddy's singing catfish plaque happens to disappear during this little rearrangement that would be perfectly fine with me."

Jackson voiced a garbled protest in the background and Milla laughed. "Just seeing if you were paying attention, darling!"

During the afternoon, Francis led a book club discussion while Scott assisted patrons in the tech corner and Fern manned the circulation desk. James offered recommendations to several mothers while their children played in the new and improved storybook area. Scott and Francis had recently built a small wooden puppet theater, and Fern, who was not only a talented photographer but apparently a skilled seamstress as well, had sewed a dozen puppets. She made the Big Bad Wolf, the Three Little Pigs, Little Red Riding Hood, Peter Pan, Captain Hook, Tinkerbell, a crocodile, a prince, a princess, and a fire-breathing dragon. She'd also set up a special display of picture books containing the characters she'd turned into puppets.

As James carried a stack of strays back to the circulation desk, he smiled at his newest employee. "Everything going okay?" he asked. "Are you adjusting to your career as a librarian?"

Fern showed him a dazzling smile. "I love it! Aside from my photography, this is the most rewarding job I've ever had. I feel like I was meant to be here."

"I was just thinking the same thing," he told her warmly.

She checked out a stack of romance books for a shy and blushing patron and then took a step closer to James. "I've been thinking about what we discussed the other day." She paused, gathering courage. "I do have feelings for Scott. I'm going to meet with the other guy and tell him I'm not interested in anything but friendship."

James nodded. "Good for you, Fern. You and Scott . . ." he trailed off, searching for the right words. "You seem to fit together. Like we all fit here in this library. Sometimes it takes a crazy chain of events to bring us where we are supposed to be."

"Waxing philosophical, Professor?" an elderly patron teased. With a self-effacing grin James wheeled the reshelving cart to the fiction section. He'd barely placed the latest Lee Child novel on the shelf when someone tapped him on the elbow. It was Lucy. James took in his friend's glassy eyes and slumped shoulders. Abruptly, the memories of the previous night he'd been able to hold at bay by concentrating on routine tasks came rushing back.

"How are you?" he asked softly.

Lucy tucked a lock of stray hair behind her ear. "It was a long and disappointing night. We found no clues. Not one!" Her mouth thinned into a line. "Sometimes this job is damned frustrating."

James had rarely seen Lucy so irritable, but he assumed that part of it was due to fatigue. "Was Tia strangled?" he whispered.

"Doesn't look like it. Someone pinned her down on the floor and held her by the neck, but that wasn't the cause of death. The ME's still working on that. With her parents being who they are, this case is the top priority of the department." She ran her finger along the spines of the books on the shelf nearest her arm. "I heard Sheriff Huckabee break the news to them this morning. They couldn't be reached last night because they're on some exclusive Caribbean Island where there's no cell phone service. They'll be here in a few hours though. Having a private plane comes in handy at times like this," she added wryly.

James guessed the reason behind Lucy's anger. "No suspects yet?"

Lucy shook her head. "None. The guy must have worn gloves. I'm assuming the killer is male because of the size of the bruises on Tia's neck. We've matched most of the prints in the room to Tia. Her mother thinks the other unknown set belongs to the cleaning woman. The parents haven't been upstairs since Tia moved in. I take it they weren't very close to their daughter. Can you imagine never having been in your only daughter's room?"

"Does Tia have siblings?"

"Two brothers. Both work for daddy, live in McMansions, and jet around the globe. They've never set foot in Tia's house." She glanced at her watch. "I need help with this case, James, and I don't have time to chase a bunch of dead ends. I'm gonna call a supper club meeting so we can bat around a few theories. Plus, I want to ask Gillian to call Kenneth's office and pretend to be a client. If anyone can worm information out of a tight-lipped lawyer, it's Gillian."

James reached out, briefly squeezed her shoulder, and then shelved the latest Booker prizewinner. "Let me make the arrangements. And don't even think about spending your last ounce of energy driving by my place. Go home and get some sleep."

"Sullie's going to do the drive-by on the way back from Luigi's. There's no way I'm cooking tonight so we're having giant plates of pasta. I plan to fall into a food coma afterward." Suddenly, she brightened. "With all this drama going on, I forgot to tell you that Luigi and Luis' mama have been spending an awful lot of time together. He's even taught her how to toss pizza dough and shape it into a pie. Word is she's a natural."

James was astonished. "They *like* each other? Romantically?"

Lucy laughed for the first time since she'd entered the library. "Stranger things have happened." She passed him a copy of Sue

Monk Kidd's *Secret Life of Bees.* "Is this any good?"

"Very. Do you want to check it out?"

"No thanks." Lucy took her keys out of her pocket. "My reading material is going to consist of the report from the medical examiner, Sullie's notes from the crime scene, and any background information I can find on Tia Royale."

"Some people have all the fun," James teased and walked his friend to the door.

After work, James, Scott, and Francis spent two hours at the Henry house moving furniture from the den to the dining room and from the master bedroom to the den. When they were done, Scott hobbled around the room on one leg, using a broom as a crutch.

"Dude, that is not cool," Francis scolded his brother.

Scott shoved his glasses up his nose and frowned. "I'm not making fun of Mr. Henry, bro. I just want to be sure he's got enough room to maneuver with his crutches." When Scott banged his knee sharply into the dresser, all three men winced.

"I'm glad you decided to put our arrangements to the test," James declared as he and Francis moved the dresser to the far side of the room. Standing back, he surveyed their work and was pleased with the results. Jackson and Milla now had a convenient first-floor bedroom and Jackson's ugly and aged den furniture had been temporarily hidden under tablecloths.

Turning to the twins, James said, "We'd better get going. Pop won't want us to see him struggling inside. I'll need to give him at least one night to get used to all of this. Now, I'd like to buy you both dinner." He reached for his wallet, but Francis held out a hand to stop him.

"You're like family to us, Professor. And Milla cooks for us all the time, so we are totally even."

Scott nodded in agreement. "Yeah, we should be paying *you.* We're always getting free treats from Quincy's Whimsies too. We are so spoiled by your family that it's like Christmas all year long."

James led them outside. "Well, just remember who your friends are when you get that big paycheck from the software company," he teased and handed Francis a twenty. "Still, I insist on a token of thanks. Go get one of Luigi's specialty pizzas."

"That's a deal!" Francis beamed and then turned thoughtful. "I kind of forgot about that monster check. We should be getting it any day now, right Scott?" He elbowed his brother, who was staring off into space. "Right Scott?"

The twin placed a hand on his flat stomach. "You had me at 'pizza'. I'd trade our future LCD monitor for a pineapple and ham thin crust."

Francis' eyes lit up. "Then let's go get one! We can eat it while watching Season Five of *Battlestar Galactica*. Again. G'night, Professor."

James waved at the twins and drove off, wishing that he too would be dining on something from Luigi's menu that evening. However, he forgot all about the pizza parlor the moment he stepped into his house.

"Hello?" he called and waited expectantly. Eliot always raced into his arms as soon as he heard the front door opening, but no footsteps sounded in the empty hall.

"Daddy! I'm cooking dinner!" Eliot shouted from the next room.

Smiling, James walked into the kitchen to find his son dressed in a fire truck apron and matching chef's hat. He was standing on a stool, filling a bowl with grated cheese. Jane was setting the table. The moment she set down the last fork and napkin she walked over and kissed James on the cheek.

"What are we having?" James asked his

son, who waved at him with a spatula.

"Pizzadillas." His little chest puffed out with pride. "Mommy and I made it up."

James cocked an eyebrow at Jane. "Please elucidate."

Jane gestured at the buffet station she and Eliot had created on the counter. "Choose your toppings, just like you would at a pizza parlor, and then Eliot will arrange them on a tortilla. I will cook each pizzadilla in the skillet and you can create 'slices' using the pizza cutter."

"Wow," James said as he made a big deal over the display. "You two should have your own food show. You could call it, *Vegetarian Creations.*"

The Henrys sprinkled cheese, black olives, mushrooms, and vegetarian sausage onto tortillas. As they ate, Miss Pickles amused herself by batting a grocery store receipt across the floor.

"That cat loves paper," Jane stated.

Eliot grinned. "Yeah, you should see what she did to the toilet paper in my bathroom!"

Jane formed her hands into claws. "Shredded the whole thing until it looked just like this bowl of mozzarella."

Snickers was lying half in the living room and half in the kitchen. When James asked Jane how the dog had fared that day, the little schnauzer lifted his head, wagged his tail, and then closed his eyes again.

"I'm a bit worried about him." Jane cast a concerned glance at Snickers. "He hasn't eaten much today and he's been moping about. Do you think he's homesick?"

Eliot stopped chewing in order to listen to his father's answer. James shot Jane a warning look. "No. He's just a tired doggie." Later, as he and Jane loaded the dishwasher, he whispered, "Snickers might be sick. Not homesick, but physically ill. Is he drinking any water?"

Jane turned the dishwasher on and waited for the noise to overpower their hushed conversation. "He's lapped up a little, but not much. Also, he hasn't done his doggie business all day. I've already made an appointment with a vet Gillian recommended. I'm sure he'll be fine, but I wanted to play it safe." She slid an arm around James' waist. "How are you doing? After all that's gone on lately . . ."

"My supper club is going to meet tomorrow night to help Lucy with her case. She hasn't got a single lead regarding Tia's murderer. There's also the matter of our stalker. We're really going to have to think outside of the box if we want to flush Kenneth out of the bushes. If this whacko really is Kenneth." He smiled at her. "But all of these things — even Pop's stroke — are much easier to bear with you and Eliot under this roof. You two chase away the shadows."

Jane squeezed him tightly and then backed away, snapping at his legs with the damp dishrag. "I'll finish in here. You go read to Iron Chef Junior. He's picked out *Green Eggs and Ham* but I've been instructed to tell you that 'ham' should be replaced by the words 'yam' or 'jam.' "

"Green eggs and jam?" James grimaced. "Dr. Seuss is going vegetarian? Somebody had better warn the Grinch." He lowered his voice until it sounded like a radio announcer's. "This Christmas, he shall carve the roast beets!"

Groaning, Jane aimed the dishtowel a little higher and shooed him from the room.

Lindy was in such high spirits over Alma's fascination with Luigi that she offered to make bean and cheese enchiladas for the supper club's gathering the following evening.

She entered Lucy's house humming a lively tune, her café au lait skin flushed with good humor. Popping the casserole dish containing the enchiladas in Lucy's oven, she performed a little twirl in the center of the floor, holding her flouncing black skirt out and clacking an imaginary pair of castanets.

"Alma's in love. Alma's in love," she sang.

"You hired a Flamenco dancer for us, Lucy?" Bennett joked as he uncapped five bottles of cold beer.

"Better open the whole six-pack," Lucy instructed. "Sullie's coming over."

Bennett paused, the opener hovering over the last bottle. "For *our* meeting?"

James and Gillian exchanged glances. It had always been just the five of them. Lindy had never thought to include Luis or James, Jane. This was their time to celebrate their friendship and to help one another solve personal problems as well as tackle eating issues. They were the Flab Five. The number five was sacred.

"It's *his* case," Lucy replied firmly. "And he knows how well we work as a team." The set of her jaw relaxed and she elbowed Bennett. "I know the newspapers give me all the credit, but I've told Sullie about every case we've cracked as a team. He'll just sit back and listen. You'll never know he's here."

Lucy's statement turned out to be false, because Sullie was a social creature. He small-talked with Gillian about her businesses, sympathized with Bennett over the subject of junk mail, told James he needed to come in to get a library card, and went out of his way to praise Lindy on her enchiladas — and James couldn't agree with the hunky deputy more.

"Have you *transformed* into a vegetarian too?" Gillian asked him, her face alight with pleasure.

James tried to ignore the thought that his friend resembled a bowl of tropical fruit with her papaya-colored hair, banana-hued blouse, and lime green skirt. She accessorized her vibrant ensemble with a pink belt and matching sandals. "I haven't officially converted," he said and carried his plate to the sink. "But I've really enjoyed the meals Jane's been making. She wasn't much of a cook before, but she's learned for Eliot's sake and I am certainly reaping the benefits."

Bennett pointed at the fridge and made a drinking motion with his right hand, indicating that James should bring him another beer. "At least you're bein' healthy, man. I've slipped on the whole no-sugar thing," he said glumly. "Ate a bunch of donut holes durin' my route yesterday. I gotta listen to those CDs more."

Gillian gazed at him fondly. "The problem is that you fall into a *deep* sleep the second the CD begins and I don't think your subconscious can hear Harmony over your own snoring. I *really* think you should try an herbal remedy such as fresh ginger mixed with honey or even some wild yam."

"Do I look like a man who's gonna eat wild yam before I go to bed?" Bennett scowled.

The friends laughed and worked together to clean up their meal. When the table was clear and the dishes were washed, Lucy produced a gallon of sugar-free frozen custard.

"Chilly Willie's created a new flavor," she announced, brandishing an ice cream scooper. "I told him about our plan to kick our sugar addiction a few weeks ago and he's been experimenting with sugar-free flavors ever since. This is called Guiltless Grasshopper Parfait."

Lindy rubbed her hands together. "Mint and chocolate? Yummy!"

"I'll read you Willie's description." Lucy tilted the gallon sideways. "It says, 'Guiltless Grasshopper Parfait is a creamy blend of mint custard, ribbons of fudge, and chocolate mint cookie crumbles. You'll be hopping across town to get your feelers on this sugar-free treat!' "

Bennett accepted a bowl and took a bite of the custard. "Willie Lamont is a gentleman and an artist. This stuff is too good *not* to be bad for us."

No one answered, being too busy licking spoons clean.

Lucy finished her ice cream first, pushed her bowl aside, opened a file folder, and uncapped a pen. She placed a yellow legal pad at her right elbow and surveyed her friend's faces. "Okay, let's get to work. The death of Tia Royale really bothers me. First of all, she was only twenty-six. Second, she was devoted to her cause. Third, her killer roughed her up, bruising her neck while he tried to pin her down, to prevent her from fighting for her life."

"And that girl had plenty of fight in her," Bennett mumbled.

Ignoring him, Lucy continued. "Tia had no official job. Her parents bought her the house where her body was found and sent her a monthly allowance. While they were generous with money, they kept their distance. According to Tia's daddy, his daughter wasn't 'a good image to be associated with their company.' And as her mother told me this morning, Tia was 'different' from the rest of the Royales."

Gillian sighed theatrically. "Poor little black sheep."

James smiled as Sullie gave Gillian a bewildered look. Turning his gaze to Lucy he asked, "Not to interrupt, but did you ask Mrs. Royale about Tia's pets?"

"Yes," Lucy said. "The Royales want nothing to do with them. Mr. Royale claimed that they travel too much to care for Tia's pets."

"It's destiny! Those animals were *meant* to be yours!" Gillian exclaimed. "Did Snickers go to the vet today?" She whispered the word *vet* as though her cat, The Dalai Lama, were present. Whenever her intelligent feline heard the threatening word, he took off for the hills, sometimes staying away for days.

"Turns out, Snickers needed minor surgery. He had stopped eating and drinking altogether. The vet said he had a blockage," James answered. "The procedure went smoothly and Jane should have picked him up by now." He looked at Gillian. "I'm glad he's mine, but I wish the Royales were footing the bill. I could have added a new deck for the cost of that surgery. And if Miss Pickles doesn't stop shredding every object made out of paper — especially toilet paper — then I'm going to have to keep a basket of leaves in my bathroom!"

Once the laughter died away, Lucy finished relaying the case details. "Tia's assailant entered her bedroom and the two of them struggled, leaving her neck bruised. However, the cause of death was heart failure. Until the lab results come back, we won't know if she was drugged or not, but the M.E. says there are no obvious indicators of the presence of drugs or poison in her system."

Sullie stirred on the other side of the table. "The Royales are big supporters of the governor. Mark my words, those labs will be done in record time. It's our only break so far."

Lindy was twirling a lock of black hair around her index finger, a sign that she was deep in thought. "The only evidence of struggle was in her bedroom. Ground or second floor?"

"Second," Lucy answered and then, guessing what Lindy would ask next, added, "There was no sign of forced entry around the windows. In fact, they were locked."

"So Tia knew her murderer. She let him inside," Lindy stated with a shiver.

Sullie's eyes grew round and he stared at Lindy. "You all are sharp! Lucy and I came to that conclusion too. We believe she was expecting this guy and that she wasn't as afraid of him as she should have been. She's made a bunch of cash withdrawals over the last two weeks. Drained her account dry."

"Yeah, Sullie got a copy of her monthly statement right before the bank closed today," Lucy added excitedly. "Tia barely had enough to live on until her next allowance check came. Her balance was down to the minimum. We think she was being blackmailed."

James used the tip of his finger to capture the last drop of Guiltless Grasshopper Parfait from his bowl. "How much money are we talking about?"

Lucy consulted the case file. "Somewhere in the neighborhood of twenty-five thousand. She made five withdrawals of five thousand dollars each."

Bennett, who was pulling on his toothbrush mustache while Lucy talked, whistled. "Whoa! But why kill your own personal ATM machine?"

Gillian put her hands over her heart, her face forming an anguished expression. "How can you talk about that tragic young woman in such a callous manner?"

Ever the peacemaker, Lindy waved her hands to stave off Bennett's rejoinder. "Let's focus on the blackmail. What would someone have on Tia? Maybe she didn't always feel so passionate about her cause," she mused. "She might have eaten a double cheeseburger every night and run over squirrels helter-skelter before she had some kind of life-changing experience."

"Her parents were of no help as far as why Tia became so involved in animal rights," Lucy said, clearly disappointed. "Tia was never allowed to have pets, and she had no contact with farmers or livestock. Her brothers had nothing to add. According to them, she left for college a self-centered, fashion-conscious girl, and came back a raving hippie activist."

"Were you able to make contact with any of her college friends?" James inquired.

Sullie consulted his notes. "We talked to the girl she roomed with for two years. The roommate says Tia got involved with any group that would allow her to yell as loud as she wanted or march in demonstrations. Defending animal rights was one of a dozen causes. The lady said that Tia's family never paid her any mind so she joined these movements as a way of getting attention and belonging to something. This girl was mighty surprised Tia didn't eventually grow tired of it all."

"She didn't! She poured all of her energy

into protecting innocent animals!" Gillian shouted. "Maybe the murderer raises cattle or works for a big chicken company and wanted to shut her up!"

Knowing Gillian's unhappy history involving one of the region's chicken plants, the supper club members remained silent. That is, except for Bennett. "Woman, not all the folks in this world who breed, slaughter, or eat meat are devils. Take yours truly, for instance. I don't lose any sleep thinkin' about where my bacon comes from. I'm gonna buy it, I'm gonna eat it, and I'm gonna enjoy it. Does that make me *bad?*" He touched her hand. "The guy who killed Tia was after money. Sure, he might be a carnivore, but this isn't about the animals, it's about the twenty-five grand."

"I agree," Lindy added gently. "Now we need to figure out who uncovered a secret she'd pay to keep hidden."

"Knowing the secret would help too," James said. "If only the killer had left a single clue at the scene."

At that moment, his phone beeped and a text message appeared on the narrow screen. James flipped open the phone and gasped.

His friends stared at him, concerned.

"What is it?" Gillian and Lindy spoke in unison.

"Jane sent a photo of the object obstructing Snickers' plumbing. According to the vet, he probably swallowed this the night Tia was murdered. Look!" He placed the phone in the center of the table and everyone leaned forward to examine the image.

"Is that a tree?" Gillian squinted at the photo.

"A gold fir tree pendant to be exact," James spoke quickly in his excitement. "We finally have a tangible clue." When his friends exchanged puzzled looks, he jabbed his finger at the screen. "You've all seen this tree before! This fir was on every landscaping T-shirt, baseball cap, and truck owned by the late Ned Woodman."

"So Tia's killer might also be Ned's killer?" Lindy seemed dubious. "But they were nothing alike. A young female activist and a middle-aged councilman?"

"There's a common thread," Lucy said, pushing back her chair. "And starting tomorrow, we're going to find it."

THIRTEEN:
WHITE CHEDDAR CHEESE
POPCORN

Grams of
Sugar
17

When James got home after the supper club meeting, he found Jane riveted to the television, her eyes fixed on the foamy ocean waves surging across the screen and her hands curled around a steel mixing bowl filled with popcorn. Miss Pickles and Snickers were asleep at her feet. They both opened their eyes when James entered the room, but seeing that he was no threat nor did he bear any food offerings, both animals immediately went back to sleep. James stooped down to pet their heads and was delighted that Snickers didn't appear any the worse for wear after the minor surgery that morning. The little schnauzer was simply sleepy, but James expected he'd be more active after a good night's rest.

"It's Shark Week on the Discovery Channel," Jane whispered and passed him a bowl of popcorn. "This episode is called 'Blood in the Water,' and it is deliciously scary!"

James glanced at an image of a Great White swimming through the water with its mouth hanging open, displaying row after row of terrifying teeth. The camera zoomed in on the shark's jaw as the narrator described the damage these triangular, dagger-like weapons could inflict on fish, seals, and humans. Nearly forgetting what he was going to say, James forced his eyes away from the awe-inspiring King of the Deep and helped himself to the cheesy, salty popcorn. "Where's the tree? The one the vet took out of Snickers?"

Jane didn't even blink. Hugging a throw pillow tightly against her chest, she gestured toward the kitchen. "In a cup next to the sink. And don't worry, it's been cleaned."

The gold fir tree didn't seem to have been damaged by Snickers' digestive system. In fact, it shone beneath the overhead lights as though it were brand new. James placed the pendant in his palm and turned it over.

There were no markings on the reverse side other than the symbol denoting that it was made of fourteen-karat gold.

"Does this look like something a man would wear as a necklace?" James asked Jane during the commercial break. "Especially Ned Woodman, a middle-aged town councilman who owned a successful landscaping business?"

Jane's mouth dropped open. "The dead man you and Eliot discovered at the food festival? You think this was *his?*" James nodded and she took the golden tree from him and examined it beneath the lamp light. "I highly doubt he wore this," she said. "After reading about him in the *Star,* I'd say he wasn't the jewelry-wearing type. Anyway, I think it's some kind of charm, like the ones you can attach to a woman's bracelet."

Frowning, James stared at a commercial for room freshener. He watched the woman gleefully spraying the curtains in her teenage son's room, her face lit with joy because the boy's room now smelled like oranges instead of dirty socks. "Could it belong to Ned's wife then?"

"Maybe." Jane plucked the gold tree from his palm. "But then how did it end up inside Snickers? Mrs. Woodman would have to have been —"

"In Tia's house." James completed the thought and then his shoulders sagged in dejection. "But why? What connection would Donna Woodman have to Tia? And how could we find out for certain? It's not as though we can invite her for dinner and the third degree." He absently munched on popcorn and watched in horror as a shark began to swim toward a lone swimmer at the Jersey Shore. As soon as he set the popcorn bowl aside, Miss Pickles jumped up onto his lap and began to knead his thighs with her prickly claws.

The shark circled once, twice, and then sank its serrated teeth into the man's thigh. "Look at all the blood!" Jane said in delighted revulsion. As the shark continued to attack his victim, she put her finger to her mouth and tapped her closed lips. "You know, there is a way to extract information from Donna. Remember the article that ran in the *Star* showing the funeral photos?"

Tearing his eyes from the carnage on the screen, James nodded.

"Well, I remember Donna being quoted as saying she and Ned met while attending JMU. I could always call her and ask for help in forming a Quincy's Gap alumni chapter."

James stared at her in amazement. "You

would do that?"

"Of course, if you think it would be beneficial. Lucy is trying her best to find who's been messing with our family, so I'd like to repay the favor." Jane hit the mute button on the remote control. "I'll have to give Donna some notice, but I'll see if she's free for lunch this weekend. You can eavesdrop while you and Eliot construct the next phase of his Lego city."

Gently removing Miss Pickles from his lap, James got down on one knee and grasped Jane's left hand. The light from the television painted her face with a soft, white glow and James' heart swelled inside his chest as he looked at her. Words bubbled up his throat, nearly catching there before launching themselves into the air. "Will you marry me, Jane?" he asked breathlessly. "Will you be my wife again?"

The remote slid from Jane's right hand and clattered onto the floor. "Goodness! What's brought this on?"

James scrambled over to the television set and turned it off. Turning back to Jane, he reclaimed her hand and said, "It's been building up since the day I spotted you in the crowd at that party celebrating Bennett's *Jeopardy!* appearance." He paused, forcing himself to slow down and speak clearly.

"There was a time I believed that I never wanted to see you again, but even when I was boiling over with hurt and anger, part of me longed for the chance to make things right again. To go back in time and stop us from breaking apart."

Jane looked down in shame and James squeezed her hand until she met his gaze once more. "I'm not trying to open old wounds, sweetheart. I'm trying, in my own awkward way, to tell you that *you're the one* who made things right. You and I are better now than we ever were. We are a family. You, me, and Eliot. I want us to be like this from now on."

"He would love that!" she whispered, her eyes shimmering.

He gripped her hand tightly. "But this is about more than our son or us living under one roof. I want *you,* Jane. Today and tomorrow and the day after that. Only you. Be my wife again. Grow old with me."

He waited while Jane sniffed back tears, too moved to speak. Finally, she slid her hand out of his, threw both arms around his neck, and cried, "Yes, yes, yes!"

Jane's tears of happiness moistened James' cheeks and her fervent whispers of assent were stilled by his hungry kisses. She pulled James down to her on the sofa, forcing Miss

Pickles to relocate. She glared at the entangled pair in annoyance and sauntered off to the kitchen.

Later, as Jane and James did their best to cover their bare flesh with throw blankets, the newly engaged couple sipped glasses of wine and discussed the future. Their faces flushed from their lovemaking, they twined their hands together and shared whispered laughter as they recalled some of the minor disasters from the first walk down the aisle.

"I still say the organist was drunk!" Jane giggled.

James recalled the wobbly notes and the congregation's startled looks. "Possibly. But there's no doubt we had the feistiest flower girl. Do you remember how she kicked her brother in the shin as she passed by his pew?"

"The highlight of the wedding video," Jane said with a smile. She then sat up on one elbow. "We've had a big church wedding with the fancy reception and the four-tiered cake. Why don't we go the Town Hall route this time? Keep things simple. Just between you and me. Quincy's Gap can marry us. I say the sooner the better too."

James considered her suggestion in a state of drowsy contentment. "How soon?"

"We can get the ball rolling during your

Friday lunch break. We'll need to drive down to the courthouse complex and apply for a marriage license."

He kissed her in reply. "We need a witness for that, if I recall. How do we choose just one person? Someone is going to feel snubbed."

"I know just who to ask," Jane murmured sleepily. "Just meet me there at high noon, okay, cowboy?"

Sighing in utter happiness, James murmured, "I could get used to your calling me that."

Stretching, James stood, hastily tied the blanket around his waist and helped Jane up from the sofa. Wrapping a blanket around her shoulders, he pulled her against him and the pair walked slowly down the hall, heads bent toward one another as they headed for bed and a night filled with blissful dreams.

The supper club members had decided to meet at the library during their lunch breaks the next day in order to discuss the details of Gillian's telephone call to Kenneth Cooper's law firm. Even Lindy, who was usually forced to remain on school grounds until the bell clanged the official dismissal time, was able to be there. The student body had been given a half-day to prepare for their final exams and as soon as the hallways had emptied of teenagers, the teachers and staff had dashed out to their cars, as drunk on the taste of freedom and the invigorating spring air as their pupils.

"So what's new in the hot love affair between your future mother-in-law and Luigi?" James teased Lindy when she breezed into his office.

Lindy tried to smooth her windblown hair with her fingers, but her dark, tangled locks refused to be tamed. Helping herself to a rubber band from his desk, she fastened the whole mess into a ponytail and smiled. "The good news is that he's mighty fond of her. The bad news is that she seems to feel right at home behind the counter of his pizza parlor. She's bossing around his kids as though she's already their step-mama."

"And why's that the bad news?" Bennett asked as he walked into the room. He brushed a paper fragment from his postal uniform shirt and sat down in the chair closest to the window.

Lindy's smile shrank. "Because she's delayed her return ticket for another month. That woman is never going to go back to Mexico! And as long as she's here, Luis can't keep his mind on *us!*"

Lucy, who had been examining a bookmark listing the top one hundred bestselling crime novels, gave Lindy a sharp look. "Someone has got to say this to you, so it might as well be me. Luis needs to pick you first and his mama second. What if she moves here permanently? What'll happen to your relationship?"

Lindy paled. "Lord have mercy, I can't stomach that thought! Alma in Quincy's Gap? Twenty-four, seven?" She nudged Bennett roughly in the shoulder. "Gimme that chair. I feel faint!"

Bennett obliged, his dark eyes sparkling with amusement. He turned his gaze toward the door as the clink of Gillian's armloads of silver bangles preceded her into the room.

"Hello, friends!" she trilled merrily. "Oh, it's so good for my *restless* and *distracted* spirit to be working on a case with you all, to be truly *focused* on truth, justice, and restored balance!"

James indicated she should sit at his desk. "Review the plan for us, Gillian."

Settling back into the comfortable chair, Gillian folded her hands together and took a deep breath. "Bennett and I spent several hours reading up on Kenneth Cooper, Esquire. He's represented quite a few drug companies and other giant corporations in lawsuits against individuals, but he's argued copyright infringement cases as well." Here, she smiled smugly. "As though the thought was *sowed* like a magical seed, the idea bloomed in the *deepest* crevices of my mind to ask for Mr. Cooper's help in suing someone who's stolen our Pet Palace plans. I will *insist* that I only want Mr. Cooper to represent me, seeing as he's won every single copyright or patent infringement case he's argued."

Lucy gave Gillian an admiring nod. "That's good! But who will you pretend to sue?"

"We called Beau Livingstone yesterday and told him about this crazy plan," Bennett took up the thread. "He got right to work settin' up a website chock full of the same Pet Palace designs shown on the real site." He glanced at Gillian. "You struck it rich the day you decided to make that man your business partner. For a former roofer, that guy's got almost as much computer savvy as those Fitzgerald brainiacs."

James edged around his desk and pointed at his computer. "We'd better take a look at the fake site."

"Surf away. You'd never know it wasn't as *real* as the touch of my hand on your arm." Gillian typed in the URL and then swiveled

305

the screen so that everyone had a clear view.

"Very professional," Lindy said as James clicked links and enlarged images of the Pet Palace designs.

"Who's this listed under the 'Contact Us' link?" James pointed at the monitor.

Gillian followed his finger with the cursor. "To order a Pet Castle, an interested customer needs to email a Mr. Jerry Brickman. Of course, ole Jerry doesn't exist. Beau set up a Gmail account using Jerry Brickman's name, so he *looks* legit, but he's just a figment of my *colorful* imagination. We used Williamsburg as the company address because that's the location of Kenneth's law firm. It's also why we didn't provide a street address."

"That's right," Bennett stated seriously. "We didn't want those pesky lawyers to call up a fake phone number or drive by some empty warehouse and call our bluff."

"You two were very thorough." James looked first at Bennett and then, Gillian. "Are all your designs actually copyright protected?"

Fluffing her hair, Gillian nodded. "Of course. Beau and I have put in *hours* upon *hours* dreaming up the Cockatiel Condo, the Pekinese Penthouse, the Siamese Suite, the —"

Lucy forced her friend to break off the list by thrusting the phone into her hand. "I recommend you speak to Kenneth's secretary first. His partners will know how to keep information to themselves. We need someone who will feel sorry for you, so get a woman on the line and then lay it on thick."

Inhaling deeply, Gillian closed her eyes and began chanting under her breath. James raised his brows and grinned at Bennett and though his friend shrugged his shoulders in befuddlement, there was a glimmer of pride in his eyes.

The supper club members perched on the edge of their chairs and listened as Gillian successfully navigated through an assortment of gatekeepers until she finally reached Kenneth Cooper's personal assistant. Her friends knew she was speaking to the right person because she gave them a quick thumbs-up before spinning her chair around in order to face the room's only window.

"Mr. Cooper's not there? Are you expecting him back soon?" Gillian already sounded as if she were on the verge of tears. "*A leave of absence!* Oh, what am I going to do?" She hesitated. "Miss?" Another pause. "It's Katherine? Thank you, it's so much easier to speak informally. Would you be willing to give some advice to a lady drowning in a pot of boiling water?"

This question was followed by a long and pregnant pause, but the answer must have been positive for Gillian's fingers, which had been curled around the telephone cord, suddenly relaxed and she began her tale. The fabrication began with Gillian running away from an abusive boyfriend and finding a safe haven in Quincy's Gap and ended with her feelings of peace and fulfillment working with animals.

"Do you have a pet, Katherine?"

The response led to a lengthy sidebar about the merits of the Boston Terrier. Eventually, Gillian was able to share her good fortune in being able to open her own pet grooming shop and after many years of loving toil, launching her second business, Pet Palaces.

"Can you imagine what it's like to have this *man* stealing my ideas? He's making money from *my* designs and I *hate* how powerless it makes me feel." Here, Gillian's voice trembled. "I searched for lawyers in the Williamsburg area because that's where this *thief* is living — probably high on the hog off *my* hard work too!" She paused and made a great show of trying to rein herself in. "Mr. Cooper's name stood out from all the *other* attorneys because he has *never* lost a copyright infringement case. Without his help, what can I do?"

James winked at Gillian. It was a smart move to end with a question, leaving the decision with the other woman, whom they all hoped sympathized enough with Gillian's plight to supply her with information.

They held their collective breath as Gillian waited for an answer, exhaling in relieved unison as she scribbled something on James' desk calendar.

"Oh, I see," Gillian spoke soberly. "That is quite a burden for you to shoulder, but Mr. Cooper is being very brave to confront his demons. You'd like to introduce me to one of his partners?" She glanced up at her friends in a panic. "Um, I'll call back! One of the dogs has hopped off the groomer's table and is shaking soap all over the mayor's wife. Thank you!" She slammed the phone down.

Leaning back in his chair, Bennett put his hands together and began to clap. Soon, all the supper club members were laughing and applauding, but their raucousness died away when Gillian pointed at the note she'd written on the calendar.

"Kenneth Cooper is *not* in Williamsburg. His medical leave translates to him receiving 'help' for a 'substance abuse problem' in Culpepper." She turned to the computer on the desktop and typed rapidly. "Yes indeed, there is a treatment center there. It would be easy for Kenneth to take a quick drive to Harrisonburg or Quincy's Gap from Culpepper."

Lindy looked confused. "Don't you have to stay inside once you're checked into one of those places? I mean, could he have just walked out whenever he wanted to write notes and kill a bird or two?"

"You'd think so," Lucy answered and placed her hands on her gun belt. "Leave it to me. I will find out exactly why Kenneth needed treatment and whether he stepped foot off the property for more than a millisecond." She moved toward the door.

Gillian also rose. "How are you going to do that, Lucy? Those places are meant to protect a person's privacy! It wouldn't be *right* for anyone at the facility to share confidential information with you!" she declared.

"If this guy were the Pope I'd still beat down the doors to discover what he's been doing!" Lucy snapped. "By threatening my friend, Kenneth has lost his *right* to keep his secrets!" Passing a hand over her face as though to wipe away the anger and frustration, she hastily apologized. "I'm open to other ideas."

Gillian waved her off. "You need to do this your way. I shouldn't feel any sympathy for this man, but I can't keep myself from thinking that perhaps the drugs have turned him into a monster and that underneath, he could be a good man."

"Maybe," Bennett said as he glanced at his watch. "But it's still no excuse to set about ruinin' James' life or scarin' his family right out of their skins." He turned to Lucy. "How are you gonna get those folks to volunteer info on Kenneth? The man's a lawyer, Ms. Deputy. He is *not* gonna stand around while you and his doctors have a nice chat about his medical file."

"That's true," Lucy agreed. "And I could lose my badge, so I'm going to assign this job to someone else. Someone who's dying to get back into our good graces."

Having made her mysterious announcement, Lucy told her friends she'd be in touch and walked out of the office.

"Okay, that's one item to check off the list. What about Tia's case?" Lindy asked, directing her question at James.

He shared Jane's idea about inviting Ned Woodman's widow over for lunch.

"How clever!" Gillian exclaimed. "We may

have to make her an honorary supper club member!"

Thinking of last night's marriage proposal, James smiled. "Yes, we just might."

On Friday, James met Jane at the Town Hall in order to present their forms of identification to the Clerk of Courts.

As she signed one of the documents the clerk placed on the counter, Jane looked over at James and whispered, "I feel like I'm twenty years old again! I have butterflies in my stomach!"

"You are so much better at forty. Smarter, sexier — a woman of the world." Ignoring the clerk's impatient frown, James kissed Jane on the lips before she could finish writing her name.

Someone cleared his throat behind them and James looked over his shoulder to see Scott and Francis Fitzgerald gazing at the floor, their hands stuffed in their pockets.

"Our witnesses are here!" Jane hugged each brother while they blushed furiously.

"We are so totally honored to be signing these papers," Francis stated sincerely. "This is a big secret, right? We're the only ones who know you two are getting hitched again?"

"Yes. Until after we make it official with

the Justice of the Peace, that is," James answered. "We'll tell our families and friends when it's a done deal." He smiled at the twins and then grabbed Scott by the arm, suddenly alarmed. "Wait a minute. If we're all here, then who is running the library?"

Scott's eyes darted to the wall clock. "Fern's manning the helm. We figured we'd scratch out a John Hancock and then dash back. She should only be alone for fifteen minutes."

On the other side of the counter, the clerk scowled. "I only need *one* witness."

Francis and Scott exchanged looks of dismay. "Paper, rock, scissors!" they shouted and commenced with a series of frenzied hand motions.

"Two out of three," Francis said as the clerk rolled her eyes.

In the end, the paperwork was completed, witnessed, and notarized.

"You should have your license in the next two weeks," the clerk droned as James paid her the required fee.

The twins shook hands with their boss, hugged Jane once more, and rushed out of the building.

"Do you need to get back too or do we have time for lunch?" Jane asked, linking her arm in James'.

"Forget about lunch. Let's go shopping!" James led her to the passenger side of the Bronco and gallantly opened the door.

Jane laughed. "Stranger words have never come from your lips. You hate shopping!"

"Not in this case," he assured her. "It's not every day that I get to buy a pair of wedding bands."

Fourteen:
Chocolate Chunk Peanut Butter Cookies

Grams of
Sugar
18

James knew that he should be focusing more of his energies on unraveling the mysteries of Tia Royale's death and Kenneth Cooper's whereabouts, but he couldn't stop thinking about Jane. He walked around the library with a light step, his mouth turned upward in a goofy smile. He greeted each patron as though he or she were his favorite person on the earth, and several older women felt inclined to pinch his cheek and tease him for being hit by an entire quiver of Cupid's arrows.

When Willie Lamont came in to pick up a

fresh stack of presidential biographies, he shook his head and made a clicking noise with his tongue. "You got it bad, my man. You're gonna break out in zip-a-dee-doo-dahs any minute."

"Stranger things have happened," James cautioned as he checked out the frozen custard shop owner's books with a flourish. "Hey! Summer's right around the corner. The song might make a good name for your next flavor."

Willie raised his brows. "Little wordy, don't ya think?"

"How about 'Second Time's A Charm'?" James slid the books and the checkout receipt across the counter.

Laughing, Willie gathered up the thick tomes. "I might just have to do some experimentin' this afternoon. Maybe I'll create somethin' like 'Wedding Bell Buttercream.' "

"Sounds perfect. Especially if you make it as guilt-free as that Grasshopper Parfait flavor."

Willie shook his head. "No way, man. We're talkin' about eternal love here. You gotta have sugar and cream and plenty of pure vanilla! I can practically hear the church bells a-ringin'!"

James found it hard to bite back his secret

at the mention of wedding bells, but he wished Willie a good day and said nothing more. The twins knew all about James and Jane's upcoming nuptials of course, and having them in on it helped James keep quiet. The toughest part of remaining mum until their vows were exchanged would be keeping the engagement from Jackson and Milla.

Though part of James wanted the ceremony to be private, another part desperately wanted to share the good news with his parents. Milla would be delighted and even though it would take Jackson time to come around, James knew that his father would approve of the family becoming a bona fide unit. What James really wanted to do was to rush to his father's side and shout that Eliot would not be going back to Harrisonburg in the fall. Or ever, for that matter. James would love to see how such an announcement would bring joy to Jackson.

James and Jane had arrived at several decisions about the future the day after their engagement. Jane had immediately called the head of her department and asked to continue teaching courses online. Because these high-tech courses were growing in popularity, she would be able to retain her position by teaching three of these. She'd have to appear on campus to attend faculty meetings and other business, but there was no longer any reason for her to reside near the university.

"As soon as we're married, I'll put my house on the market," she assured James. "Thanks to my parents, there's no mortgage. We'll put every cent of that money in savings and live happily ever after at 27 Hickory Hill Lane."

The arrangement suited James perfectly. He didn't want to give up the library or his little yellow house for Jane, but he would have in a New York minute. Instead, he and everything he loved would remain in Quincy's Gap. It was no wonder he believed he was the luckiest man in the world.

In fact, James felt so blessed that he did his best to tone down the jubilation radiating from his face when he took Eliot to visit his grandparents on Saturday morning. Jane wanted father and son out of the house so she could clean before Donna Woodman's visit, so the Henry boys ate a hasty breakfast and knocked on the back door of James' childhood home at a quarter past nine.

Naturally, Milla was cooking up a storm in the kitchen. She'd made breakfast for Jackson and was now baking a chicken casserole and a peach pie for a woman from church who'd fallen and bruised her hip. She also had a mixing bowl filled with cookie dough on the cluttered counter.

"I smell peanut butter," Eliot said after returning Milla's warm hug.

She wrinkled her nose. "That's because I'm making *you* a special batch of chocolate chunk peanut butter cookies." Lowering her voice to a whisper, she led her grandson to the mixing bowl. "Do you think it's too early in the morning to lick a beater?"

"Nope," Eliot answered hungrily.

"Me either." Milla smiled at James over Eliot's head. "I've got a beater for you too, if you'd like one."

James grinned as Eliot poked his tongue through the tines of the metal beater. "Thanks, but I'll wait for a cookie when it's hot from the oven instead. How's Pop?"

"Already painting," Milla answered proudly. "Some top-secret project."

Gesturing toward the shed behind the house, James asked, "Is he out there now?"

She nodded. "He won't use the walker, so he hobbles out there with his crutches and leans on one while he paints with his other hand. It seems to be doing him a world of good — to be working again so soon after the stroke — but he gets real tired. Can you remind him that he's got to stop and rest?

Trick him into coming in for some coffee and cookies."

"I'll try," James answered without much hope. Jackson Henry wasn't easy to manipulate.

As usual, James had to knock on the shed door and wait for admittance. It took Jackson several minutes to put down his paintbrush and palette and shuffle to the door. Poking his head out through the crack like a suspicious turtle, Jackson looked at his son. Though his mouth remained an immovable line, his eyes smiled.

James had been calling his father every day since he'd come home from the hospital, but Jackson was even more reluctant than usual to talk on the phone. His speech was still slurred and the already taciturn man had grown even more so. Milla served as Jackson's communicator, giving James updates on his father's physical therapy and general well-being, but none of the details regarding his slow and steady recovery were as rewarding as seeing that unique glimmer return to Jackson's eyes.

"I'm glad you're back at work, Pop. Can I come in or would you rather take a break and have some coffee and cookies in the house?"

Jackson hesitated, clearly uncertain

whether to let James view his unfinished painting. Finally, he stretched his lips into a lopsided grin and waved his son inside. The finished paintings were on large horizontal canvases. Jackson had always painted on vertical canvases before and never on such a large scale. The painted shapes were difficult to distinguish at first, but as James stepped closer, he saw that his father's new pieces were actually made up of dozens of small paintings, similar in style to a collage.

"The amount of detail," James breathed in awe. He leaned closer, noting the familiar features of his childhood self staring back at him. There he was in his high school marching band uniform, as an infant in his mother's arms, as a seven-year-old scarecrow at Halloween. In another square, as precise as a photograph, he was raking leaves with his father. In another, Jackson was laughing as he carved the Thanksgiving turkey. These were pictures of a happy life, but there were representations of pain and loss too. There was his mother's casket, strewn with white lilies, and a portrait of Jackson sitting on the bed with her wedding ring in his hand, his face crumpled in grief.

"Your memories, Pop." James felt a tightening in his throat. "This painting shows glimpses of your life."

Jackson nodded and reached out to James with his good arm. "It's been a good one, my boy. I need you to know that."

James turned to his father fearfully, but Jackson shook his head. "I ain't gonna drop dead. I just wanted you to know. You're a fine son and a damned good daddy to Eliot."

The two men embraced and for once, Jackson was in no rush to pull away.

Later, after a second breakfast of cookies and milk, Eliot joined his grandfather in the shed and spent the rest of the morning painting his own masterpiece using only two colors of paint. By the time he'd placed the final brush stroke and named his work, "Melted Popsicles," it was lunchtime. Knowing Jane would soon be entertaining Donna Woodman, James decided it would be wiser to spend another hour with Milla and Jackson. After all, he didn't want to arrive home just as Donna was on the brink of revealing something important.

However, as soon as Eliot had finished eating a grilled cheese sandwich and a ripe nectarine, he suddenly seemed to run out of steam. It was time to take the little boy home.

"Let's go work on your LEGO fire station, okay buddy?" James wiped Eliot's sticky chin, clapped his father affectionately on his good shoulder, and gave Milla a kiss on the cheek. In return, she handed him a baggie filled with cookies.

"These are for Jane. Tell her we're sorry we missed her and hope to see her soon." Milla squeezed Eliot and beamed as he broke free, only to wrap his arms around Jackson's neck. He whispered something into his grandfather's ear and Jackson's entire face crinkled in amusement and delight. As Eliot darted out the door, Jackson gazed after him in wonder.

"I'll be damned," Jackson chuckled and looked at James. "I never thought I'd say this but hell, I wish you'd had more kids. That one there just . . ." he couldn't find the right words, but the light in his eyes spoke volumes.

On the drive home, James considered what his father had said. Would he have another child? Were he and Jane too old? Did they have enough money or enough room in the yellow house for more children? Suddenly, the idea of a helpless infant shrieking out its wordless demands in the middle of the night filled James with anxiety. He knew nothing about babies. Eliot had come into his life eating solid foods, speaking in sentences, and completely toilet trained. But a baby! Now *there* was a mystery!

"What did you whisper to Grandpa back there?" James asked his son at the next red light.

Eliot shrugged. "I said he was my favorite play date friend." He colored. " 'Cept you, Dad."

"That was a nice thing to say," James told his son. "To both of us."

Minutes later, the two Henrys stepped through the front door of their house to the sound of a woman sniffling. "We're home!" James called out and then hurriedly followed his greeting with, "I'm going to take Eliot to his room for some quiet time."

He winked at Eliot, signaling that what he really meant by "quiet time" was an hour of design and construction using LEGO blocks. Eliot shouted, "Hi, Mom! Bye, Mom!" and dashed down the hall.

Jane didn't answer, but as James tiptoed after Eliot he heard her murmuring gently to the other woman. Donna, or at least James assumed that's who it was as he didn't dare go into the living room just yet, sounded as though she was crying.

I've got some sense of timing, James thought. He lingered in the hallway for another moment but was unable to hear distinct words, only the rise and fall of exchanged voices, soft and melodic, like two instruments playing a lullaby in *pianissimo.*

James soon forgot about the women as he and Eliot built their own version of the Empire State Building. When James heard the front door close and a car engine start in the driveway, he told Eliot it was time to rest and handed him a portable CD player and an audio CD of Curious George stories. Eliot snuggled under his covers, put on his headphones, and loaded the CD player. James was amazed at the technical savvy of today's four-year-olds and knew it wouldn't be long before Eliot ran circles around him when it came to all things electronic.

He found Jane standing in front of the kitchen sink, staring out the window into the back yard. "How'd it go?" he asked.

She sighed. "You can cross Donna Woodman off your suspect list. She really loved her husband and is genuinely grieving." She pointed at the gold fir tree on the counter. "That belonged to Ned, but it wasn't a charm for a necklace or a bracelet. Donna had it made for his key chain."

"So the two deaths must be connected! When Ned's killer came after Tia he must have dropped the charm. It was pretty dumb of him to have kept it in the first place." James picked up the shiny tree. "Did Donna mention the Wellness Village at all?"

Jane looked surprised. "Funny you should say that! When I asked her about the masseuse she visits there, she started crying. She thinks Ned was having an affair with someone who worked in the Village. She was going to confront him about it the day of the Food Festival, but Ned was killed before she had the chance."

James blinked. "An affair?" He recalled how anxious Ned had seemed before his death. "How did Donna come to that conclusion?"

"His landscaping company took care of the mowing and fertilizing for the complex — apparently, they're the only organic landscaping company in the area — but Donna said Ned went there way too often. She'd drive by and see his truck parked in the Village's lot during odd hours."

"Couldn't Ned have been a client? Maybe he was seeing Harmony or Roslyn or even the acupuncturist, but wanted to keep it a secret?" James didn't know why he was playing devil's advocate, but he felt compelled to do so.

Jane frowned. "I said 'odd hours.' We're talking after closing time, honey. If he was the acupuncturist's client, for example, then he was getting X-rated services after she put away her hot needles!"

"Oh, I see." James fell silent. Mechanically, he loaded the lunch plates into the dishwasher. He then opened a liter of Coke Zero and poured a glass over crushed ice. "Could Donna be the killer? After all, she is a woman scorned."

Jane shook her head emphatically. "No way. She was angry, but she wanted to fight for her marriage. She and Ned had a child together. Now that kid has no father. Donna is embarrassed about the missing money and she is really, really hurt, but she would give anything to have Ned back. She truly loved him."

"I trust your judgment," James answered readily, brushing a strand of hair from Jane's cheek and tucking it behind her ear. "So could the other woman be the killer?"

"That's what I've been turning over in my mind. Maybe Ned's lover wasn't as keen on him as he was on her," Jane suggested. "Perhaps her feelings were never genuine and she was using him as a source of easy money."

James took a sip of soda. "And then she disposed of him because she'd gotten all the ready cash she was going to get? That's pretty ruthless." He considered the theory.

"It also means she'd have to be strong enough to strangle Tia until she lost consciousness."

"Or, she had a partner."

Now it was James' turn to be surprised. "No one's considered that possibility." He rubbed his eyes. "Boy, this is getting complicated."

"Looks like you need to book another appointment with Harmony," Jane said, handing James the phone. "And you'll have to give yourself enough time beforehand to check out all the other women working in the Wellness Village."

Putting down his sweating glass, James dialed Harmony's number. When the office voicemail came on, he left a message saying that he was having difficulty keeping a secret from his family and friends.

"It's a good secret," he added and smiled at Jane. "Still, I'd like to make peace with myself about the whole thing. Plus, I haven't quite resolved my sugar issues either." He sighed, recalling the number of chocolate chunk peanut butter cookies he'd eaten that morning. "Honestly, life has gotten in the way of my being healthy again. I just cannot seem to stay focused on my physical fitness goals." He requested an afternoon appointment as soon as Harmony had an opening and then hung up.

Jane was studying him. "Is that true? That you feel guilty about keeping our upcoming nuptials from your family and friends?"

He reached for her hand. "Guilty, no. It's difficult because I'm having a hard time hiding how happy I am. I want to climb on top of the town's water tower and shout our news to the world." He jerked his thumb at the phone. "But I had to tell her *something.*"

Relaxing, Jane closed the distance between them. "As far as your second reason for seeing Harmony goes, I want you to know that I wouldn't change a thing about your looks. If you want to be healthier, then that's great. Eliot and I want you around for a long, long time." She wound her arms around him. "But I do like a man who can push me around in bed. I don't want some bag of bones lying next to me."

"You don't, huh?" James grinned. "Say, how long do you think Eliot will listen to his *Curious George* CD?"

Before Jane could answer, the doorbell rang.

"Lucy!" James greeted his friend loudly. Even though she couldn't possibly have heard his exchange with Jane, he felt slightly embarrassed. "Um, what brings you by?"

She put her hands on her gun belt and

rocked back on her heels looking extremely pleased. "News! Good news. Can I come in?"

Jane gave James a playful push. "Please do. I was just about to brew some coffee. Can I offer you a cup?"

"Yes, thanks." Lucy settled down at the kitchen table. "In all the crime books I read, the authors always talk about how foul the coffee is in every law enforcement agency across the country. It may be a cliché, but it's totally the truth. Ours is mixed with jet fuel, I swear it."

Laughing, Jane filled the coffeepot and got a pint of half and half out of the refrigerator. While Lucy talked, Jane placed a sugar bowl, a small pitcher of cream, and an assortment of Pepperidge Farm cookies on a tray.

"Kenneth Cooper checked into the rehab facility under a false name. Most people can't get away with that, but since he paid in cash, he didn't need to show them an insurance card." Lucy helped herself to a Milano as soon as Jane set the tray on the table. James raised his brows at his fiancé, perplexed that she was making an effort to impress Lucy. "Yum. I love these." Lucy saluted Jane with her cookie. "Anyone can get their hands on a fake driver's license and if pressed, I'm sure Kenneth would claim that he only lied because he wanted to protect his reputation as a top-notch attorney."

"You don't believe that's the reason he used a fictitious name though," James guessed.

Lucy took another cookie. "No. I think he wanted to hide his identity so he could terrorize you three more freely. We've got a record of every single second he was off the clinic's grounds." She paused dramatically, picking off crumbs from her lap. "Each time he left, one of *you* received a little love note."

Jane's hand shook as she poured coffee into mugs. Seeing her agitation, James took over the serving. "But can you prove anything? Is this going to stop now?"

"We don't have any hard evidence, but my assistant on this project has obtained permission to write an article on the clinic. She'll be sure to find Kenneth and ask him a few pointed questions." Lucy clenched her jaw in determination. "Because this is an emotional issue for him, we need to stir up those emotions and get him to confess."

James paused in the act of shaking a sugar packet into his coffee. "An article? Lucy, please tell me you haven't recruited —"

"Murphy's been searching for a way to

make peace with us," Lucy interrupted firmly. "I needed her help on this one and she was more than willing to give it. As far as I'm concerned, if she ends up getting me what I need to keep Kenneth Cooper from ever stepping foot in Quincy's Gap again, then she's forgiven." She hesitated. "At least until her next book comes out."

Breaking a shortbread cookie in half, Jane stared at the pieces. "I realize that Murphy Alistair is known for her doggedness, but how will she get him to confess? He's not a dumb man. Kenneth's going to see her coming from a mile away, even if his emotions *are* boiling over."

Lucy grinned. "That's why I'm here. I'd like your blessing to let Murphy tell Kenneth a few tall tales to get a rise out of him. For example, I thought she could mention, almost as an aside, that you two are getting married in an intimate service next week. Then, after dropping Eliot off with his grandparents in Nashville, you're jetting to Paris for a romantic second honeymoon."

"That sounds lovely!" Jane exclaimed with a laugh. "Are we flying first class?"

James avoided looking at her, for fear his face would give their secret away. "Yes, it does sound great. Except for the Paris part. I like the food better in Italy." Remembering that he wanted to tell Lucy what Jane had discovered about the golden charm found in Snickers' stomach, he retrieved the fir tree from the soap dish and handed it to his friend. Her cornflower-blue eyes grew wider and wider as he told her about Donna Woodman's visit and his plans to snoop around the Wellness Village.

"Let's have another supper club meeting right after your hypnotherapy session," Lucy said, holding the charm up to the light. "Sullie and I received an interesting update from the medical examiner today that may help us link Tia's murder with Ned's seemingly accidental death. Tia died from heart failure and her tox screen was totally clean. However, the M.E. found some burns on her chest. The kind you can get if someone uses defibrillator paddles on your bare skin."

Picturing an ugly, red welt appearing on Tia's youthful and unblemished skin, James grimaced. "Is that what happened to her?"

"We're not sure yet, but it's a strong possibility. The M.E. told me that the use of a defibrillator on a healthy person throws the heart's rhythm out of whack and can often stop it beating altogether," Lucy explained.

"We have one of those A.E.D. machines hanging in the hall right near my office!" Jane sounded shocked. "I didn't realize they could be used to kill people as well as revive them!"

"Apparently, the new models don't work that way," Lucy assured her. "Those machines test for a rhythm first so that a layperson can operate them without making a serious mistake. The one used on Tia must be an older machine or one used by professionals, like EMTs or hospital personnel. Sullie and I have been running in circles looking for the machine, but so far not one paramedic in the county has a connection to Ned or Tia." She examined the gold charm again. "But I think we need to start knocking on the office doors at the Wellness Village. Ned was killed there and if someone was dumb enough to stash their defibrillator in the back of a broom closet, we're going to find it."

"Was his chest burned too?" James asked.

Lucy shook her head. "The coroner said it wasn't, and the folks at the funeral home didn't remember seeing any marks on his chest either. Still, the M.E.'s report on Ned's is identical to Tia's. Without the bruises on the neck, that is. But we've got a pair of healthy adults dropping dead of heart failure and now we know how. We just don't know why." She took another hasty sip of coffee. "I need to get back to the station and print out a list of all the Wellness Village employees. Maybe one of them used to work around defibrillators."

"Thanks for coming over and . . ." Jane pushed out the words, "please tell Murphy that we're grateful for her help."

The sheriff's deputy pushed back her chair and rose while eying the fresh smear of chocolate on her uniform shirt with annoyance. "You two need to have a baby. That way I can borrow its bib. Look at me! I'm a mess."

She didn't notice the tinge of pink flushing Jane's cheeks, or that James suddenly reached across the table for his ex-wife's hand, but even if she had, it wouldn't have bothered Lucy. She had found her soul mate and he was waiting for her at the station, poring over the case file for the millionth time in hopes of picking out an essential detail — something they'd missed that could turn the tide in their favor.

"I've got what you need, Sullie." Lucy whistled as she hustled outside to her brown sheriff's department cruiser. "We are going to have a hell of a night."

FIFTEEN:
ICED WHITE CHOCOLATE MOCHA LATTE

Grams of
Sugar
54

James was just shutting down his computer when Fern floated into his office. At least that's how it appeared, since she danced into the room on nimble feet, completely hidden beneath a long, gauzy skirt made of crinkled white cotton.

"Guess what, Professor?" she asked, her eyes shimmering with excitement. "Some guy from the Wellness Village just paid me for *ten* of my prints! He emailed me over the weekend and asked me to bring them to work today. Look!" She waved a fan of twenty-dollar bills in front of her.

"That's great," he answered, noting that Fern had begun to call him "Professor' " in lieu of "Mr. Henry" in imitation of the Fitzgerald brothers. James snapped his briefcase closed and wiped a fingerprint smear from the brass lock. "A guy, huh? I've seen very few men around the Village. The workforce and clientele seem to be predominantly female."

"His name is Lennon, like the Beatles' singer," Fern went on. "He was *so* complimentary about my photographs and wants to give them to his girlfriend as a surprise birthday gift. Isn't that sweet?"

James nodded. "I know his girlfriend a little. Her name is Skye and I think she will absolutely love your work." He picked up his briefcase and walked around the desk to where Fern stood, illuminating the doorway with happiness over her big sale. "I've chatted with Lennon a time or two as well. A nice young man. He and Skye are well suited."

"I have to tell you something else!" Fern's smile grew even wider. "Do you remember how I mentioned that I needed to give another guy a gentle brush-off before I could get involved with Scott?"

Wondering why Fern suddenly felt the need to discuss this now, when he was clearly anxious to be on his way, James kept his impatience in check. She didn't know that he needed to leave in order to make it to the Wellness Village before his appointment with Harmony and besides, it was difficult not to fall under the spell of his winsome employee. However, just as Fern opened her mouth to continue, her attention was caught by someone at the circulation desk.

"Oh, there's Mrs. Honeycutt and her daughter. I promised to tell them all about my favorite Newbery Medal winners. I'll let Scott tell you the rest of my story." And with that, she skipped out of his office.

Scott intercepted him in the lobby. "You can't go yet! I've been dying to tell you this story all day, but I promised to wait for Fern's shift to start. Now she's going to be too busy to act as my co-narrator. The Honeycutt girl might only be in the sixth grade, but she reads five books a week. Mrs. Honeycutt wants books that are sophisticated and deep, but without too many adult themes. Fern told me she used to be the same kind of reader in middle school and she typed up a whole list to show mother and daughter."

"We do aim to please here at the Shenandoah County Library," James said, proud of the excellent service Fern was providing. Scott was gazing at Fern as though he'd never tire of looking at her. "Scott, if you're going to weave me a tale, you'd better get started. I need to be at the Wellness Village in fifteen minutes."

Scott rubbed his hands together, clearly eager to be able to share a piece of significant news with his boss. "Before Fern was hired, I told you how I really liked this person I met playing this fantasy game on the computer, but had never met her in person. So I tried to make that happen but our meetings kept getting postponed."

"I remember," James waved him on.

"Right. Well, her gamer ID was CAP-TRDMMT. Here. It's easier to understand if I write it down." He scribbled the capital letters on the back of a bookmark announcing Harlequin's new releases. "What do you think this stands for? Just take a wild guess."

James loved word riddles of all kinds, so he was happy to oblige. "Capture the moment?"

Scott's mouth fell open. "Whoa! You are *totally* correct! Guess I'm not as sharp as you are, Professor, because I was so caught up in gamer mode that I figured it was an acronym for 'Capture Dragons, Mages, Men, & Trolls.' I assumed she was an evil sorceress."

"What happened? She turned out to be a fairy godmother instead?" James couldn't help teasing Scott a little. The young man took his computer games a bit too seriously.

"Magical, yes! Evil, *no.* And she turned out to be a professional photographer. *Our* photographer! Someone who captures the moment." He beamed. "This person, this cyber goddess, was Fern all along! She and I have had this online connection for the past six months! And then, she ends up working here. With *me!*"

James was stunned by the coincidence. Forgetting about his time constraints, he leaned against the circulation desk and stared at Scott. "*Fern* was the woman you kept trying to meet face-to-face?"

"Yessir!" He whispered exuberantly. "She got cold feet the first time. The second time I canceled because Jane asked Francis and me to swing by the courthouse and watch you sign some seriously important paper-work." He looked around wildly, as though the closest library patrons might be listen-ing in on their conversation. "But then, last night, when Francis went over to Willow's place and I tagged along because . . ." He blushed.

"Because you like Fern," James finished

for him.

Scott pushed on his glasses and grinned again. "Yes, she's awesome! But anyway, I saw a screensaver shot from the game on her computer and as soon as I asked her about it and she started talking about her character, I *knew!* There, right in front of me, was my own beautiful druid priestess. A fantasy made flesh! How cool it that?"

James smiled and clapped Scott on the back. "It is very cool. Am I to assume that you two are dating now?"

"That would be correct." Scott's eyes grew dreamy. "As of ten thirteen Sunday night. That's the exact moment when I kissed my Druid slash photographer slash librarian. I've had a crush on her online for over six months and then I thought I had a new crush on the girl who walked through that door two weeks ago." He pointed toward the lobby. "I had no idea I had fallen for the same girl twice over."

"Scott, that is the best story I've heard in a long time. Congratulations, son." He pumped the younger man's hand affection- ately and then darted outside into the afternoon sunshine.

Weightier knots of air, hinting at summer's impending humidity, had snuffed out the spring breeze. Still, as James drove through town, he detected an atmosphere of anticipation. From the teenagers driving by with arms hanging out of car windows and radios pumping out bass-heavy hip hop music to the appearance of sun-loving petunias in the sidewalk planters on Main Street, the seasons were gearing up for a change.

To the teens, summer meant freedom but to James, the imminent shift created a feeling of urgency. He put aside thoughts of Scott's newfound happiness and the details of his own imminent vows and concentrated on a plan to coax information from the Wellness Village's business owners. However, by the time he stood in front of the Village's map, he realized it would be impossible to canvass each and every cottage and still make it to his appointment on time.

"What's with the glum look?" Lindy asked, appearing on the sidewalk beside him.

James was thrilled to see her. He needed help. "What are you doing here?"

"Did you really think Lucy was going to sit around twiddling her thumbs while you traipsed in and out of all these Health Houses?" Lindy rolled her eyes. "She's given each of us an assignment. I'm in charge of investigating The Soothing Touch. I even booked a hot stone massage so I'll have *plenty* of time to grill the masseuse. Lord, I hope she's some kind of miracle worker. My back is so tight you could bounce a quarter off it!"

"Alma's still giving you grief?"

Lindy sighed. "No, not really. She spends most of her time with Luigi. It's Luis I'm worried about right now. I've hardly seen him these past few days. I'm really worried that he's viewing me with his mama's eyes — that I'm just not measuring up."

"Don't think that way, Lindy. Isn't this a crazy time of year for those in the educational field? Grading final papers and projects, having those last-minute conferences, and seeing who's going to have to go to summer school while you're lazing about on a beach somewhere?" James gave his friend a sideways glance, hoping his words would prod her out of her depression.

Her dark eyes flashed. "You know I teach over the summer! We don't get paid enough to spend twelve weeks working on our tans!" She swatted him on the arm. "A-ha! You're just messing with me. And yes, the *teachers* are super busy, but what can be taking up so much of Luis' time?"

"The *Star* ran an article about a county-wide plan to prevent the spread of the latest flu strain in our schools. It sounded like all the area principals have been attending scores of meetings in order to figure out a way to implement the new system come autumn." James knew he was grasping, but he proceeded anyway. "I bet half his life is comprised of those kind of bureaucratic headaches. Miserable."

"Hey, our faculty meetings aren't exactly Mardi Gras," Lindy scoffed, but her mood had brightened significantly. "Here come the rest of our troops."

James swiveled to see Bennett and Gillian making their way over from the parking lot.

"I never thought I'd see the day," Bennett grumbled. "I gotta go talk to some twisty pretzel yoga lady. Pretend to be all kinds of interested in bending my body in ways an animal made of two hundred and six bones is *not* meant to bend."

Gillian was unfazed by Bennett's sour mood. "I have the honor of speaking to the acupuncturist. I'd love to *explore* the idea of setting up services for some of my Yuppie Puppy clients."

Seeing that James and Lindy looked perplexed, she elaborated. "Acupuncture can be a *wonderful* alternative to traditional medicine. Instead of taking drugs to relieve joint pain, a person can turn to acupuncture for relief. Avoiding prescription medicine

can also mean avoiding harmful side effects." She took a quick breath and then
continued. "There are a *select* number of
progressive veterinarians who believe that
animals can also be treated using holistic
methods."

"So a dog with an arthritic hip is gonna
sit still while some fool human sticks a hot
needle in his side?" Bennett shook his head
in disbelief. "I'd like to see that!"

The friends laughed and decided to move
ahead with their search. James now only had
to interview the natural healer, Roslyn
Rhodes, before asking Skye and Harmony if
they happened to own a defibrillator. Of
course he felt it was ridiculous to even go
through the motions of questioning any of
the even-tempered ladies. It wasn't as
though they exhibited the slightest inclina-
tion toward violence or villainy, but he had
to be thorough.

Roslyn was in the middle of a consultation when he dropped by her office. James
noted that she had no assistant but simply
hung a plaque on her door entreating visitors to make themselves comfortable and
that most consultations lasted between
fifteen and thirty minutes.

Hoping she'd be finished before his own
appointment with Harmony, James sat

down to wait. After ten minutes of trying to concentrate on a magazine entirely about herb gardens, James grew restless. He decided to take a risk and peek behind some of Roslyn's closed doors.

The first place he checked was the bathroom where he and Eliot had found Ned Woodman's body. He hadn't really taken a close look at the room at the time, but his secondary inspection revealed nothing. The room had two stalls, two sinks, a garbage pail, and a paper towel dispenser.

James darted a glance at Roslyn's closed door and then tried the handle of the door next to the bathroom. The handle refused to budge up or down. The door was locked.

There was one more door at the far end of the hall on the same side as Roslyn's office, so James treaded as lightly as he could on the carpet and was gratified that the handle moved easily in his hand. After hitting the light switch, he looked into a large, walk-in supply closet filled with dozens of boxes, glass jars, and tiny vials containing herbs and holistic medicine. He had time to read label names like Licorice Root, Milk Thistle, Bilberry, Grape Seed Extract, Fenugreek, and Thunder God Vine before he heard movement from inside Roslyn's office.

Shutting the door, James sprinted back to the waiting room and picked up a random magazine. He then felt a stab of panic. Had he remembered to turn off the lights? However, he quickly relaxed again, recalling how, on the day they'd met, Roslyn had confessed to being chronically absent-minded.

"Thank you. I have as much energy as a teenager these days," a woman said with a laugh as she and Roslyn walked toward the waiting room. "After twenty-two years of marriage things can get mighty dull in the bed —" she stopped short upon seeing James. "Oh!" Her cheeks flamed red and she shouldered her purse and hurried toward the exit. "See you soon!" She called back over her shoulder and left.

"Enjoy!" Roslyn shouted cheerfully and then smiled at James. "How nice to see you. How is your son doing?"

"Fine, thanks," James answered. "Eliot's adjusted to vegetarianism with relative ease. As a matter of fact, the whole family has been following his lead. I still eat meat, but I usually have it for lunch when he's not around."

Roslyn nodded. "It took me awhile to lose those cravings too, but I wanted to commit to veganism for a lifetime, so I knew I had to be absolutely sure about my decision. At first, I gave in to a few cravings, but eventually, I got over the taste of meat and have felt much healthier and happier ever since."

"Eliot's conversion to vegetarianism prompted me to seek you out." James indicated the framed posters showing the human digestive, circulatory, and nervous systems. "Now that the three of us are eating natural foods, I'm aware of how good they make us feel. So when Eliot started getting a little cold, probably because we wore him out at the Apple Blossom Festival, I wanted to find a natural remedy for him. Any suggestions?"

"Absolutely!" Roslyn waved him into her office. "I'd definitely recommend echinacea. It will decrease his symptoms and the length of his cold. I also have some wonderful dissolvable vitamins that include Ester-C and elderberry. They're a wonderful source of vitamins. Would you care for a sample?"

"Yes, please." James followed her into the hall. "Do you mind if I check out your stores? I've never really laid eyes on these types of medicines and I'm pretty interested in how they're packaged."

Roslyn led him into the hall and pointed at the door James had unsuccessfully tried to open earlier. "Some have to be kept cold, so I've got a small fridge in that closet, but most of my products are in here." She opened the supply room door and frowned. "Did I leave this light on?"

James did his best not to fidget and to maintain a blank expression. "Wow, look at all of this stuff! I haven't heard of half of these plants. These products are all natural?"

"Plants in their purest forms," Roslyn replied proudly.

"Were you always a holistic healer or did you start off learning about traditional medicine first?" He asked even though he knew Sullie and Lucy had spent the day running background checks on everyone in the village. James was certain that not everything made it onto a person's official profile and it wouldn't hurt to dig a little deeper.

Roslyn pulled her long, graying braid over her shoulder and twirled the end around her index finger. "Of course. In fact, I graduated from pharmacy school. It was there that I began to see that the major drug companies were really complicating plant qualities in order to make cheaper products. I began to do some research on my own and realized that the more concentrated the plant part is, the more effective it is. For those giant pharmaceutical companies, it all comes down to dollars and cents. For me, it was always about the purest product, so I started practicing holistic medicine."

"That means you have twice the knowledge of most pharmacists. You know the traditional drugs and the natural ones. Look out, Mr. Goodbee!" James referred to the town's senior pharmacist. "But there are hundreds of plants and I'd guess that most have more than one use." He pointed at a box of thunder god vine tea. "What does that one do, for example?"

The question was meant to distract Roslyn from focusing on the lights. It worked. "Extracts from the thunder god vine root can be used to treat inflammatory conditions such as rheumatoid arthritis. A study is currently being conducted to see whether it can be used on Lupus patients." She handed James a brown box covered with a print of green stalks from which dozens of tiny white flowers burst. In the center of each delicate bloom was a canary-yellow center. "Like many herbs, this one can be harmful. In ancient China, farmers used it as an insecticide and it was believed to be quite an effective murder weapon as well."

"Do not add thunder god vine to my spaghetti sauce. Got it!" James joked. "Seriously though, this is fascinating. And I honestly think death by thunder god vine sounds more dignified than death by defibrillator."

Roslyn leaned forward and replaced the tea box on the shelf. Because her raised arm obscured her face, James was unable to witness her reaction. When she turned to him again, she looked bewildered. "I'm not sure I understand."

"I don't think I was supposed to say anything about Ned Woodman's case. That just slipped out." He put on his best expression of chagrin. "I'm not very good at keeping secrets. But neither was Ned, I guess. The authorities believe he had a girlfriend and that she's sitting pretty with all that money Ned stole from the town."

Something flashed in Roslyn's eyes, but it happened so swiftly that James wasn't certain he'd seen anything after all. He blinked and Roslyn was now shaking her head, her face full of sympathy. "His poor wife. It's bad enough that she's lost her husband, but now to have to endure public humiliation too. I feel terrible for her."

The words sounded genuine and James decided that he'd grilled the friendly holistic healer enough. He purchased the products Roslyn had recommended, though he doubted he would ever use them. He'd been lying about Eliot's cold and couldn't help but feel a slight distrust of Roslyn's products. James didn't plan on giving anything to his son that wasn't approved by the FDA.

When he stepped outside into the warm evening, he found Bennett lounging on a nearby bench, engrossed in the latest edition of the World Almanac.

"Planning another *Jeopardy!* appearance?" James quipped.

"Nope, but I'll never get tired of learnin' new facts." Bennett folded down a page corner and closed the book. Seeing the look of horror on his friend's face, he quickly folded the page flat again. "Jeez, man! It's not like I killed somebody!" he protested, thumping on the fat paperback. "And neither did the yoga lady. That woman's one of those happy-all-the-time types. Not a mean word to say about anybody. She was a stay-at-home mama until hubby gave her the money to open her own studio. Says all her dreams have come true. We can cross her off the list. What about the medicine woman?"

James shook his head. "Roslyn Rhodes doesn't seem like she has anything to hide. Like your yoga lady, she's found her place in life." He hesitated. "It's just that when I mentioned Ned's having a girlfriend, I thought her eyes turned strange. But it happened so quickly that I'm not sure I really saw anything."

"Go with your gut, man. She could be sneakin' that heart shocking machine out the back door as we speak."

Though Bennett was partially jesting, a wave of doubt assailed James. "Can you stick around to see if she comes out of the office looking worried or, like you said, carrying a large box? I've got to meet with Harmony."

"Will do," his friend agreed. "Gillian's gonna be jibber-jabbin' with the needle lady all evenin' long anyhow. Why do you think I brought this book?"

Inside A Better State of Mind, Skye was humming as she watered the houseplants. She welcomed James with her customary grace and warmth, and then apologized, saying that Harmony's current appointment was running a little late and that he'd have to wait a bit.

"No problem." James settled into the chair nearest her desk and began to small talk with Skye about Lennon, her passion for running, and how had she ended up working for Harmony. They were interrupted once by a customer looking to purchase a gift certificate for his wife.

"She wants to quit smoking. Let me tell you — after living with that smell for eleven years, I'd do anything to help her stop!" he exclaimed, passing Skye a credit card.

Once the satisfied customer had gone, James used the subject of gift certificates as a segue for a discussion on birthday presents. He told Skye about the mailbox shaped like a stack of books that Scott and Francis had carved for him. He really wanted to find out whether she'd received Fern's lovely photographs so he could let his new employee know that another person had been delighted with her work. "How about you? Do you have a birthday coming up soon?"

Skye shook her head. "Mine was last month. Lennon got me a fantastic pair of running shoes. They're so light I barely feel them on my feet."

"Cool." James moved off to pour himself a glass of water, but his mind was spinning. If the prints weren't for Skye, why did Lennon pretend they were?

He didn't have the opportunity to ponder the question any further because Harmony and a pretty female client entered the reception area. The hypnotherapist bid her previous client goodbye and then smiled at James. "Come on back," she said.

Before he could settle into the recliner,

his phone chirped, signaling the receipt of a text message. James had never sent a text message in his life and wasn't sure if he knew how to read an incoming message. Luckily, the words appeared on the screen as soon as he opened the phone.

"This is from Lucy," he explained to Harmony. "I don't think we should start the session as it's bound to be interrupted."

Harmony gazed at him quizzically. "Oh?"

"She and her fellow officers are on the way here. Apparently, they've got a search warrant for every cottage in the Village."

"Does this have something to do with Mr. Woodman's death?" Harmony asked, the picture of calm curiosity.

James nodded. "And possibly Tia Royale's as well." If he'd expected to provoke a dramatic reaction by bringing up the dead woman's name, he was to remain disappointed. In fact, Harmony never broke eye contact. She stared at him with a concerned, but distinctly untroubled gaze.

"I'm afraid I don't understand," she confessed.

It was time to pull out all the stops. "Ned Woodman and Tia Royale were probably killed by the same person. The investigating deputies believe this individual may have some connection to the Wellness Village."

He paused. "I can't say anything else. All I know is they're on the hunt for a very specific object."

Again, Harmony appeared unfazed by the knowledge that her office was about to be invaded by members of the Shenandoah County Sheriff's Department. Extending her hand, she indicated James should follow her to the reception room. "We'll have to reschedule your appointment and I guess I should have Skye cancel the rest of tonight's clients. This way, we can be available to assist the deputies in whatever manner possible."

If that woman's hiding something, then she's a master of concealment, James thought. In truth, he was relieved that Harmony seemed above suspicion.

Later, after a pair of brown Sheriff's Department cruisers had disgorged six deputies bearing copies of the search warrant, Lucy met with the rest of the supper club members to get their take on the Wellness Village employees and business owners.

"The background checks were useless," she informed her friends. "Some moving violations, a shoplifting charge that was later dropped, and a few people who were late paying their taxes here and there. That's it.

Not a single red flag on our end."

The supper club members gave Lucy summaries of their casual interrogations. After James shared his experience questioning Roslyn, Bennett added that no one had entered or exited her cottage since he'd been watching her front door.

"Each house has a back door," Sullie pointed out, having just returned from examining the perimeter of the complex. "It's where the dumpsters are located and probably where they get their deliveries." He looked at Lucy. "The trash has already been picked up. The bins are totally empty. If there was any evidence in those things, it's sittin' in a heap at the landfill now."

Lucy scowled. "Seems like Roslyn would be more likely to kill someone with one of her thousand herbs than with a defibrillator, but we'll search her cottage first. I want to see what's behind that locked door James mentioned. Thanks for doing your best to flush out the perp, everyone. I'll let you know if we find anything interesting."

She and Sullie hustled off. James noticed a sulky Deputy Donovan waiting for instructions and couldn't help but smile. The combative redhead didn't dare start trading insults with Lucy when Sullie was around. Donovan might look like a bulldog, but Sullie still towered over his fellow officer and was a solid mass of muscle. James cast an envious glance at the snug fit of Sullie's uniform shirt and then hastened out to the parking lot. He still had one more errand to complete before heading home for dinner.

A half hour later, James left the local jewelry shop with a small bag containing a pair of gold wedding bands nestled inside red velvet boxes. As he waited for the clerk to shine the bands until they twinkled, he strolled over to the coffee shop next door and ordered an iced white chocolate mocha latte. Taking a sip, the jolt of sugar covering his tongue and washing over his teeth shocked him. It had been so long since he'd ordered such a sweet treat that he was unprepared for how unbalanced it tasted. It was, amazingly, too sweet.

James knew that he should stop sipping the cold coffee drink then and there, but he'd paid four dollars for the thing and couldn't make himself throw it out. Slowly, as he became distracted examining and paying for the rings, he grew accustomed to the taste. By the time he crossed the street and headed in the direction of the public parking lot, the plastic cup was empty.

Irritated with himself, James chucked the cup into a nearby garbage can from several feet away and was surprised when someone applauded his successful shot.

"He shoots and he scores! Would you like to coach our JV basketball team next year?" James turned to see Luis Chavez grinning widely at him. "They didn't *exactly* have a winning record this past season."

James reached out and shook the principal's hand. Lindy's boyfriend was good-looking and charismatic with dark, intelligent eyes and a ready smile. James hid the bag from the jewelry store behind his back and fell into stride next to Luis. Together, the two public servants headed toward the parking lot. "School's almost out for the summer," James said as they walked. "Do you have any big plans?"

"Besides shipping my mama back to Mexico?" Luis laughed loudly. "Always. I'm a man filled with big plans." And before James could ask him to elaborate, Luis dug around in his pocket and pulled out a handful of tickets. "I was going to drop these by the library, but now that I've bumped into you there's no need. These are tickets for our musical this Friday night. I'm asking you, as a special favor, to come to our play with your family, staff, and all of Lindy's supper club friends. Can you do that for me?"

His curiosity piqued to its highest level, James accepted the tickets. "Is this some kind of special performance?"

"Absolutely!" Luis clapped James heartily on the back. "It's at *my* school, after all! And, it's Shakespeare. A musical version of *Much Ado About Nothing.* I promise that it will be the most memorable dramatic performance this town has ever seen."

James raised his brows. "In that case, I wouldn't dream of missing it."

Luis waved and took off in the opposite direction. Even though his pace was brisk, the light timbre of the song he started to sing drifted through the warm air and seemed to hover about the sidewalk. It was like the pleasant scent left behind by a woman's perfume. James smiled. He couldn't hear any of the song's words, but he recognized the emotion underlying the tone: Luis Chavez was singing about love.

SIXTEEN: WEDDING CUPCAKE

Grams of
Sugar
33

The official search of the Wellness Village proved fruitless. Lucy found Roslyn quietly filling out paperwork in her office and, after taking a cursory glance at the proffered search warrant, the holistic healer was more than happy to unlock the supply closet in which she kept organic medicines chilled in a small refrigerator.

"I've never met a bunch of people so eager to help after I've informed them that we plan to rifle through every inch of their stuff," Lucy informed James as he shelved books in the new release section. She pointed at a James Patterson hardcover. "Does this guy ever sleep? Seems like he churns a book out every six months."

"There are some critics who would agree with your choice of verb." James handed Lucy two tickets to the Blue Ridge High production of *Much Ado About Nothing.* "I've been told by Principal Chavez that attendance is mandatory. Are you bringing Sullie?"

Lucy shrugged. "I don't think plays are his thing, but he's got another reason to be there."

Perplexed, James was about to ask Lucy to clarify her statement when Fern finished assisting a patron and joined them in front of the display. "You wanted to ask me something, Professor?"

"Actually, I did," Lucy answered with a friendly smile. "Don't mind the uniform. This isn't official. I'm just trying to satisfy my own curiosity about something."

Fern visibly relaxed. "For a second there, I thought you were here to scold me for parking in the loading zone in front of Quincy's Whimsies, but I swear I was only helping Willow with a delivery."

Lucy laughed. "I try to leave the dispensing of parking tickets to Deputy Donovan. Nothing perks him up like a row of cars with tickets stuck under their wiper blades. No, I wanted to ask you about the photographs Lennon purchased. Can you describe the prints and repeat the conversation for me?"

"Sure." Fern pointed at the computer behind the reference desk. "It's easier for me to show you the photos online. My boyfriend created a gorgeous website for me."

Curious, James followed the two women behind the counter, leaving Francis to man the circulation desk. Scott was busy in the tech corner and was likely to be there for some time, considering Mrs. Withers was back with a tote bag full of Beanie Babies and a digital camera.

"I'm ready to sell these on eBay!" she'd announced upon entering the library and grabbed James by the elbow.

Scott had witnessed the encounter and had quickly intervened. "I can show her the ropes, Professor. Francis and I have been on eBay since the dawn of online trading. I know a trick or two to get Mrs. Withers the best price possible."

As the pair sat down in front of a computer, Mrs. Withers reached over and ruffled Scott's hair. "You're such a nice boy. I'm mighty glad I baked up a batch of my homemade peanut butter brownies for you and your sweet brother. I know the both of you go outta your way to help us old coots and we sure do appreciate it. Besides, someone needs to put a bit of meat on your bones! When are you gonna find a good girl to cook for you?"

"Oh, I've found the girl, Mrs. Withers," Scott declared happily. "And she might not be a whiz in the kitchen, but she is a shining star in every other way!"

Returning his focus to the present, James turned away from the tech corner and peered over Lucy's shoulder just as Fern was pointing at some images on the computer screen. Fern's website was beautifully designed. The background was a soft, moss green framed by her photograph of a purple rhododendron flower. Fern clicked on the thumbnails showing more close-ups of plant parts.

"I took these shots when I was working as a part-time park ranger," Fern explained. "All of these plants grow wild throughout Virginia."

"How many photos did Lennon buy?" Lucy inquired.

"Ten," Fern said. "They were all framed prints costing one fifty apiece. It was the biggest paycheck I've ever gotten for my photographs. Actually, it wasn't a check. Lennon paid me in cash."

Lucy drew back and rubbed her chin. "That's fifteen hundred dollars — a big chunk of change for the Wellness Village maintenance man. And he said the photographs were a gift for his girlfriend?"

"Yes. He was really excited about giving them to her." Fern searched Lucy's face. "Why would he pretend to be buying the prints for her birthday when he really wasn't? Unless," her lips scrunched up in thought, "he has more than one girlfriend."

"Unfortunately, two-timing's not against the law." Lucy thanked Fern and saluted James. "Food for thought," she whispered to him. "I think I need to look a little closer at Lennon's spending habits. See you at the play." She moved a few steps away and then paused. Walking back to the desk she added, "We haven't stopped driving by your house. I may be nose-deep in this case, but I haven't forgotten about Kenneth."

Neither had James. In fact, his dreams the previous night had been tormented by hundreds of sinister crows. Reminiscent of Alfred Hitchcock's *The Birds,* the feathered assailants gathered on tree branches, telephone wires, and on the roof of Eliot's tree house. They squawked and ruffled their black feathers, but never took their dark eyes off James' bedroom window. He knew they were only waiting for a signal, but from what or whom he couldn't tell. It was as if their master remained hidden in the shadows of the distant trees, waiting and watching.

"James!" Jane had finally shaken him awake. "If you don't stop thrashing around, I'm going to be black and blue by dawn!"

Despite his anxiety, the workweek passed without incident. No one in the Henry household received strange letters and there were no dead birds left on the property. By the time Friday rolled around, James was immersed in thoughts of his upcoming marriage ceremony. It was to be performed by the justice of the peace that very afternoon. Their marriage license had arrived by mail on Wednesday and Jane had wasted no time in securing the last available spot in the JP's schedule.

"It'll be tight," she told James Wednesday evening. "We need to be ready by five-thirty. Our marriage officiate, whose name is Frank Love (if you can believe that), says we'll be man and wife by six o'clock. Then we need to eat dinner and high-tail it to the school by seven."

"Our first appearance wearing our wedding rings," James mused and then asked, "What are your thoughts regarding our vows?"

Jane, who had been stirring spaghetti sauce at the time, stood still. "I believe we should write our own. We went by the book last time. Let's make this ceremony really personal. Oh, and I forgot to tell you. We're getting married right here, in our house."

"That's wonderful! You, me, Eliot, Snickers, and Miss Pickles. We could tie the rings onto Snickers' collar."

"And put a basket of tissue paper flowers on the floor. Miss Pickles would scatter those in a heartbeat!" They'd chuckled at the idea. After passing James the wooden spoon so he might taste the sauce, Jane said, "The more I think about it, the more I believe your parents should be here too."

"But won't your folks be hurt when they find out they weren't included?"

She'd shaken her head. "No. They'll just be happy we made things official. Besides, we're not taking pictures or having a cake or anything like that, so there really won't be any details for them to hear about later on. I'm wearing a blue and white sundress and sandals and you can be just as casual." She'd put an arm around his waist. "We're stripping away all the trimmings this time around. On Friday, it's all about the promises we make to one another. Nothing else matters."

However, by the time the Fitzgerald brothers finished with their lunch breaks that Friday, James had already thrown out page after page of rejected wedding vows. He spent his entire break surfing wedding websites and flipping through books stuffed with sample vows. None of them felt right.

By the afternoon coffee break, James was nearing a state of panic. The twins knew something was amiss with their boss, so when James ducked into the kitchen to start the coffee machine, Francis trailed after him.

"Professor?" The younger man said. "Do you need a hand? An ear? A shoulder to cry on? A punching bag? Scott and I have watched the clouds gathering over your head all day long."

James, who had been staring at the tin of coffee grounds as though he might see his future written there, jumped at the sound of Francis' voice. The scoop in his right hand jerked sideways and grounds went everywhere. "Blast!" He dampened a paper towel and waved at Francis to stay back. "It's not your fault. My mind is a tangled knot today." He glanced at the younger man. "Jane and I are getting married in two hours and I haven't written my vows yet!"

"Ohhhh," Francis whispered and squatted down to push the grounds on the floor into a tidy pile. "But you're good with words, Professor. Can't you just tell her you love her and that you'll take care of her for the rest of your life?"

Shaking his head, James dumped the paper towel in the trash-can. "I need to promise more than that. I need to make her realize that she is the only one in the world for me, that she makes my dreams come true, and that she's given me a second chance at happiness." His eyes grew distant as he thought about Jane. "I want her to know that her love is a gift to me and that my love for her is, and always will be, the forever kind. She is my friend and my partner and my soul mate and together, we can make all the days of our lives whatever we want them to be. As long as she's with me, no matter what happens, I'll have hope and I will face each new day with gratitude and joy in my heart."

Francis had stopped cleaning. Sitting back on his heels, he stared at his boss open-mouthed. "Wow, Professor. *I* would totally want to marry you if you said that to me!"

"That was okay? It wasn't formal or grammatically correct or —"

"Forget about that stuff! It was awesome!" Francis leapt up, dashed from the room, and returned with a pen and scrap paper. "Write it down. Quickly! And then post a copy on YouTube for the rest of us hopeless guys."

James sat at the table and wrote his vows, smiling all the while. As soon as he was done, he wolfed down a peanut butter and jelly sandwich and then called his parents. He would later swear that Milla squealed in delight for a full thirty seconds.

He failed to accomplish even the most menial tasks that afternoon. It wasn't nerves. James wanted nothing more than to recite his vows and slide a ring onto Jane's finger. Now that the ceremony was almost upon him, he found he couldn't concentrate on books. When a female patron asked for a light beach read, James handed her *The Color Purple.* Right after that, he gave Dan Brown's *The Lost Symbol* to a patron who despised books having anything to do with conspiracy theory. Fortunately, Scott remedied both blunders as soon as James turned away to collect the wrong amount of money for an overdue fine.

At four-thirty, Francis tapped James on the shoulder. "Scott and I think you should go home, Professor. You've got a big evening ahead. We'll see you at the play tonight. If anything work-related comes up, we can always fill you in then."

James gave his employee a crooked smile. "You're right. I've never bumbled about the library as much as I have this afternoon. If I stay here any longer, I'm going to let some seven-year-old check out a Laurel Hamilton novel."

Scott walked over and, one at a time, the twins embraced their boss. "Congrats, Professor. Now go get married." They smiled and pushed him out the door.

When he got home he found Jane in the backyard, weaving a daisy chain. She'd already made several for Eliot and wore one around her head like a crown. When she saw James, she finished the chain in her hands and placed it around his neck. He closed his arms around her back and planted a soft kiss on her mouth. She smelled like grass and sunshine. As he released her, Eliot bellowed a pirate's "Arggh!" from his tree house and waved at James with a plastic sword.

"You go in and change," James told Jane. "Or you could just stay like this. I think you look like a queen in your tank top and bare feet. And the crown of daisies is very bridal."

Jane laughed. "I'd keep it on, but then I'd look like an aging hippie. Perhaps a single bloom tucked behind the ear is more fitting. See you at 'the altar'."

"I'll be there!" James waited for her to go inside before scooping Eliot up in his arms. "Now, you're mine! Consider yourself pirate-napped!"

For the next thirty minutes, James and Eliot raced around the yard, alternating between warring pirates and co-conspirators in search of buried treasure.

"Arggh, I wish I could remember where we left our booty!" James growled out of the side of his mouth while squinting one eye shut.

Eliot poked at the base of the birdhouse pole with a sharp stick. "It was those robbers! They stole our treasure!"

James stood as tall as he could and put his hands on his hips, surveying the yard with a fierce glower. "Let's make 'em walk the plank!"

Together, he and Eliot prodded a plastic Velociraptor and a wind-up robot to the end of a narrow wood board jutting out over the deck railing. On the ground below, they'd placed a rubber crocodile and a pair of Halloween vampire teeth on a blue towel.

"You must pay for your treachery!" James snarled.

"Yeah!" Eliot echoed with glee.

Once the sea monster had devoured the toys, the Henry men went inside and clinked glasses of ice water, signifying their victory over the forces of evil. By the time James showered and changed into fresh khakis and a light blue polo shirt, the wedding officiate had arrived. James welcomed him inside and introduced him to Eliot. Milla and Jackson weren't far behind and James was unsurprised to see Milla carrying a large cardboard box into the kitchen.

"I didn't think you'd have enough time to bake anything," James complained. "You were just supposed to show up and enjoy yourselves. No gifts, no food, just a simple champagne toast."

"Fiddlesticks!" Milla exclaimed. "I was *not* going to let this occasion pass without contributing in some way. You were so wonderful to Jackson and me when we got married. How could I sit around and twiddle my thumbs when I knew I had the chance to whip up something for you and Jane. Believe me, with only two hours I was forced to make a simple dessert."

Jackson snorted. "You should see what she's callin' 'simple'."

"Hold the box for me, dear." Milla smiled at her husband.

Placing his good arm around the base of the box, Jackson looked on with pride as Milla lifted out a small tower of cupcakes. The cupcakes were vanilla frosted and rimmed with white sugar crystals. In the center of each cupcake, Milla had drawn a heart using silver icing. The top cupcake featured the bride and groom's initials, J & J in elegant silver script.

"How lovely!" Jane cried upon entering the kitchen. "Thank you, Milla!"

Milla embraced her future daughter-in-law and elbowed Jackson in the ribs. "Go on, dear. Tell Jane what you wanted to say."

Jackson spoke slowly, making a powerful effort to form his words clearly. "I'm right glad you and my son are puttin' your lives together." He glanced at James and though his face appeared impassive, there was a twinkle in his eyes. "It's a real gift to this old fool to have you all livin' close by. You three and Milla here give me reason to get this bag of bones outta bed in the mornin'." He hesitated, gathering the needed strength to finish his speech. "Guess what I'm tryin' to say is I'm right honored to be here today."

Jane threw her arms around Jackson and kissed him heartily on the cheek. As she led him into the living room James turned to Milla and whispered, "He's walking much better this week."

Milla nodded. "Your daddy's been working real hard in therapy. He wants nothing more than to get on his hands and knees and play with his grandson. The nurses say they've never seen someone Jackson's age make such speedy progress."

Indeed, Jackson barely limped as he walked into the living room to shake hands with Mr. Love. Snickers had made himself at home on Eliot's lap while Miss Pickles perched like a gargoyle behind his shoulder on the sofa back. James had to laugh when he noticed that the animal's collars had been replaced by daisy chains.

"All set?" asked Mr. Love.

James and Jane smiled at one another.

"We've never been more ready," James answered and took hold of his bride's hand.

Sitting in the auditorium of Blue Ridge High School, James kept touching the gold band encircling his left ring finger. Even though it had been years since James last wore a wedding ring, he was surprised at how wonderful it was to feel the warm metal against his skin and to be able to display his status as a married man to the entire world.

Next to him, Jane glowed. James had never seen her looking more beautiful and he couldn't stop repeatedly leaning over and whispering in her ear or kissing her on the cheek.

"Ease up on the PDA, kids!" Lucy teased as she took the reserved chair next to James.

With flushed cheeks, James craned his neck toward the back of the room. Nearly every available seat had been taken and the noise level was rising exponentially. "Is Sullie here?"

"He wants to hang out in the parking lot for a bit," Lucy answered cryptically. "Where's Eliot?"

"With his grandparents," James said. "We're having a date night."

Bennett and Gillian walked briskly down the carpeted aisle and settled in the two seats next to Jane. The two women immediately fell into conversation about what they planned to purchase at the farmer's market the next morning while Bennett frowned over the paper program in his hands. "I could be watchin' baseball!" he moaned and James chuckled.

"Luis promised us a night we'll never forget," James reminded his friend.

"He did?" Lindy asked as she took the last open seat in the row. She reached across

Lucy to poke James in the leg. "When did you run into him and what *exactly* did he mean by that?" Her eyes darted around the room as she waited for his answer. "Where is his mama? She could be up to no good."

"I saw her sitting right in the middle." Lucy pointed at the opposite side of the room. "With Luigi and his brood." She shook her head. "Call me crazy, but she seemed to be thoroughly enjoying herself with his kids."

Lindy brightened. "Those darlings might just save me! If Alma gets wrapped up in *their* lives, she won't have enough spare time to meddle in *mine!*"

Suddenly, the lights blinked and the clamor from the audience died down. A teacher walked up to the piano positioned offstage and began to hammer out a lively melody. The heavy red curtain parted and a pretty young girl dressed in contemporary clothes began to sing. Soon, the crowd was completely absorbed in the blossoming romance between Claudio and Hero and the antics of Beatrice and Benedick. Just when things seemed to be going smoothly for both couples, the treacherous Don John appeared at the back of the auditorium, singing in a bold, bass voice about his plans to ruin Claudio and Hero's wedding. As the spotlight followed the teenage thespian down the aisle, Jane suddenly gasped and jabbed her fingertips into the flesh of James' arm.

"It's Kenneth!" she hissed fearfully. "I saw him when the light shone on the section near the fire door!"

James desperately tried to distinguish the shadowy faces in the far back rows, which had been pitched into darkness once the spotlight had passed. He leaned over to Lucy. "Jane says she saw Kenneth! Sitting near the fire door. What should we do?"

Lucy's shoulders stiffened. "Sullie was right. He had a hunch Kenneth might come around tonight — said he was about due for another appearance. You stay here. I'll handle this jerk."

When Lucy left, Lindy slid into her vacant chair. "What is going *on?*" she asked James and was angrily shushed by the older woman seated behind her. Onstage, the girl playing Hero sang a duet with the boy cast as her father, Leonato. As their voices intertwined, the pair walked with extreme slowness down a red velvet aisle, the train of Hero's wedding gown being carried by her maid, Margaret. Suddenly, it became painfully apparent from his balled fists and hostile glare that the groom was waiting in a state of extreme anger and the joyful melody abruptly morphed into a song filled with discord and strife.

The disharmony of the music spurred James into action. "Come on!" he whispered urgently to Jane. "What if Kenneth goes to the house . . . ?"

"Eliot!" Jane's eyes flashed with fear. Ignoring the rumblings of the woman behind them, James told Gillian and Bennett what was happening and then jogged up the aisle.

"His chair is empty now," Jane said as soon as all five of them were gathered in the school hall.

Lindy's face was stormy. "This creep is going down! No one runs around *my* school bullying people without getting in trouble. Kenneth Cooper is about to serve the longest detention of his life!"

Minutes later, armed with aluminum baseball bats taken from the school's P.E. supply closet, they moved down the empty halls, rattling each and every classroom door, but all were locked.

Outside, the night sky blazed with brilliant stars and a luminescent half moon. The parking lot, which formed an L-shape around the building, was eerily quiet. James looked around, trying to discern the shape of a man's body in the darkness surrounding the parked vehicles. The glow from the parking lot lights added to the confusion, refracting off hundreds of windshields like mirror images of the stars above. More than once, James was certain he'd seen movement in the periphery of his vision, but it turned out to be merely a wink of light bouncing off a car window.

Deciding that subtlety was not necessary, James shouted, "LUCY! WHERE ARE YOU?"

"AT YOUR TRUCK!" Lucy's voice rang out through the parking lot.

James broke into a run, Jane and the rest of the supper club members close on his heels. He'd parked near the football field and as he approached the Bronco, he could see the beam of a flashlight playing over his truck. Sullie was barking terse orders into his cell phone while Lucy examined the Bronco's hood.

"What the — !" Bennett began and then stopped.

Kenneth had formed a heart made of black feathers on the hood of James' Bronco. But what made the women gasp in horror and rendered James and Bennett speechless was the blood splattered over the feathers and in wild zigzags across the windshield.

"There's more." Lucy gestured at the back of the truck. There, tethered to the bumper, were three dead birds. Ropes were tied around the crow's necks and they dangled midair, heads lolling and dark eyes set in fixed stares.

James put a protective arm around his wife.

"It's like a twisted version of the tin cans people put on a newlywed's car," Lindy murmured in repulsion.

James and Jane exchanged fearful looks. "Do you think he knows?" Jane gulped. "Could he have *been* there?"

Lucy was observing Jane closely. "Been where?" she demanded.

"This isn't how I wanted to tell you." James held out his arms to indicate that he was addressing everyone. "Jane and I were married by the Justice of the Peace earlier this evening." Taking Jane's hand in his, he showed his friends their rings. "We didn't want it to be a big deal. We just wanted to quietly make things official."

"Second time's the charm," Jane added with a nervous smile.

For a moment, his announcement hung in the air, but as the supper club members wrapped their minds around the news, their grim and anxious expressions were transformed into smiles.

"Mazel tov!" Gillian shouted and embraced the couple.

Lindy was next to congratulate them. "You really *are* meant to spend your lives together!"

"Way to go, man." Bennett clapped James on the shoulder and then kissed Jane on the cheek.

Lucy touched each one of them on the arm and said, "I'm happy for you both," while Sullie beamed at them briefly before turning businesslike again. "Okay, so this event must have prompted Kenneth into action. And he hasn't gone anywhere. He's hiding." He crossed his arms, making his biceps appear even bigger than before. "No vehicles have entered or exited this lot since the play started. Our guy went in with the rest of the crowd and since I didn't see him come out, I bet he plans to wait and leave when everyone else does."

"But we're not going to let that happen," Lucy stated with authority. "This nonsense stops right here, right now." She turned to Jane. "I have to be blunt; this is all about you. For some reason or another, your ex is going crazy because you've moved on. To draw him out of hiding, I need to use you as bait."

"No!" James protested, but Lucy held out her hand. "I'll be with her. It'll seem like we're two vulnerable women alone in the parking lot, but I can handle anything this guy's got to dish out. Sullie, you take Lindy and Gillian and do a sweep of the area near the bus drop-off. James and Bennett, you guys check every row of this lot." She handed James a flashlight. "Don't forget to sweep under the cars too. A grown man can easily stay out of sight beneath a jacked-up truck or some of these other SUVs."

"If we find him, how will we signal you?" Bennett asked. Lindy dug around in her purse and came up with a whistle. "Here. I always have one with me."

Before the groups moved off, James touched Lucy's holster. She apparently kept a weapon stashed in her Jeep. "Do you think Kenneth is armed?"

She shook her head. "I don't, but be ready to swing those baseball bats just in case. Let's go people, I don't know much about Shakespeare, but it seemed like the play is nearing the final act."

Lucy was correct. As the two deputies and the supper club members spread out across the parking lot wielding flashlights and baseballs bats, a double wedding was taking place onstage. Before the cast raised their voices to belt out the final number, Luis Chavez jogged up to center stage, his hand gripping a cordless microphone.

"Sorry to interrupt, folks, but the students have graciously allowed me a minor speaking part in the wonderful conclusion of this year's stellar musical. Like Claudio and Benedick, I too need a partner to complete my scene." He smiled at the crowd, unable to see clearly with the spotlight bathing his face. "Lindy Perez, would you join me onstage?"

The student actors cast knowing glances at one another and an air of strident expectation filled the room. When Lindy didn't appear, Luis shielded his eyes against the light and stared at the section where she'd been sitting minutes before. "Don't be shy, Lindy. I've got a quick question to ask you."

"SHE'S GONE!" Luigi's voice boomed out from the middle of the auditorium.

Luis sagged, his buoyant face deflating, the sparkle in his eyes extinguished. Glancing at the diamond ring in his palm, he waved at the students to continue and managed to slink off stage right. He kept walking, numbly, past pieces of scenery and members of the chorus waiting for their moment to dance onstage. Music exploded around him and his precious students sang their hearts out, as though trying to erase their principal's awkward moment.

On any other night, Luis would have savored the experience, his chest swelling with pride. On any other night, he would have presented the pianist and the drama teacher with a bouquet of roses. Even now, the flowers were carefully tucked beneath his auditorium seat. On any other night, he would have shaken hands with every audience member and would have stayed until every last person had left the building. But tonight, the night he'd planned on proposing marriage, he could no longer be himself. He hadn't realized until that long minute onstage that he'd waited far too long to ask for Lindy's hand; that his mother's approval wasn't as significant as he'd thought; and that nothing mattered until he found the woman he'd taken for granted for years and dropped to his knees before her.

With renewed purpose, Luis burst from the emergency exit at the back of the building, flinging open the heavy metal door with the passionate impatience of a man consumed with the desire to gaze upon the face of his lover. Unbeknownst to Luis, a person had chosen that unfortunate moment to try to gain access to the building. The door hit this stranger like a sledgehammer and he crumpled in a heap to the ground.

"¡*Dios Mio!*" Luis shouted and sprang to the aid of the unconscious man. He reached into the man's pockets in search of a cell phone in order to call for help, but found nothing but a handful of sticky black feathers.

Seventeen:
Granola Bar

Grams of
Sugar
17

Luis dropped the feathers on the ground and stared at the blood on his fingers. Believing that he'd hit the man so hard that he was now bleeding from the impact, Luis yelled, "HELP!" at the top of his lungs.

He was relieved to hear the echo of footsteps approaching. A woman with a camera slung over her shoulder dashed around the corner of the building and came to a sudden stop when she saw the body on the ground.

"Do you have a cell phone?" Luis asked Murphy Alistair. "I smacked him with the door when I was coming out. I think I knocked him unconscious."

Murphy pulled a phone out of her purse. Reaching the emergency operator within seconds, she calmly requested an ambulance to meet them at the back of Blue Ridge High. After placing the call, Murphy scuttled around the man's body to get a closer look at his face.

"Kenneth Cooper! I'll be damned." She raised her camera and immediately began to take pictures of the unresponsive man and then took several close-ups of the black feathers scattered on the ground around him.

Luis was initially startled into immobility by her actions, but as the light of the camera flash created a strobe over the unconscious man's still form, he leapt up and put a hand in front of the lens. "What's wrong with you? This man is injured!"

Murphy lowered the camera. "Before you get too judgmental, allow me to introduce you to the person who's been terrorizing James Henry and his family for the past month." Shocked, Luis took a step away from Kenneth Cooper. "And that blood on your fingers?" Murphy continued. "That's from the dead birds he killed and hung on James' truck. I got some beautiful photos of that little artistic display. This guy is truly imbalanced. It's a good thing you took him out."

Luis gaped at the slumped form in silence, but it wasn't long before the sound of more footfalls caught his attention. Two groups converged on the scene. First came James and Bennett, panting from exertion, followed by Lucy and Jane. Jane looked frightened, but Lucy's eyes glimmered as they alighted on Kenneth.

"Nice work, Principal," she praised Luis after he explained what had happened. She then called Sullie, who appeared shortly afterward with Lindy in tow. Lindy lagged behind in order to flag down the ambulance, and before Luis could even speak to her, the sound of boisterous applause emanating inside the building signaled the end of the play. Knowing that it was his duty to direct the flow of traffic away from the exit the ambulance would need to take, Luis asked Sullie for help and the two men hustled off, flashlights in hand.

"I like a man with leadership qualities," Murphy murmured to James as she stared after the two men. "Dark, handsome, and authoritative. I might have to schedule an exclusive interview with the charming Principal Chavez."

James scowled. "He's spoken for and you know it. He and Lindy —"

"Hey, there's no ring on *his* finger," Murphy said with a sly smile as she stepped aside to give the paramedics room. Turning to Lucy, she pointed at her camera. "Do you want a ride to the hospital? I'm going to try to get a comment from Kenneth as soon as he wakes up."

"Only after *I'm* done with him," Lucy stated firmly.

Murphy gave a little bow. "Naturally. On the way over, I thought we could discuss our strategy."

Lucy's expression was inscrutable. "Our strategy?"

"Yes. Kenneth and his lawyer buddies are going to argue that the evidence in this case is too circumstantial for a conviction. If you and Sullie can't coerce him into making a confession, then I have another idea of how to rid ourselves of this menace to our town."

"In that case, I'm all ears," Lucy said.

Bennett watched the women walk away. "I wouldn't trust that woman for all the donut holes in the bakery."

Gillian took his arm. "I believe Murphy is trying to make amends. Did you hear how she said 'our' town? I think we need to *open* our hearts to the possibility that she is truly capable of selfless acts of kindness."

"We'll see when her next book comes out," Bennett muttered. "Come on, woman. The long arm of the law has nabbed the bad guy and I'm right sure our newlyweds wanna get on home." He pointed at James. "And don't think you've wormed your way out of havin' some kind of party. No friend of mine ties the knot without booze and a speech or two."

Gillian beamed at Bennett. "You are *so* right! At least let us throw you a little dinner party. Nothing fancy, just the supper club, the library staff, your parents, and Eliot. A nice vegetarian reception!"

"That would be lovely, thank you." Jane accepted and then sagged against James' chest. "This has been quite an evening. Let's go back to the house, relieve your folks, and spend the rest of the night watching TV in our pajamas."

Holding hands, the married couple navigated the busy parking lot. They were both glad to be among the presence of the animated crowd, to have to maneuver around bumper-to-bumper traffic, and listen to half the town shout greetings to James or wave to him out of car windows.

"Boy, I feel like the wife of a movie star,"

Jane teased when they finally reached the Bronco.

James sighed happily. "Thank goodness I'm just a small-town librarian. I'm so exhausted after all this drama that I can only hope to have enough strength to carry you over the threshold."

"I'll settle for a piggyback ride," Jane replied saucily, leaned back against the headrest, and closed her eyes. "Do you think we'll live peacefully ever after now that Kenneth's been caught?"

Easing the truck into the stream of blazing red taillights, James shook his head. "There's still a murderer at large in Quincy's Gap." Stalled in the knot of traffic, he gazed out the windshield, lifting his eyes to the dark shape of the mountains looming above. "We've got miles to go before we sleep."

The house was quiet when Jane and James tiptoed inside. Jackson was watching a television program on the most destructive car chases ever filmed while Milla embroidered Eliot's Christmas stocking. She'd been working on the stocking since February and had already warned Jane that it would be a miracle if she had the project completed in time for Christmas Eve. When

James saw the tiny stitches and the intricate pattern of Santa Claus removing toys from his sack, he marveled at Milla's skill.

"How was the play?" she asked James, easing a piece of silky thread from beneath one of Miss Pickles' paws.

James smirked. "Dramatic." He told his parents every exciting detail while Jane went down the hall to peek in on Eliot. When he was finished, Jackson turned off the television and struggled to his feet.

"If this Kenneth fellow comes 'round here again, you need to scare the tar outta him, son." Jackson's brows furrowed in anger. "I'd best loan you my shotgun."

James shook his head. He had no intention of keeping a gun in the house. "Thanks for the offer, Pop, but Lucy will deal with him."

"That *is* a comforting thought," Milla said and patted James on the back. "You can have a nice, carefree summer now." Gathering her things together, she paused at the front door. "Oh, I almost forgot! A lovely woman stopped by with some herbal iced tea. She said it would help with Eliot's cold, but that you might want to taste it first to see if he'd find it too bitter."

"Roslyn Rhodes was here?"

Milla nodded. "Yes, that was her name. I

told her Eliot seemed right as rain and she said you'd probably given him some of her products already and that the tea would be good for you too. She said you must come in contact with all sorts of germs handling those library books and this tea would help rev up your defenses."

Slightly bewildered by the healer's house call, James wished Jackson and Milla good-night and crawled into bed, too tired to even open the fridge and investigate Roslyn's gift.

The next morning was Saturday. That meant cartoons, pajamas, coffee, and James' famous pancake faces. He got up before the rest of the family and set about brewing coffee and making Eliot fresh-squeezed orange juice. He was just folding blueberries into the pancake batter when Eliot shuffled into the kitchen. The little boy rubbed sleep from his eyes and hugged his father. He then pulled a stool over to the counter and watched as James used a ladle to spoon the batter onto the hot skillet.

"Can we have alien pancakes today?" Eliot asked.

"Aliens with blue spots," James agreed. He cooked one oval-shaped pancake and two silver-dollar-sized pancakes. The bigger pancake formed the alien's face while the smaller ones served as his eyes. Strawberries cut into triangles formed a sinister mouth while half a banana cut lengthwise became the nose. James added two chocolate chip pupils and presented the plate to his son with a flourish.

"Earth has been invaded by aliens with blue spots," James announced in a robotic monotone. "Only one boy can save the day. Eliot Henry, will you rescue our planet by destroying the mean, spotty-faced aliens?"

"I will!" Eliot shouted and stabbed the banana nose with his fork. James howled as though wounded and then they both laughed. Jane entered the kitchen and headed straight for the coffeepot. James knew better than to start a conversation with her until she'd had at least three sips, so he merely smiled at her and continued making pancakes.

"I have the best husband in the world," Jane declared. "Makes his pancakes light and his coffee strong."

Kissing Eliot on the top of his head, she took her cup out to the front door and retrieved the newspaper. The Henrys batted around proposals on how to spend the rest of the day. James had to mow the lawn while Jane needed to do laundry, work on her summer class syllabus, and get groceries at the farmer's market.

"I want to build a fairy house today!" Eliot announced and ran to his room. He returned with one of the dozen library books he'd checked out during the week. "See? This little girl makes one and the fairies love it. You have to use stuff you find outside. If you buy stuff that's cheating."

James examined the illustrations of the small structures crafted from pinecones, twigs, and stones. "I think we can make time for this project," James told his son. "It's going to be hot today, so let's take a walk in the woods after we get dressed. Maybe Snickers would like to come with us."

Hearing his name, the miniature schnauzer raced into the room, his tail wagging. Jane got ready first and then left for the farmer's market. James and Eliot headed out back with both Snickers and Miss Pickles trailing after them. It was James' job to carry the hemp bag that would hold the fairy house materials Eliot found.

"Okay, bud. Enough rocks." James protested as Eliot tried to add another heavy stone to the bag. "How about some nice, lightweight sticks?"

It took another hour to construct the house and then Eliot sat back on his heels and brushed the dirt from his hands. "All done! When do you think they'll move in?"

James shrugged. "Fairies are very shy. They don't usually let people see them."

Eliot pouted. "Then how will I know if they liked my house?"

"Oh, they have a way of letting you know that they were here." He thought frantically. "Um, they might make a heart using flower petals or leave you some other gift."

"Like what?" Eliot's eyes shimmered.

Now James really was stuck. He glanced around the yard, stroking Miss Pickles as he tried to come up with a plausible answer. "A lucky four-leaf clover or an empty robin's egg. Something from nature."

"Cool." Eliot seemed satisfied. "When should we look for presents?"

Knowing he'd need time to sneak back to the fairy house and plant an item there, James waved Eliot away from the edge of the woods. "Tomorrow. We need to give them time to discover their new house. Plus, I heard they come out with the sun. *Very* early. Let's go inside and see what Mom got from the market."

After a snack of celery sticks and peanut butter, Eliot went to his room to play with the train set Jackson had bought him. James donned a baseball cap and went back outside to mow the lawn.

"Take your shoes off before you come

397

back in!" Jane warned. "I'm going to vacuum and mop since neither of my men are underfoot."

The Henrys passed an industrious morning. James finished with the front and side yards and stopped the mower, his shirt soaked with sweat. He'd drained his water bottle and wanted a refill and a bite of lunch before attacking the large expanse of lawn behind the house. He also wanted to check in with Lucy and find out whether Kenneth Cooper had been charged with a crime or had spent the night in the hospital, making phone calls to his firm and practicing the statement he'd make to the authorities.

Mindful of Jane's request, he kicked off his sneakers on the front porch and shook the grass from his socks. Frowning at the green tinge discoloring the ankle area of his white socks, James wiped his face with the old dishrag he used as a gym towel and stepped into the blissful cool.

In the kitchen, he refilled his water bottle, noting that an unfamiliar plastic pitcher containing a brown liquid had been left out on the counter. A tumbler with what James assumed was the tea given to them by Roslyn sat next to the pitcher. He picked it up and gave it a sniff. Normally, he wouldn't be suspicious of the holistic healer's odd visit the night before. After all, he lived in the South and it was an everyday occurrence for the townsfolk to help one another out, but why would Roslyn stop by when James had already purchased the products needed to cure Eliot's false cold?

He found Eliot still in his room. Train tracks snaked across the floor while library books, wooden blocks, and Lincoln Logs formed a series of tunnels. "Just a few more minutes," his son pleaded, assuming it was lunchtime.

"Where's Mom?" James asked, but Eliot just shrugged and continued to play.

Peering into the bedroom, James recalled that laundry had been on Jane's to-do list. He walked back down the hall to the tiny room next to the garage and found a pile of clean clothes partially folded on top of the dryer. The T-shirts had been placed neatly in the laundry basket, but the family's socks and underwear were scattered on the floor. The sight of the freshly laundered clothing dumped on the tiles caused a stirring of anxiety in James. He quickly checked the garage and, finding it empty, hurried out to the deck.

Jane was there, hunched over the railing, retching violently.

"Honey! Are you okay?"

She couldn't answer. Each breath was a desperate gasp as her body tried to inhale oxygen in between convulsions. One hand kept her balanced on the rail while the other clutched at her stomach.

"Oh, my God!" James stared at her in fear. "Did you drink the tea?"

Jane managed a nod and James flew into action. He raced into the house and dialed 9-1-1. With a tremulous voice, he told the operator that his wife had likely been poisoned by a herbal tea.

"Which herb, sir?" the woman asked serenely and James was exasperated by her calm. He wanted her to speak rapidly, to hastily tell him what to do, to promise that all would be well.

"I-I don't know," he stammered, picturing the shelves and shelves of products in Roslyn's storeroom.

The operator spoke again. It took a moment for her words to pierce the buzzing in James' head. "What are your wife's symptoms, sir?"

Suddenly, James felt that he was wasting precious time fielding questions from the composed woman on the phone. He slammed the handset down and yelled, "Eliot! Get in my truck!"

"But I wanna —" the little boy whined.

"*NOW!* DO WHAT I SAID RIGHT NOW!" James so rarely shouted that his son responded immediately.

James grabbed a bucket from under the kitchen sink, ran back out to the deck, and gently lifted Jane into his arms. "You're going to be fine, baby." He rushed through the house, gently set Jane into the passenger seat, put the bucket on her lap, and belted Eliot in his car seat. He then raced inside once more, grabbed the pitcher of tea from the counter, and jumped into the truck.

The drive to the hospital was hell. Eliot sat in wide-eyed silence in his seat, his large pupils dark with fear. Jane retched several times, but then dropped the bucket between her feet and grabbed her belly with both hands, moaning in pain.

Her agony made every red light and slow driver James' agony. Somehow, Eliot's mute presence in the back seat kept James from taking too many risks, but each passing minute filled his mind with a series of torturous questions. How powerful was the poisonous herb in the tea? How much did Jane drink? Would he get her to the hospital in time?

James screeched to a halt in front of the Emergency Room entrance, unbuckled Eliot and told him to stay close. Lifting Jane out of the car, he left the Bronco where it was, doors open wide, the key-left-in-ignition alarm sounding.

Ignoring the reception area with its enclosed desk, sliding glass window, and sign-in clipboard, James carried his wife right up to a man in scrubs, who was loitering near the vending machines.

"Please, my wife's been poisoned!"

To the man's credit, he leapt into action immediately. He slammed a nearby wall button, automatically opening a set of double doors leading to the treatment rooms. Gesturing for James to put Jane down on an empty gurney in the hallway, he removed the stethoscope from around his neck and listened to Jane's breathing.

"Do you know what she ingested?" He spoke to James without looking at him.

"An herbal tea. But I think it was deliberately brewed to do us harm. I've got it out in the car."

The man gestured for a pair of his colleagues to come to his aid. "Go get it, please."

James took Eliot's hand to fetch the pitcher and then he stopped. "Thunder god vine," he said. "Check for thunder god vine."

The man removed the stereoscope stem

from his right ear. "Thunder god vine?" His look of astonishment was quickly replaced by a nod. "Okay. But get the pitcher anyway."

Murmuring words of comfort to Eliot, James grabbed the pitcher of tea from the Bronco and handed it to the nurse stationed outside the double doors. "You've got to move your car and check your wife in," she directed. "They're not going to let you back in here until you do."

Too blinded by worry to realize that Jane wasn't the only patient the emergency room team would see that hour, James stalked off to move his car to the nearest lot. He completed the paperwork as fast as possible, his handwriting an anxious scrawl. Shoving the clipboard in the glass reception window's slot, he pointed at the double doors. "Can I go back now?"

"Your wife might have been moved, sir. Let me find out where she is." The woman picked up her phone and dialed a number. She then glanced back at James. "I've paged the doctor. I'll call you as soon as I have more information."

James controlled the rage surging through his body. He knew it stemmed from his feelings of helplessness and that he needed to press it back down. Only the warmth of

Eliot's small hand in his kept him from erupting. He led his son over to the vending machines and bought him a bag of pretzels and an apple juice.

"What's going to happen to Mommy?" Eliot asked, his lips quivering as he held his untouched snack.

Gathering the boy in his lap, James whispered. "She was sick, but the doctor's going to make her better. Don't you worry."

Deciding to funnel his anger, he called Lucy on his cell phone. "Roslyn must be the murderer you've been looking for! She tried to kill *us!* Me or Jane . . . maybe all three of us." The horror of his own statement sank in. "My God, she would have knowingly poisoned my son!"

"I'm on it." Lucy answered after James ran through the details. "She must have been worried that you discovered something in her office and that, eventually, you'd put two and two together and turn her in. Think about why you spooked her, James. When I catch her, I'm going to need as much information as possible to toss her in a cell."

Sensing Lucy was about to hang up, James called, "Wait! What about Kenneth?"

"He's denying everything. Says that he had the feathers in his pocket because he took them off your car." There was a smile in her voice. "Don't give him a second thought. He had cocaine in his system. First thing Monday morning, we get a restraining order for you and your family and go from there. He's never going to bother you again, James. I promise."

James saw the receptionist pick up the phone and then glance in his direction. She pointed at the wall button and gave him a nod of consent. "Gotta go," he told Lucy and moved toward the double doors. A nurse took James and Eliot back to the treatment area and had them wait while she went inside a room with a closed door. Several minutes passed before a doctor emerged from within, explaining that Jane had been given activated charcoal and seemed to have successfully purged the contents of her stomach.

"The good news is that your wife ate a meal before drinking the tea, so the harmful qualities of the poison were absorbed at a slower rate." He eased off a pair of clear disposable gloves. "We'll be watching her closely over the next few hours, but I believe she'll be just fine. Her throat will be sore and she may have other side effects such as headaches and cramping, but we'll make her as comfortable as we can."

"Can I see her?" James asked, his voice

full of yearning.

The doctor flicked his eyes at Eliot. "You might want to wait a bit. Let her get everything out and then get cleaned up. Trust me," he clapped James on the shoulder. "No one wants to be watched at a time like this. Honestly, it wouldn't help her to know you're in the room. She can only focus on one thing right now."

Heeding the physician's advice, though not without feelings of guilt, James entertained Eliot by telling him as many Aesop's Fables as he could remember. At the end of "The Fox and the Grapes" Lucy called again.

"Roslyn's gone. Anything of value has been removed from her house and office." She cursed under her breath. "With all the money she got blackmailing Ned and Tia, she could be anywhere by now, on a first-class flight to paradise."

"I take it you didn't find a defibrillator under the floorboards either," James responded with equal anger and dejection.

"I'm with the team at her house now, but Roslyn was no dummy. She was prepared for flight. Hold on, her phone is ringing." James heard Lucy speaking, but her low voice was garbled. After a rustle, Lucy returned. "That was a gallery in New

Market. They called to tell Roslyn that her framing job was ready to be picked up. She'd commissioned custom frames for a series of ten nature photographs."

James stood up abruptly, nearly dumping on the floor. "Fern's? The photos Lennon bought for his *girlfriend?*"

"Maybe she's not his girlfriend. I *cannot* picture them together. No, I'm thinking Roslyn is Lennon's mom."

A light bulb went off in James' mind. "Lennon's new SUV! He told me a generous relative gave him a bunch of cash. Roslyn must have given Ned's money to Lennon, to her son . . ."

"He might have been involved in the murders too. Remember the prints on Tia's neck? They were made from a large hand? And I could see her letting Lennon inside without worrying about being hurt. With his gentle hippie act, he might have had us all fooled. You sit tight," Lucy commanded. "I've got to track down that rock-raking bastard!"

Having no plans to leave the emergency room area, James and Eliot wandered back to the vending machines. He bought a package of Fig Newtons for Eliot and a granola bar for himself. The receptionist came out from her glass enclosure and gave Eliot a coloring book, crayons, and a sheet of rescue vehicle stickers.

"How's Mama doing?" she asked Eliot.

Putting a fire truck sticker on his shirt, Eliot thanked her for the goodies. "Daddy said she's going to be okay. He's always right."

The receptionist winked at James. "I bet he is."

Eliot had colored three pages when a nurse came out of Jane's room and told her husband and son they could go in and see her.

"She's a bit dehydrated and her throat hurts, but by the time she goes home tomorrow she'll be good as new," the nurse said and then lowered her voice. "The cops are going to want to talk to you."

"Fine. The more the better," James replied, and then walked to his wife's bedside. She smiled weakly and he felt the fear, which had clung to his chest like a parasite, release its grip and scuttle from the room.

Later, after Eliot was in bed and James had listened to the frantic phone messages left by his friends, he sat in the dark living room and thought. With his pets nestled beside him, James turned over all the details of the two murders. Pieces were still missing. How did Roslyn get Ned in her power in the first place? Who used the defibrillator and where had it come from? Why would Roslyn perform such hideous acts of violence? As a moneymaking scheme to provide for her son? And what hold did she have over Tia?

It was difficult to think clearly without experiencing spurts of rage and indulging in fantasies of revenge. After all, Roslyn Rhodes had poisoned his wife. If one little sip had been so harmful to Jane, James couldn't stand the thought of what the tea could have done to Eliot.

"To protect her son, she would have willingly killed mine," he whispered, the anger flooding through him like an intense heat.

He'd saved his phone call to Lucy for last. When he reached her, he wanted to hear that it was all over. The culprits had been apprehended, there was irrefutable proof that they'd murdered two townsfolk and had attempted to kill a third. and they'd be spending a long, long time in prison.

"I wish I had better news," Lucy said as soon as she heard his voice. "But the governor's pulling out all the stops on this one. He's got the state and local police involved. Photos are being shown during every news broadcast and for once, the media's skill at sensationalizing might work to our advantage. I already saw a segment about our manhunt during the six o'clock news."

"What about their cars?" James tried to rein in his frustration, but failed. "Are they broadcasting their license plate numbers? Lennon's was pretty hard to miss. Green SUV with a vanity plate reading, VEG OUT."

"We found his car on a CarMax lot. Lennon sold the truck four days ago and deposited a check for over twenty grand in his bank account. He was smart," Lucy grudgingly admitted. "He waited for that check to clear and then withdrew all his funds. He's run off with at least forty thousand in cash."

James sighed and Snickers raised his head in concern. "That kind of money makes it easier to hide."

"Hey, my neck is in the noose here. If they get away I look totally inept! Trust me, James. I am *very* motivated to catch those two. And I'll start tomorrow by going over every possession, every piece of mail, and every detail people can recall about Roslyn and Lennon. It also means I'm giving you an assignment."

"What's that?"

"Think back on the conversations you've had with both mother and son. If I gather enough data from enough conversations, I believe we'll get a clue as to where they've gone."

James smoothed the fur on his dog's neck. "I'm way ahead of you on that front. That's what I've been doing for the last hour. Between Roslyn and Kenneth, I've got scores to settle." He hung up.

A summer thunderstorm was brewing outside. The wind curled around the tree-tops and clouds blanketed the moon. At the sound of a branch tapping against a window, Snickers cocked his head and growled. In the dark and silent living room, James growled too.

EIGHTEEN:
GILLIAN'S ZEN COCKTAIL

Grams of
Sugar
18

A week later, the Henry family arrived at Gillian's colorful Victorian for what their hostess had dubbed a "Union of Souls" fête. Gillian had tied white and silver balloons on the porch railings and fastened crepe paper sculptures of kissing doves on the sconces flanking the wooden doors. A little sign taped to the brass knocker directed guests to head straight for the back yard. Gillian had outdone herself in creating a romantic atmosphere. She'd decorated her gazebo with more balloons and curtains of white streamers while twinkling white lights hung from the rafters in loose, graceful swags.

It was a perfect summer night. The humidity was blessedly low, a soft breeze flowed down from the mountains, and the first fireflies of the season were speaking to one another in their magical language of light.

The women were clad in cool sundresses and the men in shorts and polo shirts. The Fitzgerald brothers played croquet on the lawn as Lindy adjusted the volume on a battery-powered radio. Tony Bennett serenaded the party goers who exchanged small talk until Gillian asked them to congregate for a toast.

The table she'd set was beautiful. Scott, Francis, Bennett, and Gillian had somehow wrestled her dining room table out the back door. Gillian had then covered it with a cloth so pristinely white that it glowed beneath the periwinkle sky like a new moon. Tall pillar candles protected by hurricane glass and posies of white roses in silver vases created a line of flickering light and heady fragrance down the center of the table. Rolled white cloth napkins were fastened with ivy vines and a silver tray bearing glass tumblers filled with a bright green liquid and sprigs of mint rested at the head of the table.

"A green toast!" Gillian shouted. "To the bond between man and woman and parent and child! May your future together be filled with joy, adventure, and an *endless* stream of love!"

The newlyweds clinked glasses with the other guests and even Eliot, who was given a limeade in a "grown-up glass," participated in the toast.

Bennett cleared his throat. "To James Henry. The best friend a fellow could hope to have. And to Jane, for bringin' my man happiness. Lord knows he deserves it!"

"To the couple that makes me believe that love is forever!" Lindy cried.

The toasts continued for another five minutes. Eventually, most of the women were in tears and even Jackson's eyes were shining.

"What is this stuff?" he grumbled, holding out his glass and struggling to maintain a gruff expression.

Gillian interpreted his question as a cue to pour refills all around. "It's a Zen cocktail. I didn't want anything *traditional* like champagne. A *whole* family has been united by this marriage. By going green, I was able to truly include Eliot and to celebrate how he's influenced his parents to embark on a healthier, vegetarian lifestyle." She performed a little curtsy in Eliot's honor.

Bennett gestured at the grill. "Is he the reason we're eatin' mulch burgers tonight?"

Gillian elbowed him roughly in the side. "You can have a non-vegetarian patty if you want. I prepared both, but I'm grilling the bean burgers first so they're not *tainted* by the meat."

"Leave the grillin' to me," Bennett insisted. "I don't want to ingest any more carcinogens than I have to."

While the pair bickered over cooking time and temperature, Fern and Willow escorted Eliot away from the table and showed him how to play horseshoes. Gillian had thoughtfully purchased several lawn games perfect for a boy his age. However, it was the Fitzgerald brothers who got the biggest kick out of the putting green, the beanbag toss, and the croquet set.

The rest of the adults settled at the table and continued to sip on their refreshing green cocktails. Eventually, the conversation led to the subject of Kenneth Cooper and the unsolved murders of Ned Woodman and Tia Royale.

"Kenneth is out of our hair," Jane explained. "We were granted a strict restraining order. I've heard he's also lost his job."

"I hope he gets disbarred," James murmured.

Milla rubbed her dimpled chin thoughtfully. "What about official charges? He's not going to have to do any time?"

Lucy fidgeted with the sprig of mint in her glass. "We couldn't charge him with possession. He didn't have any cocaine on his person or in his car — just in his body. And there wasn't much we could do as far as his affinity for leaving dead birds around Jane and James. But no one wanted to see him go unpunished, so we decided to put Murphy's idea into play."

"Ah ha! Her plan was to make the official inquiry public, right?" Lindy declared. "She splashed Kenneth's history of cocaine use all over the front page. Every news service in the country picked up that story. No wonder that jerk's law career is over!" She grinned. "Luis was certainly at the right place at the right time! It's funny though; he keeps telling me he wasn't. He's being very mysterious about the big finale I missed. Even my students are acting weird. They won't even talk about the play!" She shrugged. "Guess that's what final exams will do to you."

James nodded, recalling how uncannily quiet the campus of William and Mary could be during finals week. "How did Murphy ever get inside information from an employee in the rehab center?"

A wry smile spread across Lucy's face. "She never did tell me the whole story there. All she would say was there was a young orderly working there who's real dream was to be a writer. Apparently, he's now a *Star* employee."

"You see!" Gillian's voice was triumphant. "She made a personal sacrifice to come to our aid. Without her help, Quincy's Gap might never have been rid of Kenneth Cooper."

Bennett grudgingly agreed. "I suppose she's made amends."

Satisfied that her faith in Murphy's goodness had been proved true, Gillian put a hand over Jane's. "Are you *completely* restored after your ordeal last week? I will *never* be able to look at my herbal teas in the same light!"

Jane laughed. "Don't give up on chamomile and peppermint because of me. Your teas aren't mixed with pure thunder god vine root. I'm fine, really. James saved me. He's my Superman."

"Speaking of the bad guys, are you getting closer to catching them?" Scott asked as he trotted over to the table and gulped down half his drink in one swallow. "Yum! I *love* going green!"

All eyes fixed on Lucy. "Roslyn and Lennon have not been apprehended." James could tell that the admission caused her a great deal of displeasure. "We've chased down dozens and dozens of false leads. Now that Tia's parents have offered a fifty thousand dollar reward, the phone calls and emails have been flooding in at a ridiculous rate. Even with other law enforcement agencies helping, it's taking all our manpower to sift through them. Despite the monetary incentive, we haven't received a single useful clue."

Lucy went on to give examples of the most preposterous tips the Sheriff's Department had received, including a caller who swore mother and son had been abducted by aliens and another who claimed to have seen the pair, disguised as Elvis impersonators, dining on Grand Slams at Denny's.

When the laughter died down, Lucy glanced down at the table and began to toy with the ivy wrapped around her napkin. "Sheriff Huckabee's been breathing down my neck like a dragon. Sullie and I don't do anything but work. This is my first real break in a week." She glanced apologetically at James and Jane. "I've read the case files until I start seeing double, but when I lie down to sleep at night, I still feel like I've let everyone down. Even my dreams are focused on this case."

Gillian reached over and put an arm around Lucy's shoulders. "You're only human. Have faith in yourself. Someone will experience an unexpected moment of clarity and an answer will be revealed."

"I can't stop until I've set things right. You see, I made a mistake," Lucy looked at Gillian's kind face. "When I looked in the pasts of those working at the Wellness Village, I wasn't thorough enough. If I had been, I would have discovered that Lennon had changed his name at age eighteen. After making sure he didn't have a juvenile record I concentrated on his adult years, calling former employers and stuff like that. He didn't go to college and has worked a series of maintenance jobs. No one had a bad word to say about him. I found no financial red flags. In my mind, he was low on the suspect list! Yet he was the killer!"

"You were researching backgrounds on dozens of people," James said. "What you did was logical."

The assembly agreed, soothing Lucy with their words and sympathetic looks.

"You're gonna get them, Lucy even if

they're out there, preparin' a new scheme and sniffin' around for fresh victims to blackmail." Bennett's dark eyes flashed with righteous anger. "You're gonna make it right."

That being said, Gillian and Bennett excused themselves to prepare the food. The partygoers agreed not to talk about the case anymore and, after another round of Zen cocktails, they became quite jolly. Most of the company enjoyed Gillian's dinner of black bean burgers, fruit salad, and edamame. Bennett, Lucy, and the Fitzgerald brothers opted for traditional burgers and for once, Gillian didn't chastise them for being unwilling to explore new tastes. Later, Willow and Fern served dessert: chilled white chocolate mousse embellished with a white chocolate dove. It was rich, creamy, and utterly decadent.

"We girls wanted to contribute in some way," Willow said, smiling shyly.

Fern handed Jane a square package wrapped in brown paper. "And here's the rest of our joint gift."

Jane opened the package, revealing the photograph of the purple rhododendron flower James had planned to buy for his wife. "It's beautiful!" Jane exclaimed.

Gillian and Bennett gave them a gift

certificate for a couples massage, Lindy made them a stunning pottery fruit bowl, and Lucy presented them with a generous gift certificate to Dolly's Diner. The Fitzgeralds waited until all the other gifts and greeting cards had been opened before handing James a shoebox wrapped in the funny pages.

"Did you give them each a single shoe?" Bennett teased.

The box was stuffed with tissue paper and did not contain footwear. Nestled at the bottom of the box was a glossy brochure featuring a cruise ship. Inside the folded brochure were two tickets for a five-day cruise from Norfolk to Bermuda on a massive ship called *Grandeur of the Seas.*

James was flabbergasted. "You got us a *cruise?* To *Bermuda?*"

The twins bobbed their heads enthusiastically.

"This is too much!" Jane protested and James quickly agreed. "Scott, Francis. We are *really* touched, but —"

"Non-refundable, Professor!" Scott announced with delight.

Francis gestured at Jackson and Milla. "We've lined up the dates with your babysitting service here and worked it out on the library staff vacation calendar too."

"We also called your department head to see when your summer semester would start, Mrs. Henry." Francis wore a mischievous grin. "He says to tell you, 'Bon Voyage.'"

"I don't know what to say . . ." James broke off, too moved to continue. He and Jane bent their heads over the brochure, excitedly pointing at photographs of pink beaches. They then embraced the Fitzgerald several times until the younger men finally pulled away.

"Seriously, we're not going to be late on our rent because of this. See, we finally got our check from the gaming company," Francis explained. "It was *big*. Scott and I bought a pair of awesome mountain bikes for some off-road adventuring, a killer flatscreen, and two new computers with more gigs than the Pentagon's entire database." He and Scott exchanged high-fives. They waited for their boss to respond, but his eyes had turned distant. "Professor?"

Something Francis had said triggered James' memory. Suddenly, he gripped Scott by the sleeve. "Do you have a map of area mountain bike trails?"

"There's one online," the startled twin answered. "Why?"

James turned to Gillian. "Can we use your

computer?"

The Fitzgerald brothers followed their boss inside and spent several seconds arguing over which site was best, but Francis finally won out and began typing. A map of Virginia covered by green bicycle symbols appeared onscreen.

"Can you zoom in on our area?" James asked and Francis quickly complied.

James read the names of the trails until he saw the one he recognized. "That's it!" he shouted. "Brandywine Lake!" Leaving the befuddled Fitzgerald twins staring at the computer screen, James raced outside. He found Lucy at the beanbag toss, engaged in an intense match with Fern.

"Brandywine Lake!" He shouted again, grabbing her elbow.

Lucy scowled. "Hey, you're throwing off my aim!"

"Lennon loved to mountain bike. Skye told me he went every weekend without fail. It's what he lives for. I had a short conversation with him in which he invited me along one day. He said it's what he does to relieve stress and his favorite trail is Brandywine Lake."

Lucy squeezed the beanbag in her hand, her eyes glinting with excitement. "We need to circulate his photo around every trail in the region. We have a new composite showing him with and without the dreadlocks, so even if he's changed his looks another rider might still recognize him." Her face shone. "Good work, James. This might be that obscure clue that ends up with me slapping handcuffs on those two fiends!"

Pausing briefly to thank Gillian for a lovely evening, Lucy jogged around the side of the house and disappeared from view. James returned to the table and explained what had transpired to the rest of the ensemble.

"There's something I don't understand," Jane said to him as everyone broke into animated chatter. "Why was Roslyn so anxious during the food festival if she was the one blackmailing Ned?"

James mulled over her question. "I don't know. Maybe Ned refused to pay her any more, forcing Lennon to get involved." He could see Roslyn's panicked face in his mind. "Could she have actually cared about Ned? Perhaps murder had never been part of her original plan."

Jane considered this theory. "Tia also looked scared when we saw her at the Apple Blossom Festival. If Lennon caused her to run away like that, then she would have been too frightened of him to let him in her house later on. So what happened? Tia found Roslyn standing on the doorstep and invited her in with Lennon nearby hiding in the bushes?"

"Again, maybe Roslyn was trying to get money out of Tia without harming her. Tia would have viewed Roslyn as a potential friend — a vegetarian and animal rights' sympathizer. She would have let the older woman into her home without having any idea that Roslyn was Lennon's mom. Nobody knew. After all, they don't look alike and they have different last names."

The couple fell silent, sipping the decaf coffee Gillian had brought to the table. They watched Lindy, Willow, and Fern play croquet while Eliot and the Fitzgerald twins chased after fireflies. Milla and Jackson said their goodnights and headed home. Jackson gave his son a brief hug and told him that he was still busy creating the couple's wedding gift. Thrilled over the thought of receiving one of his father's masterpieces, James teased, "You'd better get some rest then. I've got a blank wall in the living room that could do with a classy painting by Virginia's premier country artist."

James and Jane carried dishes into Gillian's kitchen but she immediately shooed them away. "We are *not* going to waste this heavenly evening washing dishes. Out! Out into the night with you!"

So it was that they found themselves in a pair of wicker rockers on the back porch. Laughter floated up from the lawn; Eliot's high notes mingled with the low timbre of Scott, and Francis' voices. The three women smacked mallets against croquet balls, their comfortable prattle circling lazily upward where it caught in the tree branches.

Reaching for Jane's hand, James lifted his eyes to the indigo sky and sighed. His exhalation was filled with contentment. "Gillian was right. This is heaven."

AFTERWORD

It took two weeks for a rider on the Elizabeth Furnace Trail southeast of Strasburg to phone the tip line, saying that he believed he'd seen the man in the photograph he'd been given by a park ranger the week before. The man was unloading his bike from the rack of a dark green Jeep Compass.

"If it's your guy," the cyclist said to the officer fielding calls from the tip line, "you can catch him when he comes back out. It's a grueling, thirteen-mile trail. Even the most experienced riders have to stop for a water break, so you've got time. He might go for a dip in the reservoir too. It's a great way to clean the sweat off before pumping the pedals again. Just be careful, because if other riders see a bunch of cops hanging in the parking lot, they might warn your guy. Not because they think murder suspects are cool," the cyclist added defensively. "But because in general, they don't care for authority figures."

Lucy heard about the tip and within minutes, she and Sullie were in his Camaro heading north. "It's him. I can feel it in my gut," Lucy said, twisting her hands in anticipation.

"You're so sexy when you're on a manhunt," Sullie answered and then focused on speeding around any vehicle, the magnetic siren on his roof screaming out a warning.

Arriving at the trail entrance slightly breathless and pumped up with a surge of adrenaline, Lucy and Sullie had a quick conference with the local deputies and together, came up with a strategy to ensure that the wanted man wouldn't slip from their grasp.

Later, Lucy would tell the supper club members how Lennon had dismounted in the parking lot, his young face flushed and full of satisfaction. He'd clearly had an amazing ride. The lawmen almost felt sorry for him, for it would be the last time he'd experience the sweet, invigorating taste of freedom for many years to come.

His head was completely shaved, leaving only a hint of light brown stubble bleached gold by the sun, and he wore a pair of mirrored sunglasses. A sheen of sweat glistened on his smooth skin and when Lucy and Sullie stepped up to meet him, he bolted. A dozen local deputies and police officers were waiting at the ready for the suspect to flee, and he was quickly flattened by a young deputy who'd been a track star in college. His glasses flew off in the scuffle and his eyes glimmered with rage.

Lennon/Curt Snyder denied everything, but his capture forced Roslyn to surrender of her own volition. The *Star* was loaded with photographs of her being escorted inside the sheriff's department building by Huckabee himself.

"Roslyn tried to take the fall for both of them," Lucy told her friends. "She and Ned Woodman had a brief affair and when he tried to break it off, Roslyn threatened to tell his wife and talk about his indiscretions to the press unless he bought her silence."

"So that's how the blackmail began," Lindy stated.

"Yes, but Ned wanted to come clean. He was going to tell Donna everything and then present himself to the authorities with a confession regarding his embezzlement of town funds. It was at the Food Festival that he told Roslyn he was no longer in her power. That's why she looked so frantic."

Bennett snorted. "She was losin' her free ride — that's why she was sweatin' like a fry cook durin' a breakfast rush."

"Except she didn't keep a single dime of the money," Lucy explained. "Every cent went to Lennon. With her line of work, she'd struggled financially as a single mom and she was tired of the struggle. Go on, someone ask me why she was single."

"Because she's a duplicitous blackmailer?" James guessed.

Lucy paused, letting the dramatic tension build. "Because her ex-husband is spending thirty years to life in prison! He killed someone in a bar fight. It started as an argument about sports and then punches were thrown, but Lennon's daddy took it to the next level by smashing his opponent's head into the jukebox."

"Ow!" several of them said at once.

Gillian clucked her tongue. "I cannot understand why that angry young man chose Lennon as his false name. John Lennon was an advocate of *peace.* How it pains me that his memory is disgraced by having his name associated with such a *twisted* soul."

"That's not how people will think of him," Lindy stated, hoping to comfort her friend. "Murphy referred to him as Curt Snyder in her articles and so has the rest of the media. I don't think anyone wants to use his fake name and the term 'double murder' in the same sentence." She turned to Lucy. "Tell us about the defibrillator."

"Roslyn purchased it years ago through an online medical auction. I gather that when hospitals or medical offices upgrade to new equipment, they often put the old stuff up for sale."

Bennett put a hand on her arm. "You mean I could just go online and buy a blood pressure machine? See what happens to my numbers after Mrs. McDougal's bloodhound chases after me like I'm wearin' Milkbone aftershave."

"I think a stethoscope might be more handy in that scenario," Gillian said with a saucy wink. "Really Bennett, you need to hire a dog whisperer. Perhaps I should look into that for you."

Before the couple could engage in an argument over befriending all the pooches on Bennett's mail route, Lucy continued her narrative. "Lennon was storing the device in the closet where Roslyn kept her refrigerated products. You were right to be suspicious of that locked door, James. Lennon lured Ned into Roslyn's office, saying that he knew about the blackmail and could show Ned where Roslyn had hidden the cash."

"Of course Ned followed him!" Lindy cried. "He could return the money to the town's account and not face jail time, divorce, or public humiliation. But why believe Lennon?"

Lucy shrugged. "Because Lennon had access to all the buildings with his master key. Also, many of Roslyn and Ned's trysts had taken place in her office, so Ned probably found it plausible that the young man knew all about their affair. Lennon led Ned into the bathroom by claiming that the cash was in the toilet tank. He then quietly locked the door and used the defibrillator on the unsuspecting councilman. Afterward, he put the device back in the closet and returned to the festival."

The friends fell silent as each of them pictured the surprised look Ned Woodman must have worn as he turned to find the person he'd hoped could rescue him wielding a pair of charged paddles.

James wondered what it felt like to be blasted with an electric current powerful enough to change the rhythm of a beating heart. Did death occur so rapidly that Ned had no chance to process the betrayal or was there enough time for him to register shock and then, a second later, horror?

Sensing the mood shift of her audience,

Lucy grew more solemn as well. "Roslyn claims to have been distraught over Ned's murder. She didn't care that her lover had been killed, but that Lennon was exhibiting his father's violent tendencies. She begged Lennon to leave Quincy's Gap right after the festival, but Lennon had already started blackmailing Tia and he had genuine feelings for Skye."

"What hold did he have over Tia?" James asked. "We've never been able to guess."

Lucy shook her head. "You'll never believe this, but Tia was in a commercial for a fast-food restaurant when she was a teenager. I've seen the footage. Tia takes three bites of a cheeseburger and then smiles at the camera."

"Where did Lennon see the commercial? It's gotta be older than my shower curtain." Bennett frowned in confusion.

"On the Internet. Apparently, one of the other kids on the commercial went on to become a famous singer in a Grateful Dead cover band, so the clip was posted on a bunch of sites," Lucy answered. "The second Lennon found out Tia was one of the rich Royale kids, he started digging around and he stumbled across the commercial."

"Poor girl," Gillian sympathized. "She was

probably afraid that no one would support her animal rights' campaign if they knew about that silly ad, but she was wrong. She was still a child when that was filmed!"

"She was still a child when she was *murdered*," Lucy added with an undercurrent of anger. "Roslyn went to Tia's place to warn her to get out of town, but Lennon followed Mommy Dearest. Inside, Roslyn accidentally dropped Ned's fir tree charm and because she'd had it in her skirt pocket, where she was also keeping a small wedge of cheese, Snickers swallowed it. Lennon snuck in when the two women were talking and hid in Tia's closet. He tried to get more money out of her and when she didn't produce any right then and there, he grew enraged. They struggled and when she was weakened by strangulation, he zapped her with the paddles."

James felt his mouth go dry. "What a monster."

"Yeah, he's messed up. And he and Roslyn have never had a healthy relationship. She said that throughout Lennon's childhood, she went without so he could have nice things. She gave him too much power and spoiled him rotten, thinking that was how a loving parent acted."

"I feel a little sorry for her," Lindy admitted. "She has to live with the weight of so many regrets."

Lucy nodded. "At least she feels remorse. Lennon is just ticked off that he got caught."

"Well, that boy is in for a rude awakenin' when he gets to prison," Bennett concluded with satisfaction in his voice. "Not too much peace, love, and harmony in the ole slammer. Maybe he'll learn a little bit about the value of freedom when he only gets to see the sky through a barred window. Maybe he'll learn what he stole from Ned and Tia when the life he took for granted comes to a screechin' halt."

There wasn't much more to say after that and the supper club meeting broke up shortly afterward. The friends were tired. Each of them felt glad to be welcoming the new season, as though the heat of the summer sun could burn away the damp, dirty residue left behind by a spring marred by stalking, blackmail, and murder. By mutual agreement, they all signed up for more sessions with Harmony. This time, however, no one was interested in treating sugar addictions. Instead, they wanted help in letting go of their repressed guilt for not discovering Lennon's foul deeds earlier. They also had another shared goal: they wanted to kick off the summer feeling in control of their bodies, their minds, and their futures.

"And a sense of calm," James added when he made the appointment with Harmony's new assistant. Skye was long gone and though James didn't know where the young woman went, he wished her a quick recovery from what was no doubt a deeply wounded heart.

A few weeks into the month of June, James was reading emails on his home computer when Jane entered the tiny third bedroom he used as an office. The walls were lined with bookshelves and books filled every available nook and cranny. There were books piled on his desk, on the side tables, and in boxes and chest-high towers within the closet.

Jane walked into the room wearing a smile. "I forwarded you the email I received from Fay Sunray. Did I ever mention that I'd written her complaining about how she'd upset Eliot during the Nashville show?"

"No, you didn't, but I thought about writing her myself." He scrolled down his list of emails. "Here it is."

"Dear Mrs. Henry," the email began. "I definitely owe you, your son, and everyone at that concert an apology. That was not the time, the place, or the means to deliver my message to people about converting to a vegetarian lifestyle. In fact, my behavior may have done a cause near and dear to my heart more harm than good. We've had the offending song cut from the DVD version of the show and I've mailed you a free copy of the edited work along with a signed photograph and a selection of Fay Sunray Friends puppets. I know these items don't make up for my poor judgment, but it is still, and always will be, my hope to bring a smile to your son's face. Yours, Fay Sunray."

"She sounds very sincere," James said when he'd finished reading the email. "You know, she and Tia Royale would have gotten along well. But Fay seems to have realized something that Tia didn't. You don't have to be vulgar or crass to get your point across. A few farm puppets and a gentle manner can go a long way."

Jane laughed. "You need to shut down that computer and start packing. We've got an early start tomorrow."

"I know," James answered without moving. "I still can't believe we accepted a cruise from my employees. It feels so wrong and yet," he glanced up at her with a smile, "*so* right."

"We'd better have a vacation now, while

we can." She handed him a small package wrapped in white tissue paper.

"What's this?" James asked and began to tear at the paper. Parting the tissue, he saw that Jane had bought him an ebook reader. "Jane!" He looked stunned and not just a little taken aback. "I'm a librarian. I . . . I can't read books on a machine. I need to hold them, turn paper pages, leave a bookmark inside." His eyes were anxious and Jane could see that he was concerned about hurting her feelings.

"It's just for you to use at home or on trips," she explained soothingly and gestured at the books. "And because we're going to need to get rid of all these."

James leapt from his chair. "WHAT? WHY?"

Ignoring him, Jane put her index finger on her chin and tapped. "A yellow paint would do nicely. Or maybe a calming moss-green."

"Why do we need to paint this room? It's fine the way it is!" James spluttered indignantly.

Jane put her arms around her husband. "Beige is a bit boring for a nursery. I think we'll go with the green." She drew James' hand to her belly and smiled as his face began to glow with astonishment and joy. "Or we could just take a chance and paint it pink. I've got a powerful feeling that this one's a girl."

RECESS

RECIPES

DOLLY'S BLUEBERRY DREAM PIE
Ingredients:

4 ounces cream cheese, softened (Dolly prefers *Philadelphia*-brand cream cheese)

1/2 cup confectioner's sugar

1/2 cup heavy whipping cream, whipped

1 (9-inch) pie shell, baked

2/3 cup granulated sugar

1/4 cup cornstarch

1/2 cup water

1/4 cup lemon juice

3 cups fresh blueberries

Directions:

1. In a small bowl, blend cream cheese and confectioner's sugar until smooth. Gently fold in whipped cream. Spread in a pre-baked pastry shell.

2. In a large saucepan combine sugar, cornstarch, water, and lemon juice. Stir with wooden spoon until smooth, and

then stir in blueberries. Bring to a boil over medium heat. Cook, stirring constantly, for 2 minutes or until thickened. Cool. Spread over cream cheese layer. Refrigerate until ready to serve. Garnish with a sprig of mint (optional).

MILLA'S CHOCOLATE MOCHA CAKE

Cake Ingredients:

2 cups cake flour
2 cups granulated sugar
2/3 cup unsweetened cocoa powder
1/2 cup vegetable oil
2 eggs
1 cup buttermilk
1 teaspoon baking powder
2 teaspoons baking soda
1/2 teaspoon salt
3 tablespoons instant coffee powder
1 cup hot water

Directions:

1. Preheat oven to 350 degrees. Grease two 9-inch cake pans. (Milla likes PAM Baking spray)
2. Measure flour, sugar, cocoa, oil, eggs, buttermilk, baking powder, soda, and salt into a mixing bowl. Dissolve instant coffee in hot water. Add to mixing bowl. Beat at medium speed for 2 minutes until smooth;

batter will be thin. Pour into prepared pans.

3. Bake 35 minutes, or until a toothpick comes out clean. Cool in pans for 10 minutes, and then turn out onto racks to cool completely.

4. Frost with Milla's Coffee Icing. For garnish, sprinkle outside edges of cake with dark chocolate shavings.

MILLA'S COFFEE ICING

Frosting Ingredients:

4 cups confectioners' sugar

1/2 cup unsalted butter, softened

6 tablespoons strong brewed coffee

2 teaspoons pure vanilla extract

Directions:

Beat together sugar, butter, coffee, and vanilla until smooth. To thicken frosting, add more confectioners' sugar.

JANE & ELIOT'S VEGETARIAN PIZZADILLAS

Ingredients:

Package of flour tortillas or mini flour tortillas

Small jar of marinara sauce

2 cups mozzarella cheese, shredded (Jane and Eliot also enjoy the Italian blend avail-

able in the dairy aisle)
1/2 cup mushrooms
1/2 cup black olives
2 tablespoons butter

Directions:

Spread 2 tablespoons of marinara sauce on each tortilla. Sprinkle 1/2 cup shredded cheese on top of sauce.

Add sliced vegetables (mushrooms, black olives, or any veggie you enjoy).

Place a plain tortilla on top and press down slightly.

Melt butter in skillet.

Place pizzadilla in a warmed skillet until cheese melts and tortilla turns golden brown.

Flip pizzadilla over to evenly brown other side.

Remove from skillet and allow pizzadilla to cool slightly. Cut each pizzadilla into quarters using pizza cutter.

GILLIAN'S ZEN COCKTAIL

Mix one part ZEN Green Tea Liqueur with two parts white cranberry juice.

Serve over ice with spring of mint as garnish.

GILLIAN'S BLACK BEAN BURGERS

Ingredients:

1 (15-ounce) can black beans, drained
1 small onion, chopped
1 tablespoon finely chopped jalapeño pepper
1/4 cup bread crumbs
1 egg, beaten
1/2 cup shredded Cheddar cheese
2 cloves fresh garlic, minced
1/4 teaspoon pepper
1/4 cup vegetable oil

Directions:

1. In a large bowl, mash black beans. Mix in onion, jalapeño pepper, crushed bread crumbs, egg, cheese, garlic, and pepper. Divide into 4 equal parts. Shape into patties.

2. Heat vegetable oil in a large, non-stick skillet over medium-high heat. Fry patties until golden, about 6 to 8 minutes per side. Top with cheese slices or a splash of taco sauce.

GILLIAN'S SUMMER FRUIT SALAD

Ingredients:

1/4 cup honey
4 tablespoons lime juice
2 teaspoons poppy seeds

1 cup halved fresh strawberries
1 cup cubed fresh pineapple
1 cup fresh blueberries
1 cup cubed seedless watermelon
1/4 cup slivered almonds, toasted

Directions:

In a blender, combine the honey, lime juice, and poppy seeds to make dressing. In a serving bowl, combine the fruit. Drizzle with dressing; toss gently to coat. Sprinkle with the almonds.

ABOUT THE AUTHOR

J. B. Stanley has a BA in English from Franklin & Marshall College, an MA in English Literature from West Chester University, and an MLIS from North Carolina Central University. She taught sixth grade language arts in Cary, North Carolina, for the majority of her eight-year teaching career. Raised an antique lover by her grandparents and parents, Stanley also worked part-time in an auction gallery. An eBay junkie and food lover, Stanley now lives in Richmond, Virginia, with her husband, two young children, and three cats. Visit her website at www.jbstanley.com.

We hope you have enjoyed this Large Print book. Other Thorndike, Wheeler, Kennebec, and Chivers Press Large Print books are available at your library or directly from the publishers.

For information about current and upcoming titles, please call or write, without obligation, to:

Publisher
Thorndike Press
295 Kennedy Memorial Drive
Waterville, ME 04901
Tel. (800) 223-1244

or visit our Web site at:

http://gale.cengage.com/thorndike

OR

Chivers Large Print
published by AudioGO Ltd
St James House, The Square
Lower Bristol Road
Bath BA2 3BH
England
Tel. +44(0) 800 136919
info@audiogo.co.uk
www.audiogo.co.uk

All our Large Print titles are designed for easy reading, and all our books are made to last.